JO JAKEMAN

What His Wife Knew

VINTAGE

1 3 5 7 9 10 8 6 4 2

Vintage is part of the Penguin Random House group of companies
whose addresses can be found at global.penguinrandomhouse.com

Penguin
Random House
UK

Copyright © Jo Jakeman 2022

Jo Jakeman has asserted her right to be identified as
the author of this Work in accordance with the Copyright,
Designs and Patents Act 1988

First published in Vintage in 2022

penguin.co.uk/vintage

A CIP catalogue record for this book is available from the British Library

ISBN 9781784709266 (B format)

Typeset in 11.4/15.2pt Bembo Std by Jouve (UK), Milton Keynes
Printed and bound in Great Britain by Clays Ltd, Elcograf S.p.A.

The authorised representative in the EEA is Penguin Random House Ireland,
Morrison Chambers, 32 Nassau Street, Dublin D02 YH68

Penguin Random House is committed to a sustainable future
for our business, our readers and our planet. This book is
made from Forest Stewardship Council® certified paper.

MIX
Paper from
responsible sources
FSC
www.fsc.org   FSC® C018179

For Mum

*Let death stalk my enemies; let the grave swallow them
alive, for evil makes its home within them.*

Psalm 55:15 (New Living Translation)

*The five stages of grief model (or the Kübler-Ross model) postulates
that those experiencing grief go through a series of five emotions:
denial, anger, bargaining, depression and acceptance . . . The model
was first introduced by Swiss-American psychiatrist Elisabeth
Kübler-Ross in her 1969 book* On Death and Dying, *and
was inspired by her work with terminally ill patients.*

Wikipedia

Stage One of Grief

DENIAL

CHAPTER ONE

Beth Lomas

Sorry.

Just one word on the back of a discarded envelope. I told the police that no way, never, not in a million years was that a suicide note.

I said, 'You're going to have to trust me. I know him better than you do, and I know that Oscar would never take his own life.'

His writing was as familiar to me as my own. There was a cat's tail swirl on the S and the Y, followed by a single X. A kiss. Perhaps he'd used the last of the milk, or forgotten to take the bins out. Something silly and forgivable that we'd laugh about in time.

'You idiot,' I'd say, punching his shoulder. 'You scared me half to death.' And he'd wrinkle his nose in that way he did when he was embarrassed, and I'd rest my head on his chest.

I shouldn't have told the detective about the note on the kitchen table, propped between the salt and pepper grinders. The slump of her shoulders and the downturn of her mouth made it clear that DC Lowry Endecott's mind was made up.

'I know what you're thinking, but it isn't that,' I said.

'Then why's he apologising?' she asked.

'We argued. No, not really, that sounds too strong. We'd

had *words* on Friday night. He left the house before I got out of bed yesterday, making the most of the last day of good weather, you know. He told Gabe – that's our son – that he was going for a hike and he'd see him that evening. The note was an apology for the argument, you see. That's all. Please, I beg you. You have to find him. What if he's hurt? Don't give up on him now.'

'Can I ask what the argument was about?' Endecott said.

She was tenacious, I'll give her that, but I couldn't allow her to get side-tracked.

'It was something about nothing. One of those silly spats all couples have from time to time. I can't even remember what started it.'

Was that the first lie I'd told her? Of course I could remember the argument, I could remember it word for word, and that's why we had to find Oscar so I could take it all back.

We'd been inseparable since the day we met. Beth and Oscar. Oscar and Beth. You couldn't have one without the other because we came as a pair. People envied us because Oscar and I, well, we were still going strong after all these years. My heart fluttered, and I caught my breath, every time I saw him unexpectedly in a crowd. I didn't know who I was without him. So much of me was tied up in him that it made no sense to me that he wasn't here by my side as the storm clouds tumbled in, talking about making sure the drains were clear of leaves.

Endecott was dishing out platitudes she'd learned on a training course that were meant for other families, not people like us. She was trying to prepare me for the worst but she should have saved her breath. I had to believe they would find him while I stayed home and waited.

And waited.

4

Waited, while the rest of the world carried on laughing, and bickering, and attaching importance to matters that were so insignificant I wanted to scream, 'How can you pretend the world isn't in turmoil?' And so I prayed, I pleaded and I begged. If Oscar could be delivered safely home, I would never take him for granted again. Never snap, never scold, never nag.

I wanted to be out there looking for him, but I was no asset to the search party of two dogs, the Peak Rescue Team, and a drone. Oscar's car was in a lay-by in the shadow of Wilders Pass. The keys were in the ignition, which wasn't like Oscar at all. Me? Sure, I often leave keys in the outside of doors or the insides of cars, but I'm forgetful like that. Oscar remembers everything; the names of his employees' kids, the number plate of his first car, even the way someone slighted him eight years ago. He'd never forget to come home to us.

Endecott assured me they were searching in the right area now. It was a matter of time, and a matter of clinging on to the little hope we had left. But with plenty of crags and caves, Oscar could be anywhere. The Peak District was treacherous terrain for those who weren't familiar with the landscape but Oscar and his brother, Harvey, had made these hills their playground from the moment their mother cut her apron strings. The Limestone valleys of the White Peak with stepping-stones across rivers, and the dramatic ridges and gritty moorland of the Dark Peak made up over five hundred square miles of land, and somewhere, in the midst of it all, my husband was waiting for me to find him and bring him home.

Harvey was heading up the search party. Though he volunteered for the Peak Rescue Team, and had located countless climbers who were injured or lost, he'd never imagined that, one day, he'd be looking for his own brother. If anyone could

5

find Oscar, it would be Harvey. He was the level-headed one of the two. He and Oscar shared that unbreakable bond that meant they loved and fought fiercely, and Lord help anyone who got between them. The Lomas brothers were a team to be reckoned with. They climbed together, holidayed together, and ran a business shoulder to shoulder. They were terrible practical jokers, always setting the other one up through prank phone calls and in-jokes. Though they were equal business partners, it was Oscar who captained that ship. Harvey preferred to take a less visible role, but you couldn't have one without the other. Oscar was as extroverted as Harvey was introverted. Oscar was flamboyant where Harvey was measured. They each needed the other for balance. Harvey was the one who talked about projected income and cost-saving measures while Oscar went after orders they couldn't fulfil and expanded their premises without planning permission. Harvey knew as well as I did that the possibility of Oscar taking his own life ... well, there was no possibility. It was ridiculous the police were even considering it.

The coming storm was all anyone was talking about. News reporters would have us believe that three months of rain would be falling in the space of forty-eight hours. Flood warnings were already in place. People in picturesque market towns were dragging sandbags into doorways and driveways, buying in extra milk and bread with tins upon tins of store cupboard essentials. But Oscar knew all of this, we'd watched the news together, commented on how impossible the roads would be. Oscar took risks, it was one of the things I loved about him, but never with the weather. I knew he would've been home by now if it was within his power.

Judge me if you must, I don't care, but I didn't report him

missing until lunchtime even though I hadn't seen him since Friday night. Though I was concerned, and tried his phone twice, I didn't immediately assume the worst. Why would I? I supposed Oscar had taken himself off somewhere to sulk, still angry with me for the way I'd reacted to our quarrel. He could have stayed the night with Harvey and Miriam after one too many brandies. It wouldn't have been the first time.

'Have you checked with family and friends?' Endecott asked.

'No one has heard from him since Friday night when his brother spoke to him on the phone. His parents are on their way up from Cornwall now. They've not heard from him at all this week. There's not really anyone else to call. They're a tight-knit family. Sorry, not *they*. I mean *we*.'

DC Endecott said I had to be patient and, as anyone who knows me will tell you, patience is something I excel at. There's power in my patience. No one can bide time, fill time, or spend time as I do. Patience brings all good things to bear and, as my father used to say, *time has a way of burying your enemies*.

I'd just taken a dozen lemon and blueberry muffins out of the oven. They were cooling alongside the tray of chocolate brownies. Oscar would be hungry when he came home. I bake. It's what I do. I bake to celebrate, to console, and to nourish. You can chart my stress levels by how much time I spend in my kitchen.

It might've been the heat from the oven, or the tension in the house, but there didn't seem to be enough oxygen left in there for me. I flung open the door but the air was just as thick outside. My clothes were sticking to me as I slipped into the garden, pulling at the neck of my T-shirt. My bra strap was twisted and digging into my shoulder but I didn't alter it. The pain was a welcome focus; a domestic cilice.

Clouds gathered over the hills, dark heads together in collusion, plotting destruction. The wind ruffled my hair as I sat heavily on the bench. I looked over my shoulder and saw our daughter at the window on the second floor. Honey's face was intent on the horizon as if she could spot her father and guide him home. She was the beacon in the window. If anyone could bring Oscar back to us, it's her.

The patio door slid open and I snapped my eyes shut.

'Mrs Lomas?'

The first drops of rain fell on my head.

'Beth?' Louder this time. The detective's feet tapped down the three steps towards me but I didn't look at her. I could tell that she judged me for not reporting Oscar's disappearance soon enough, and for baking cakes while rescue teams risked their lives. The slight arch of her right eyebrow had suggested she thought me careless for misplacing something as precious as a husband. She was everything I wasn't. Organised, resilient, strong, authoritative. I bet she'd never gone to pay for groceries and realised she'd left her purse by the kettle, or put petrol in her diesel car, never forgotten that the clocks had gone back and ended up an hour late for an important meeting. I would hazard a guess that she'd never been late for anything, whereas I couldn't remember when I'd ever been on time.

I opened my eyes.

'Sorry,' I said. 'Just needed a moment. Is there any news?'

It was the same question I'd asked half a dozen times already.

But this time the answer was different.

'Yes,' she said. 'I'm afraid there is.'

Sorry.

CHAPTER TWO

Molly Ingram

'Will you?' he asked.

Molly looked down at Vijay. His keen eyes shining with a hint of tears. He was on bended knee, and there was a small blue velvet box in his hand. Molly's stomach lurched as if she was on a rollercoaster. It was the pause after a long climb to the top.

This was what she'd hoped for through all the tedious trysts, the dead end dates, and the embarrassing encounters with the friend-of-a-friend whose ink hadn't yet dried on their decree nisi. When she'd imagined this moment, she'd seen herself crying happy tears, but in a pretty way of course, saying 'yes' as her voice caught in her throat at the over-whelming emotion.

She'd never wanted to be anybody's other half. Didn't need the kids, the cul-de-sac, the sensible car that was economical and good for the environment. She wasn't cut out for domes-ticity, but she wanted to be loved. Accepted. Maybe, occasionally, looked after. She felt like she was missing out on a world that was only open to couples. You had to collect all the stamps on your social passport before you got invited to the bank holi-day barbecues and the New Year's Eve dinners. As a singleton, she was treated as a liability. The odd number who'd corrupt your children and run off with your husband, given half a chance. She wished she knew what was stopping her from answering what should have been the easiest question of her life.

'Well?' he prompted.

God, why wasn't she saying something? *Anything*.

Vijay had been a fortuitous encounter at work. He should have been meeting with someone else about recruiting a Director of Finance for his company. Molly had shaken Vijay's hand and said, 'Change of plan. Valerie isn't well today; you'll be meeting with me. Molly Ingram, Chief Executive. Can I get you a coffee?' Five months later and here they were in Tuscany and there was a balcony, a sunset, and a ring.

'Vijay, I don't know what to say. Are you sure?'

Vijay smiled, 'I've never felt more sure about anything in my life.'

Molly put her hand on the railings of the balcony and looked over the side. She could jump down without much difficulty, a slight bend of the knee, hope to avoid a twisted ankle, and then run for the hills. And then what? She couldn't keep running every time things got uncomfortable. She hadn't told him everything there was to know about her. Would he still want to marry her if he knew what an absolute mess she'd made of her life? What would he think when he found out the business was going under? That she was damaged goods?

Look at him, on one knee, with the most beautiful diamond ring she'd ever seen. If she said *no* to him now, he'd be humiliated. But on the other hand, to say *yes*?

Vijay swayed a little in front of her. He really should have proposed in a carpeted area. She had to give him an answer if only to save his knees.

'Vijay ...'

She couldn't take her eyes off that diamond. She did love pretty things. And she loved long weekends in Tuscany. Would it be so terrible to say yes and make a kind man happy?

A phone rang.

It took her a second or two to realise that the noise was coming from her mobile on the table. She frowned and thought, *Can't you see we're having a moment here?*

She snatched it up to silence it, but saw that it was Beth calling.

'Sorry, Vijay, do you mind? I need to get this.' She turned her back on him. 'Beth? Is everything okay?'

CHAPTER THREE

Beth Lomas

No.

He couldn't be dead, not my Oscar.

Honey had watched from the window as I'd shrunk from the piercing words of 'body' and 'too late'. She was at the door and throwing herself at me before I could get out of the rain. She felt small and frail in my arms. Even as I'd told Honey that her father's body had been found at Cloud Drop, the words stuck in my throat like lies. I stuttered and stumbled over the impossible lines that had been fed to me by the police.

At fifteen years old, Gabe towered above us both as he appeared behind his sister with an emotionless face and clenched fists. I reached out for him but he stepped away. He lifted his chin, a question without words.

'They've found your dad, Gabe. He's ...'

There was only a slight change in Gabe's facial expression as he braced himself for the next word. 'Gone.'

His lips parted to let out a long sigh. His fists unclenched as if knowledge was a relief rather than a millstone. 'What happened?' he asked.

His voice was controlled. More like his father than me.

'I don't know,' I answered. 'They're trying to piece it all

together. He must have fallen. Uncle Harvey will be able to tell us more when he gets here.'

Honey leaned away from me and towards her brother. Her tormentor, her protector, her best friend, and her sworn enemy. He pulled her to him and turned his back on me as if he was shielding her from my cruel words. Her cries were anguished and raw.

I shouldn't have been surprised that the children had reacted to the news in the same way they responded to most things in life; Gabe with silence as the shutters came down on his feelings, Honey all noise and emotion.

'It's okay,' I said. I touched Gabe's back and I felt his muscles tense across his shoulders.

'No, Mum, it's not,' he said. His voice was muffled by Honey's golden crown of hair.

I shook my head. Of course it wasn't, but what else could I say? There was nothing I could do. Words were all I had.

Nothing felt real anymore. I wished I could cry if only to show them – to show Endecott – that my heart was breaking, that I was broken beyond repair. But instead, I stood in the rain, wondering why there was a hole in my chest where my heart used to be. I should have been gathering the children to me, squeezing them tight, but instead I watched them as if the mere inches between us were a gap of miles.

'C'mon Honey,' Gabe spat. 'Let's leave Mum to her *grief*.' He was angry with me and I couldn't blame him. Without the energy to stop them, I let them go. I'd make it up to them later but, for now, I turned my face to the sky and opened my mouth to catch raindrops on my tongue.

Endecott was still there, still talking in my ear, telling me what would happen next, who to call for assistance. When she said, 'If there's anything you need . . .' I turned to stare at her. We both knew she couldn't give me what I craved.

'I'd like you to leave,' I said.

But before she could, Oscar's parents arrived in a shake of umbrellas and a stamping of feet. Esther knew that Oscar was gone before she even asked, I could see it in the set of her face. Lowry told them everything she'd told me, saving me the job of repeating her assumptions, before she left the house in a head-down dash to her car.

Vince and Esther huddled. Their tears were silent but I could see Esther's hands shaking, and hear her breath catch on the jagged corner of her grief. She was 'doing her best' as if awards would be given out for the best stiff-upper-lip, best supporting role, best costume. She was sure to sweep the board. I wasn't even in the running.

I wanted to say to them, *Don't cry. This is all a big mistake. Just you wait. Oscar will walk back through that door by dinner-time.*

Vince carried their bags to the top floor, to the place we ambitiously called the Guest Room, while Esther and I stood side by side at the front window watching rain bounce off the pavement. I didn't comment on her tears, she didn't comment on my lack of them.

My mother-in-law was dressed entirely in black, and not the faded milky black of half my wardrobe, but jet-black, razor-sharp black, impenetrable. Had she known that her missing son was on his way to becoming her dead son when she set off in the car for the long drive north? Had she packed alternative outfits for good news? All that was absent was a veil, and then she'd be the perfect picture of grief.

She'd never liked me, though Oscar said I imagined it. She was protective, he'd said. No one was ever going to be good enough for her boy. I didn't believe it was as simple as the clichéd tensions between mother and wife because she had no such problems with Harvey's wife, the marvellous Miriam. This was personal and would have been the same whether or not I'd married her favourite son. As soon as I'd admitted that I didn't know the difference between a white wine and a red wine glass, I was judged unsuitable. Bad breeding was not to be tolerated. Nor was being scatty. It was fair to say that everything about me brought Esther out in ugly red blotches on her chest and neck. I was the human equivalent of hives.

To hear Esther speak, Oscar was a handful. A cheeky chap who always fell on his feet, while the rest of the world lay at them. To me, he was strong and decisive, charming and confident. He was easily frustrated and ruthless in getting his own way, but he had such conviction that he was doing the right thing that he never felt guilt or shame.

Poor Harvey. I wonder whether he ever felt second best. Quieter, less handsome than his older brother, Harvey used to joke that his parents only had him in case they needed spare parts for Oscar.

The relationship between Oscar and his mother was complicated. With adoration came frustration. Both of them were colossal personalities who never backed down. She envisaged him going off to university and becoming a doctor or lawyer; something that would give her bragging rights at Tuesday night Bridge. But Oscar preferred to take a relaxed attitude to his exams and follow his dad into the family lumber business.

As a girl who left the local comprehensive with a handful of mediocre A levels – and general studies and art don't count, apparently – I was a big part of the problem. Esther said I held him back, but she wildly overestimated my power.

Oscar went on to prove her wrong. He had a real interest in the family business and worked hard with Harvey to grow and expand it. She forgave him but, somehow, not me. It wasn't that she was outright rude – her impeccable manners wouldn't allow it. Most of it was done under the guise of being helpful; such as paying for a cleaner for six months because the housework was 'obviously too much' for me. And sending books on child-rearing to help with Gabe's 'discipline problems'. And, generously, each Christmas she bought me a new cookbook – for weight loss. But now she was here, we were united in our grief and she was the one person who felt Oscar's loss as deeply as I did. And until Molly got here, Esther was all I had.

I felt like I should apologise to Esther because when Oscar had been living with her, she'd kept him safe. I didn't. I never stopped to ask why he'd been acting strangely recently, or why he was working later and later every day. Why? The question was in every look that Esther gave me. Why didn't I stop him? Why didn't I do something?

Why did he ever marry me?

We gravitated towards the kitchen and began the endless cycle of boiling the kettle and drinking tea. I opened the cupboard doors and closed them again, looking for a sign, a miracle, anything to stop the nightmare. Esther kept telling me to sit down, drink, eat something. But if I stopped, I'd never start again. I kept thinking that Oscar must have left me a message. Something beyond the '*sorry*' note to explain what was going on.

The rain lashed against the windows, but the night had fallen and I couldn't see anything beyond my own reflection. I ran hot water into the sink and washed up so carelessly that I broke a wine glass, slicing the fleshy part of my hand between my thumb and forefinger. I waited for pain but it didn't come. How curious that the numbness in my heart had spread to my hands.

Blood bloomed in the water. I watched, fascinated by how easily a life source could drain from a person. How long would it take for me to lose consciousness? I lifted my hand and watched the blood snake its way down my wrist. I stretched my thumb away from my finger and the cut gaped like a mouth mid-scream. Esther yanked my hand towards her and tutted.

'You'll need a plaster,' she said, wrapping my hand in a tea-towel.

'I need stitches,' I said, averting my eyes.

'Nonsense.'

She used that word around me more often than I liked. When I was worried about the pressure of exams on the children; *nonsense*. When I was considering starting my own catering business; *nonsense*. When I suggested I wasn't too old to wear a miniskirt in the summer; *absolute nonsense*.

In this case, she was right. A cut was irrelevant. Physical pain was no competition for emotional anguish. The human body was designed to heal from cuts and breaks, but there were no assurances that emotional wounds would ever heal.

I heard the front door open and spun around to see the top of a man's head as he shook the rain off his shoulders. Time froze; my heart lifted; my head swam. I opened my mouth to yell Oscar's name but, as he raised his head, I saw the pale, lined face of his brother and all I could say was, 'Oh.'

Harvey's steps were slow and heavy along the hallway and into the kitchen. He left a trail of dark footprints on the tiled floor.

'Harvey?' I said.

With that one word, I urged him to tell me that the police were wrong, that it wasn't my husband they'd found at the bottom of Cloud Drop. Just a misunderstanding. A prank taken too far.

He shook his head. 'He's gone, Beth. Oscar's gone.'

He covered his face with his hands and hunched his shoulders. His fingers were red. Blood had dried on the knuckles of his right hand. Vince and Esther were at his side in a second to *coo* and to *shush*. Harvey's whole body seemed to shake and, though his grief came like a torrent, he made no sound. I backed away, closing my eyes and gripping my bleeding hand to my chest. Harvey couldn't be Harvey without Oscar. I couldn't be me. Watching Harvey crumble at the loss of his brother was yet another cut. Oscar wasn't only mine to lose.

Oscar's body had been 'recovered', Harvey said. It sounded as though he was a broken-down vehicle at the side of the road, or a forgotten password, rather than someone we all depended on. In a person, *recovered* gave the impression of getting better, or moving on from illness. A recovered alcoholic. A full recovery.

'But it can't be him, Harvey. I'd know.'

Harvey didn't look at me, only spoke to his parents to tell them that he'd found Oscar crumpled on a ledge towards the bottom of Cloud Drop.

One of the most photographed spots in the Peak District, it was as if the water came straight from the rock beneath your feet, arching outwards and disappearing again into the gaping cavern below. The underground rivers were too dangerous to explore, though that didn't stop people from trying. There were rumours that some had thrown themselves off

18

the top of Cloud Drop but their bodies were never found because of the vast underground caverns. Though you could still walk through the valley at the foot of Cloud Drop, the way to the top was blocked twenty years ago by iron railings and signs warning of danger.

'They think he's been dead for twenty-four hours,' he said. 'No,' I said. 'No.'

There was the saying that 'if something sounded too good to be true, it probably was'. I'd like to think the same could be said of news that was too painful to bear because that kind of thing can't happen to us. We're not *those* kinds of people. We have two kids, a mortgage, and we holiday in the same place on the south coast every year. We're predictable – some might say boring. We don't do death, drama and detectives. We're too normal to be the subject of a newspaper headline.

How could I accept that Oscar was dead when it had taken me long enough to even notice that he was missing? On Friday night he'd slept in the home office at the bottom of the garden. We liked to call it 'the Cabin' so it sounded more luxurious than a shed with electricity. He'd been just metres away from where I slept, but it may as well have been another city. I didn't know what mood he'd been in when he'd left the next morning and I hadn't been able to say which clothes Oscar had been wearing when he disappeared, even when I looked in his wardrobe to see what was missing. He owned more clothes than I did. He'd always been a peacock of a man, my Oscar. Gabe hadn't paid attention when his father had said goodbye, his eyes glued to a phone screen, no doubt.

I'd noticed that Oscar's walking boots were gone, but only because of the gap they'd left in the shoe rack under the stairs. I'd often looked at them, noticing the greater signs of wear and tear on the left heel. He always wore through his left shoe first. A slight twist of his foot, a heavier stride. His other shoes were replaced regularly, but his tatty old boots had served him well and he was putting off the day they would finally hang up their laces.

'Any distinguishing marks? Tattoos?' the police had asked when I first reported him missing.

'No. His mother would kill him.'

'How heavy was he?'

'I don't know. I mean he wasn't fat or skinny. He was normal. Average.'

'Height?'

'Oh, I know this one. He liked to say he was six-foot tall but he was actually an inch short.'

A whole life, and a whole man, reduced to facts and figures on a sheet of paper. But there would never be enough words to sum up what we'd lost. Absent was the man who used to get on all fours so that the kids could ride him like a pony. The man who'd camp out in the garden, build forts and have water fights, always letting the children catch him in a game of tag. Vanished was the storyteller, the shoulder to cry on, the joke-teller, our rock. There'd be no more cups of tea brought to me in bed while I was half asleep, doors wouldn't be opened, and no one else would be able to quote eighties films at me or make me feel safe in the dark the way that he did.

But, more than that, our certain future had disappeared. Oscar wouldn't walk Honey down the aisle, cry at the birth of his first grandchild, or help decorate new houses. Anything that any of us did from now on would only highlight how much was missing.

CHAPTER FOUR

Beth Lomas

Miriam Lomas burst into the house without knocking. I recognised her steps in the hallway. My sister-in-law was the only person I knew who always wore high heels regardless of weather or terrain.

'I can't believe it,' she said, looking frantically around the room. 'Harvey phoned and said . . . I mean, is it true? Oscar's dead? Where's Harvey? I need to see him.'

'Harvey's on the phone, love. Letting people know the news.' Vince nodded towards the closed door of the living room. He got to his feet and opened his arms wide. Miriam went to him. In her heels, she was taller than him.

'Oh, Vince . . . Esther. I can't believe it.'

'None of us can,' Esther croaked.

I watched Miriam as she played the role earmarked for me. Vince wiped a tear off her cheek and Esther reached out and took her hand. They were united in their grief, yet I felt removed from them because of mine. I could see their grief but I couldn't feel it. I couldn't understand why they'd accepted the worst without a fight.

'Where are the children?' Miriam asked me. 'I should go to them.' They were the first words she'd said to me since she'd arrived. No sympathy. No hugs. I'd known Miriam for nine years – ever since she'd started working for the family business as Head of HR and Harvey had fallen hard for her. We'd never known Harvey in love like that before. We thought he was a perpetual bachelor, and then in walked Miriam with her long legs, her sharp mind, and Harvey was lost. She was responsible for taking Harvey away from us, even if it was only by degrees. He had been like the brother I'd never had, until thoughts of Miriam occupied his every waking moment.

'Gabe and Honey are upstairs,' I said.

I don't know why she pretended to be the doting aunt when all she ever did was buy them gifts that I'd forbidden. Games for Gabe that were rated for eighteen-year-olds when he was still only a boy, make-up for Honey back when she was still playing with dolls.

'This will destroy them,' she said. 'And Harvey ... Imagine finding your brother like that.' Her voice cracked and Vince placed his hand on her bony shoulder.

'I know, love. I know.'

'I only saw Oscar on Friday. There was nothing that suggested ... We all know the strain he's been under at work with these redundancies, but I was dealing with that. What made him take off on his own like that? And in this weather. Something must have happened to ...' She stopped speaking abruptly and covered her mouth.

I didn't tell her about the argument, or the fact that I hadn't seen Oscar since Friday. They already had a low enough opinion of me.

'They're saying he did it on purpose,' said Vince. 'Jumped.'

Miriam's heels clacked across the floor and back again. 'No,' she said. 'Oscar wouldn't. He just wouldn't. They can't say things like that without evidence.'

I touched my neck where it felt like ants were crawling up and down my spine. I needed a *proper* drink to calm my nerves.

'He would have said something if it had got that bad,' Miriam said. 'There was nothing, was there? Nothing that made you think . . .'

I looked up, surprised to find she was talking to me. 'No,' I said. 'Nothing.'

She nodded, satisfied.

Harvey came into the kitchen saying, 'I've done all I can for now.' He looked surprised, but not happy, to see Miriam. For a moment, they stared at each other and we all stood in silence. I saw Miriam's gaze slip to Harvey's bloodied knuckles. He must have noticed it too because he folded his arms, tucking his hands out of sight. 'I'm done in. Might head home.'

'The police think it was suicide, do they?' said Miriam. 'I hope you told them that was ridiculous.'

'I told them everything I know, but they'll come to their own conclusions based on the evidence, not because of what I say.'

'Right,' said Miriam folding her arms to mirror Harvey.

'Right,' Harvey repeated.

Miriam and I didn't often share a point of view, but she and I were sure of the fact that Oscar hadn't taken his own life.

'When do they think it happened?' she asked.

'Saturday morning,' Harvey said.

'But you were with him on Saturday morning,' Miriam said.

Harvey glared at her, shook his head a fraction. 'I told you. I didn't meet him in the end. I went straight to the office.'

'Right.'

'Right.'

I watched them intently. Something was going on between them, a friction I hadn't seen before.

'Are they at least considering that this could have been an accident? That he slipped?' Miriam said.

'For goodness' sake!' Esther stood up and brushed non-existent crumbs from the front of her pleated black trousers. I cowered and stepped backwards. She looked from Miriam to Vince. 'If no one else is going to say it, I will.'

'Don't, love,' Vince said. 'We're all tired, let's talk about this tomorrow.'

'I don't believe in leaving things unsaid.'

I braced myself against the edge of the sink, pushing my plaster and feeling the skin split open again. I was already shaking my head. I looked up at the window over the sink and the rain that was lashing down. I flinched as I caught sight of a face staring back at me, but it was only my reflection.

'The only logical explanation,' Esther continued, 'is that someone pushed him. Can't you see what's in front of you? Oscar was murdered.'

I didn't sleep that night, and from the noises I heard downstairs, I guessed that Esther and Vince were the same. Grief wasn't how I expected it. This felt more like fear. I jumped at every noise, my hand to my heart which wasn't beating to the right rhythm anymore. A knot in my stomach stopped me from eating, stopped me from standing up straight. I couldn't get warm, couldn't re-engage with the world around me.

Oscar wasn't meant to die first. We'd talked about this over too much wine and too little sleep in the early days of parenthood. We agreed that he'd be well looked after if I died before him. He had friends and family to rally round him and make sure he wanted for nothing. I told him I'd want him to remarry, and I pretended not to be offended when he readily agreed. We didn't talk about what would happen if I lived longer than him, because it was inconceivable that the world could be so cruel. Ours was a good life, no better or worse than anyone else's, but it was good enough for me, that's for sure.

I was already sitting at the kitchen table when Gabe and Honey came downstairs in their school uniforms. Gabe's shirt was untucked, his tie was loose, and his hair unbrushed. Honey was every inch the school prefect. Her skirt was regulation length, shoes shined, hair pulled off her face into a neat ponytail. It could have been any other day; a normal day. And we could have been a normal family.

'What are you doing?' I said.

'What's it look like?' Gabe took two clean bowls from the dishwasher.

'You're not going to school, are you? You know you can stay home as long as you want?'

Gabe said, 'And do what?'

He was right. What could we do? The accepted norm was that we would sit in rooms where the curtains were closed, bundled up tissues in our hands, trying to understand what had happened to us, and why. I had no desire to do anything else but sit and stare into space but, for the children, normality was to be hounded until it was commonplace.

Gabe offered Honey a bowl but she shook her head. 'Not hungry'.

'You have to eat something, sweetie,' I said. 'How about some toast?'

'I can't.'

'Some fruit then?'

Gabe said, 'Mum, leave it, okay? She'll eat when she wants to. We're not kids. We can look after ourselves.'

I bit back a retort and turned away. I heard him mutter under his breath. 'Which is a good job, really. Seeing as you're pretty much useless.'

Honey poked Gabe's arm and pursed her lips. A slight twitch of the head warning him to stop.

'Actually, Gabe, d'you know something?' I said. 'I might not get it right, but I am trying. And right now, this is all we've got; the three of us. Your dad would want us to pull together.'

'No, he wouldn't. Dad didn't give a shit about anyone but himself.'

He stormed out of the kitchen. I tried to follow but I'd been sitting still for so long that my legs had grown stiff and, before I could stand up, Gabe was already at the front door.

'Gabe. Wait! Don't you dare leave this—'

The door slammed behind him, reverberating through the house like a cannon shot.

'. . . house.'

I sank back into my chair and rested my head on my hands. Was I meant to give him space, or bombard him with love? I felt Honey's arms snake around me. 'I can stay home if you like,' she said. I would have sat like that all day if I could, breathing her in, thanking God for her. So conscientious, my girl. More like me than Oscar. A rule follower, a good girl.

I would only let them go to school – or anywhere – on the

understanding that they came straight home afterwards. If they didn't answer their phone when I rang, or were as little as fifteen minutes late, I would immediately call the police. I wouldn't make the same mistake again.

'It's up to you, darling,' I said. 'I don't want you to stay home for my sake. But if you'd like a few days to come to terms with things ...'

She nodded. I noticed then how tired she looked. Honey hadn't slept last night either.

'Mum?'

'Yes?'

'I heard you all talking last night. Is it true that Dad killed himself?'

'No, it's not. It was just a terrible accident.'

No matter how many signs pointed to suicide, I wouldn't accept it. It was hard enough to accept that Oscar had died, but impossible to consider what they were suggesting. When Esther said he'd been pushed, I felt a spark of hope like someone had lit a match in a dark room. I moved towards it before it burned out. Even when it extinguished, I could still see the imprint when I closed my eyes.

What kind of woman actually *hopes* that her husband was pushed to his death? I'll tell you who – a woman like me, who can't cope with the guilt for one second longer. Whose only hope is that she couldn't have seen this coming, couldn't have done something differently, and couldn't have stopped it. If someone else had done this to him then I could be angry with *them*, not Oscar. Not myself. But if it really was suicide, then who could I blame except myself?

I was the custodian of Oscar's memory now and he had to be remembered by his life, not his death. We all knew about the gold standard end – the one where you pass peacefully in your sleep at a ripe old age, with loved ones crouched, weeping, at your bedside. We aspire to slip away quickly and painlessly in our sleep. You get extra points for being in your own bed when it happens.

Oscar managed none of those things, and now his death would be held against him like a character flaw.

And the part I played in his death would be mine.

CHAPTER FIVE

Molly Ingram

Five gin and tonics and one commercial flight later and, to be honest, Molly was feeling a little bit groggy. She wrestled her suitcase onto two different trains to get to Hellas Mill. It crossed her mind to abandon the case at the station and buy all new clothes when she got to Beth's. But then she remembered that a) she had no money to buy new clothes with, and b) unattended cases at stations led to the appearance of the bomb disposal unit.

She missed the days when she would have jumped in a taxi and to hell with the cost. This train didn't have a first-class carriage even if she could have afforded to travel in it. She'd forgotten the grubby reality of rural trains rattling along at speeds that a granny on a mobility scooter could outpace.

Molly checked her forehead for a fever, but her hand was so clammy it was difficult to know whether there was more to this headache than a racing mind. She ran her tongue over her teeth, half-expecting to feel the braces that had been a fixture throughout her school years. Every mile bringing her closer to where she grew up seemed to pile on puppy fat and social awkwardness. Molly didn't have a nostalgic bone in her whole body. If she never visited Hellas Mill again, she wouldn't mind. Honest to God, she wouldn't give it another thought.

The bad memories were enough to taint everything around her. And what do you do with bad memories? You bury them, you pretend you can't hear them calling your name.

The news still hadn't sunk in that Oscar had died. It didn't sound like the kind of thing Oscar Lomas would do. Christ, she would have been less surprised if he'd had himself cryogenically frozen so that future generations could marvel at his perfection. He wasn't the kind of man who would slip quietly into the night. There had to be a twist.

A mistake.

A big old joke.

Perhaps this was one of his elaborate ruses. Surely he would burst out of the coffin at the funeral and say, 'Gotcha!' And everyone would laugh and say 'Ah, Oscar. You got us good that time.'

Before she saw Beth, Molly would have to rearrange her face into an acceptable mask of sadness. It shouldn't be that difficult, she *was* sad for Beth and the kids. As far as Oscar was concerned though, her overriding emotion was anger. She was furious with him for breaking her best-friend's heart, leaving her godchildren without a dad, and – perhaps this sounded selfish – ruining a perfect marriage proposal. And that was before she even let herself think about how much unfinished business she and Oscar had. Typical of him to check-out before he had to face the music. Molly couldn't help but think that, as the *proverbial* was about to hit the fan, Oscar had been gifted a get-out-of-jail-free card. She wondered whether Beth knew that Oscar owed Molly money. If not, she could hardly bring it up now, could she.

'Bastard,' she said aloud. Molly's voice carried across the train aisle and a woman with a young child turned in her seat to scowl. Molly resisted the urge to flip the woman her middle finger. She wasn't completely without decorum.

Molly took her mobile phone out of her Birkin bag and scrolled through her texts. It took her a couple of minutes to find Frazer's number because she'd saved it without a name associated with it. They'd decided it was better this way. Very cloak and dagger.

Call off the dogs she typed. OL died at the weekend. Nothing for us here. Don't suppose I could get a refund?

She knew she'd been mistaken to pay up front without so much as a handshake to seal the deal. But, to be fair to the guy, she was asking him to take on risky – perhaps even illegal – work and she'd already told him she was close to bankruptcy. She'd offered him a percentage of whatever he managed to get out of Oscar but, for some reason, he didn't trust her.

While she waited for a reply, Molly looked out of the train window. The river had burst its banks and fields were flooded, glistening in the late afternoon sunshine, looking more like glass than the patchwork of grass she was used to seeing. The blue skies held no hint of the catastrophic storms of the last twenty-four hours. She really should have called her dad to check he was okay. But if she phoned him, she would have to admit that she was coming back to Hellas Mill for a few days and he would expect to see her. There was only so much she could cope with.

Instead, she was on a rickety train heading to comfort a woman who was yet to realise that she was better off now her husband was dead. Even as a widow, Beth had better prospects than Molly who had no idea if she would still have a boyfriend, or a job by this time next week. This wasn't how she envisaged coming back 'home'. The only way to return to the place you grew up was in a blaze of glory to show your old school friends how rich, skinny and successful you were. Well, one out of three wasn't bad. They wouldn't call her roly-poly Molly ever again.

'The next station,' came a tinny voice over the tannoy, 'is Hellas Mill. Hellas Mill your next station.'

Molly bent forward in her seat as her stomach cramped, wishing she could put it down to an exotic illness rather than nerves. Standing up she checked her phone before stuffing it into her bag. No response from Frazer and nothing from Vijay either. She'd promised him that they would talk soon. He understood that the timing was all wrong. Her oldest friend had just become a widow. But, in her heart, she knew that the moment had passed, and if Molly was going to say yes, she'd have done it already. Oscar Lomas was still pulling strings from beyond the grave. Just when she thought she couldn't hate him more, he went and bloody died.

From the train station, her feet traced a well-worn path across the main road by the antique shop and past a new café which used to be a bank. Molly stood at the top of a narrow lane that led to Hellas Mill park and took three deep breaths. What did you say to someone who'd lost the love of their life?

As she looked about her, Molly realised that Hellas Mill hadn't changed much. This was both a curse and a blessing. At least she knew where she was going, but it was like stepping back in time, to a place where she'd been desperately unhappy. She walked down the familiar street and took the bridge over the impossibly fast-flowing river, her handbag over her arm and her case on wheels behind her. The park opened up, though it looked smaller than she remembered. Kids were playing football and a small train chugged backwards and for-wards giving five-minute rides for two pounds fifty.

The band-stand had been repainted white and green, but still looked largely the same. She used to hang around in the park in her teenage years, sipping on cans of pop, and sharing bags of ready salted. It was here she tried her first cigarette, her first swig of vodka. Both made her feel sick. It was also where she used to meet Barnaby Flint-Stanton. Thinking about him now made her feel more nauseated than cigarettes and alcohol ever did. This was why coming back here was such a bad idea. Too many memories.

Apart from her dad, who was largely oblivious to her exist-ence, Beth and the children were the only reason she would ever set foot back here. Everyone else had moved away, or died, or weren't worth bothering with. Hellas Mill was the kind of place you grew up in and retired to, but most of the living happened elsewhere. After Molly left to go to univer-sity, she never called Hellas Mill home again.

She'd met Beth at primary school. Cat Clarke had pulled Beth's pigtails and Molly had rushed to Beth's aid by barrel-ling the other girl over in what can only be described as a rugby tackle. They used to be so easy in each other's company – but, as they got older, they'd developed edges that didn't fit together anymore. They'd never admit it because they couldn't help but be drawn to each other, bonded by things that they never talked about. They understood each other in ways no one else could. And Beth was the most loyal and kindest per-son that Molly had ever met. Molly was sorry that Beth couldn't say the same about her.

As young girls, they had sleepovers at each other's houses where they'd eat jelly babies at midnight and share cans of warm lemonade. They'd whisper and giggle until tired parents in firm tones told them to '*keep it down in there!*' They told each other all their secrets, and – something more precious – their dreams.

They sniggered over first kisses and tried to make sense of overwhelming emotions. When their hearts were inevitably broken, they cried together, hugged, wrote poems about those who'd wronged them. And then under moons that always seemed to be full and low in the sky, they hatched their plots.

Innocent childhood memories ended when Barnaby's sister, Hattie, threw a birthday party, and called it a soirée. It was here that Barnaby took more than he should, that Molly lost more than she wanted, that Beth taught Barnaby a lesson he wouldn't forget. They promised to never say a word about that night. Not even to each other. But it was the thread that bound them still, even when they might have otherwise drifted apart.

Twice a year, they met up in London. Molly drank too much because she couldn't find the right words when she was sober. They talked of work, of love, of the children. They gossiped about so-and-so from their old school going to prison and that woman who used to work in the pub being a drug addict. For two afternoons a year they pretended their lives were perfect.

Beth had remained in the town where they grew up, while Molly had flown to a Russell Group university and soared into a job in the city. After starting her own recruitment consultancy, Molly's life revolved around fine meals and expensive champagne. She used to pity Beth, silently mock her narrow life. And then one day she realised that she was searching for something that Beth had had all along – a family; a place where she belonged.

CHAPTER SIX

Beth Lomas

The night of the argument

Beth had been watching the clock but she could have sworn the hands slowed until they almost stopped. Time was a tricky devil; it slowed when you wanted it to go faster, and sped up when you needed just a little bit more of it.

She'd practised what she was going to say to Oscar, mumbling and rephrasing words as she diced onion and fried spices. But when he came home – late – the kids were claiming starvation, dinner was ready, and the moment to '*have a quick word*' had passed. He hadn't noticed her being quiet through the meal, or the way she flinched when he leaned in to kiss her cheek. Otherwise, it was the same as every other Friday night. He was acting like a man with nothing to hide and Beth was starting to wonder whether she'd imagined the whole thing.

Oscar liked routine and so, like every week before it, Friday night was curry night. He didn't care whether it was Indian, Chinese or Thai, as long as it was highly spiced and served with an ice-cold beer. Friday was the one night of the week when neither of the children had clubs to attend after school. Dinner as a family was non-negotiable. It was where they caught up on each other's weeks and told funny stories.

No phones allowed at the table, no television on in the background. It was Beth's favourite night of the week.

Usually.

Gabe tutted. 'I was only asking.' He dropped his fork onto the table, spraying grains of rice over the white tablecloth.

'And I,' said Oscar, 'was only saying no. There will be no band practice in this house.'

'It's my house too!' Gabe shouted.

'Tell me that when you're paying the mortgage.'

Gabe was a growing teenage boy with a biological imperative to show who was top dog, and lately Oscar could do nothing right in his eyes. It never used to be like this. They used to be close enough for in-jokes that Beth didn't understand, but now it was the antagonism that she couldn't fathom. It was as if turning against his father had happened as he'd blown out the candles on his fifteenth birthday cake.

'Daddy,' Honey said, 'I got my speech and drama results today. I got a distinction.'

Honey was long past calling Oscar 'Daddy', but the more combative Gabe was, the more that Honey became Daddy's little girl. She was an expert at defusing difficult situations, but Beth wished it wasn't necessary.

'Well done, sweetie.' Oscar picked up her hand from her lap and kissed the back of it. 'Proud of you.'

There was a line drawn down the middle of the family. On one side Gabe and Oscar said – and did – whatever they wanted, and on the other side, Honey and Beth tidied up the destruction their performance left behind. What behaviour was she modelling for her daughter? Because she was certain that was where Honey had learned to cajole and to appease. Beth wasn't unhappy with her life, but she wanted something better for her children. She couldn't let Honey see her being a doormat, otherwise she'd never expect better for herself.

Gabe pushed his chair back from the table and stood up.

'Where are you going now?' Oscar asked.

'To my room to practise guitar. I assume that's still allowed. Or is it only mine if I pay rent?'

'Can you give the attitude a rest for once?' Oscar said, shaking his head.

As Gabe stormed out of the kitchen, Beth heard him mutter 'arsehole!'

His big passion in life was music. Making music was all he wanted to do, but Oscar said it was a dream for wasters and druggies. No son of his was going into the music business.

'Have you got much homework?' Beth asked Honey.

'Nope. Only revision for my history test.'

'Why don't you get on with that now?'

'Can I do it tomorrow?'

It was reasonable to expect a rest after a busy week at school, but Beth needed some time alone with Oscar.

'I'd prefer it if you made a start tonight.'

Honey moved silently from the room, but without complaint. Oscar drained the last of his beer and asked, 'Is there another one of these?'

Beth opened the fridge and pretended to take a moment to locate a bottle, steadying herself, putting off the conversation she was dreading. She'd misplaced the words she'd so carefully set aside.

'Osc?' she said, closing the door and taking the top off the bottle.

'Hmm?'

He looked tired, older. Why hadn't she seen it before?

'Harvey came round earlier,' Beth said.

'Oh yeah? What did he want?'

She handed him the beer. Froth pulsed at the mouth of the bottle and threatened to spill down the sides. Oscar sucked it away. She'd noticed that there were more beer bottles and wine bottles in the recycling bin than she remembered buying. Beth wondered how many of Oscar's late nights working in the Cabin at the bottom of the garden were fuelled by a bottle of red.

'Harvey was looking for you. He said you'd gone home early and your phone was switched off. He was worried.'

'Harv worries too much.'

'That's what I said. I said you must've had a meeting or something, and he'd got the wrong end of the stick.'

'Hmm.'

'Is that what happened?'

'What?' Oscar looked up from reading the label of his beer bottle.

'Is that what happened?' she asked. 'Did you have a meeting?'

'Yeah. These aren't my usual beers, are they? Tastes metallic.' He licked his lips and considered the bottle once more.

'They're the same ones we always get. You said I wasn't to buy anything else.'

Oscar shrugged and took another swig of beer, swilling it around his mouth like a fine wine.

'Anyway,' Beth said. 'You were saying that you left work early to go to a meeting?'

Beth stood in front of Oscar with folded arms, then decided it looked too confrontational and dropped them to her side.

'And? There's not much else to say. You know how work stuff bores you.'

She nearly turned away. Could've done. It would have saved so much heartache if she'd chosen to stay in the dark. But then she thought of Honey, and the example she was setting her. She and Oscar were partners. His problems were her problems too. She could help him, if only he'd let her.

'I was just wondering if something's going on that I should know about?' She grimaced as if she were embarrassed to bring it up.

Oscar sat back in his chair and tilted it until he was balancing on the back two legs. He put the bottle on the table so fiercely that it frothed over the neck again. Beth felt the colour rising in her cheeks.

'There have been late-night calls that you don't want me to hear. I see you talking on the phone in the Cabin after I've gone up to bed.' She pointed to the window, unnecessarily.

Still, Oscar remained silent. Beth had hoped he would be relieved to unburden himself of the secret that was eating him up, but he wasn't going to make it easy for her.

'I'm not stupid, Oscar.'

Oscar raised an eyebrow as if to say '*really?*'

'I know when something isn't quite right.'

'What exactly are you saying?' Oscar asked. His eyes narrowed and his jaw tensed.

'You've been ... preoccupied lately. I was worried about you and so I started looking into ...'

Beth looked over her shoulder, checking that neither of the children had reappeared.

Oscar was quick to interrupt. 'What? You started checking up on me?'

Beth put up her hands in front of her. She needed to calm him down before he lost his temper. 'No, darling, it's not like that at all. Harvey's worried about you too. He says you've been acting strangely at work and . . .'

'So, you and Harvey have been talking about me behind my—?'

'No! Not really.' She closed her eyes for a moment as if by doing so she could start over. 'I know when something is on your mind, and all I've been trying to do is work out what has been bothering you. I thought, maybe, I could help.'

'A regular Miss Marple, aren't you?' Oscar stood up and took his phone out of his pocket. He used his thumb to unlock it. 'Want to read my texts? There are emails too. Here, why don't you look through them?' His voice was getting louder.

'Oscar, no, that's not what I . . .'

'Go on, you obviously don't trust me.'

'It's not that.'

'What is it then? What is it that you think you know?' He slammed his phone onto the table between them. The silence that followed seemed louder than all the shouting. All Beth could hear was the slow ticking of the kitchen clock. A sound that she'd never noticed until now.

She cleared her throat. 'Harvey wasn't the only visitor I had today.' Beth touched the back of her neck and rubbed her shoulder. 'There was someone else.'

Oscar frowned. 'Who?'

Beth knew that face – loved every inch of it – so, as much as he tried to look like he had no idea what she was talking about, she recognised the start of panic behind his eyes.

'It's okay,' she said. 'I know. I should've guessed earlier. I just wish you'd have felt able to talk to me before it came to this. So, I suppose the question now is what are we going to do about it?'

Oscar scratched the back of his head. Beth thought she saw the moment he considered playing dumb, but then realised he was left with no choice but to come clean. His shoulders sagged. 'For God's sake, Beth.' He shook his head. 'It's not that big a deal. Especially when you've been married as long as we have. I suppose you believed everything she told you, did you? Didn't stop to think that she had an agenda here? You're such a bloody mug.'

'What?'

'You're going to pretend that everything in our marriage is perfect, are you? I didn't tell you because I knew you'd over-react. I've been under pressure at work, and she was there for me when I was having a bad day. That's all. It doesn't have to change anything. Grow up.'

Beth sank into the nearest chair before her legs gave way. For a moment she thought she might faint and seconds passed before she was able to breathe evenly again. How had they turned into one of those couples? How had she turned into one of *those* wives?

'An affair?' she said, looking up at him. Perhaps this was one of his sick jokes. Yes, that's it. And then he'd tell her, 'Nah, but the house is being repossessed,' and she'd be relieved because, of the two options, that was the one that wouldn't kill her.

Oscar held her gaze. No shame. No regret. No more excuses. She almost laughed at the absurdity of it. Why would he have an affair? And who with? For a start, when would he find the time? Or energy? She could barely find the strength to sleep with her own spouse, never mind someone else.

'I'd hardly call it an affair.' He shrugged as if it really was nothing. 'I don't know what she thought she would achieve by telling you. She's only done this to split us up because, if she can't have me, she doesn't want you to have me either. Don't let her win, Beth. You're playing right into her hands.'

'Who?' Beth asked. 'Don't let who win?'

He tilted his head, considering her for a moment. 'You said she came round earlier.'

'No. I didn't say it was a woman.' Beth's voice was scratchy. She took a deep breath. 'The person this morning was here about your debts.'

'Debts?' The colour drained from his face. It was impossible to know whether this was because Beth knew about the money, or because he'd inadvertently let slip he'd been having an affair.

'The man this morning was a debt-collector. He said you owed a lot of money and it was time to pay up. I thought Lomas Lumber was going under. I thought we had money problems. I was worried that we were going to lose the house. I was going to talk to you about me starting up the catering company I've been thinking about.'

'A debt-collector turned up here?' Oscar asked. 'At the house? He had no right to do that. I told him ... Look, I'll make sure he doesn't come here again.'

'Really, Oscar? Really? I think we've got bigger problems than debts, don't you? What about me? What about your family?'

Oscar flung out an arm and knocked the beer bottle over. 'C'mon. You've done pretty well out of my money so don't give me that shit.'

She flinched at his raised voice. 'Shit? That's what our

family is, is it? Shit?' Beth's voice was getting louder and shriller. She was on her feet now, though she couldn't remember standing up. The bottle rolled off the table and its contents foamed over the floor. Why was he shouting at her? She hadn't done anything wrong.

'Don't try twisting my words,' said Oscar. 'You know exactly what I mean. I work fucking hard while you stay home and bake cakes and—'

'You've told me time and time again that you don't want me to get a job. That, by staying at home, I'm supporting you to support us.'

'You didn't put up much of a fight though, did you?'

'When do I ever fight? I've always thought you had our best interests at heart. Sacrificing having a career was small compared to the sacrifices you were making. That's what you always said. I thought we were in this together.'

'Career? What the fuck do you think you could do? You'd be lucky to get a job at the supermarket.'

Beth was inches away from his face now as she leaned over the table. 'Yes, I would. Because at least then I'd get paid for the work I do and I wouldn't have to rely on you for everything and be taken for granted every single day.'

Oscar stood so that he towered over her. 'You'd be nothing without me.'

Beth wanted to move away from him but instead, she straightened up and looked him in the eye. 'Yeah? Well maybe I'd like the chance to find out.'

CHAPTER SEVEN

Beth Lomas

They wouldn't let me see him.

Harvey, Esther, the police. They said it wasn't possible. Harvey had formally identified the body so I wasn't required. But I needed to see Oscar, or I'd never believe what they were telling me. Just one last time, that's all I was asking.

'No.'

'Harvey, I need to hold his hand. I need to kiss him.'

'Beth!' Harvey had never raised his voice to me before and it made me flinch. He rubbed his hands over his face, dry hands catching on three days of stubble.

We were sitting on the stairs while Esther cleaned out my kitchen cupboards. Honey was at school, but I didn't know where Gabe was. The school had called to say that, while they understood the pressure I was under and really, it wasn't a problem, but could I confirm – for their records – that Gabriel wasn't in school because he was taking some time out following his father's death. To his credit, Gabe answered his phone within two rings. He was safe but he wouldn't tell me where.

'Miriam said that you were meant to be with Oscar the morning he died. Why did she think that?'

He sighed. 'Oscar asked me if I wanted to meet up on Saturday morning. I went to work instead.'

'Why didn't you tell me?'

'Tell you what? That I could have stopped him if I hadn't been so focused on work instead of family?'

We sat in silence but I could feel the distress coming off him in waves.

'Do you think he did this on purpose?'

Harvey nodded slowly. 'When have you ever known him to do anything half-heartedly? Just accept it and let it go.'

'But without seeing him for myself—'

'Beth,' Harvey said, quieter this time. 'Believe me, you don't want that image in your head. He was pretty messed up. An accident like that . . . Shit. I don't want to upset you Beth, but his face . . . the impact of the fall . . . You know what I'm saying, yeah?'

'I don't care. I still want to see him. The undertakers can do things to make it look—'

'For Christ's sake, Beth! There is no *him*. His skull is bashed in. His face is a fucking mess.'

I shrank away from Harvey, pushing myself against the stairs, turned slowly and began crawling. All I could hear was my own breathing. It was shallow and jagged. But then the sickness came to me in a wave and I scrambled up the stairs on hands and feet. Running now, slipping, flinging myself into the bathroom just as the vomit came.

As I retched for the third time, I heard the front door slam. I thought Harvey had gone, and perhaps he had but, more importantly, someone had arrived.

I felt hands pulling my hair back from my face, holding it at the nape of my neck.

'Just like old times, eh babe? But this time, no tequila.'

Molly put me to bed and climbed in beside me, stroking my head as I curled into a ball and sobbed. Mouth open, eyes clenched. Raw sobs that splintered my ribs and grazed my throat. All I wanted to do was sleep, or at least lie in bed staring at the wall as the hours passed by. I didn't care, as long as I could keep my mind empty and my heart beating just enough to stay alive. But then I'd catch the smell of Oscar on the bedcovers, or hear his voice, or see him out of the corner of my eye and I would dissolve into heaving, chest-sucking howls.

Oscar's face was everywhere. Our wedding photograph, Honey's first Christmas, our trip to Bath for our anniversary. Smiling, laughing, gazing at each other. Not knowing the heartache that was waiting for us. Oscar had always been the strong one, the backbone of our tribe. I was exposed and vulnerable without him. I didn't even know if I had a place within the Lomas family anymore. I'd always felt like an add-on. Without Oscar, where did I belong?

'Let it all out,' Molly said. 'Scream if you need to.'

'Moll, he's gone. Really gone.'

'I know, babe.'

The square of light from the window moved from one wall to another before Molly said, 'Shower.'

'I don't want to.'

'Did I ask what you wanted? Now get in the shower. I'll make us a cup of tea.'

'Can't I just—'

'No. The kids will be home soon, right? They need you to be more ...' She waved her hands trying to grasp the right word. 'Present.'

What did it matter whether I wore clean clothes? Who cared if I'd brushed my teeth today? But Molly knew that my Achilles heel was the children and had used it to good effect. She reminded me that I couldn't go to pieces. They'd lost their father and they needed their mother now more than ever.

I missed Oscar with a force like my heart was being torn from my chest. A desperate empty longing that would suck me into the void. I could barely cope with the physical agony of the loss. I wanted my mind to quieten down for a moment, to leave me in peace to work out how to fit my life back together. The cog that had made it work for the last twenty years was missing.

I struggled to sit up, my head spinning. I couldn't remember eating anything since Sunday.

'I'm allowing you two sessions of crying per day for no more than ten minutes at a time,' Molly said. 'Three sessions on the day of the funeral. And only one of those can be in front of Gabe and Honey. Do you hear me?'

'But ...'

'No buts. What do we say is at the heart of every "but"? That's right; an arsehole. Now, you get in the shower and I'll be back in a tick with a nice cup of tea.'

I went through the motions of washing my hair, letting my tears mingle with the hot water. If Molly didn't know about my clandestine sobbing, it didn't count towards my two-a-day quota. I'd been desperate to see her, hoping she'd help me make sense of things, but now she was here I wanted her to leave me to wallow.

47

I was leaning my head against the tiles when she reappeared holding a clean towel.

'You haven't asked me how I'm holding up,' I said.

'No offence, babe, but I've got eyes in my head and I can see exactly how you are. I'm here for as long as you need me, so we've got plenty of time to talk about how you're feeling. For now, your emotional state doesn't matter. We need to put one foot in front of the other.'

'But everyone asks how I am,' I said. 'Everyone.'

'No one expects an honest answer, because there's no answer to give. What they're saying is, "Christ almighty, this is the shittiest day in the whole history of shitty days", and they want you to know that they understand that. None of them believe they can make it any better. Mostly they're just glad it's not happening to them.'

She reached around me and turned off the shower. 'Come on.'

She held the towel open and I stepped into it, letting her wrap it around me.

Molly was a free spirit, unencumbered by social norms or expectations. She had a fluid love life, her own business, a flat in London, and could drink pretty much anyone under the table. A party wasn't a party without Molly. In many ways, she was similar to Oscar. She took risks that I'd never dream of, and yet it always seemed to work out for her. Molly was the cat that always landed on her feet.

She used to poke fun at me and call me 'Mum' because I liked to look after people and only ever dreamed of getting married and having kids. She thought I was grown up, mature, when the opposite was true. I didn't want to move away from home. I didn't want the responsibility of getting a job. I didn't want to be on my own. I was scared of growing up and having to make my own decisions.

My parents were older than everyone else's and, in my late teens, I'd been their carer. They died within weeks of each other and I married Oscar in the same church where we'd had their funeral, with the smell of their memorial lilies still in the air. I would have married anyone who asked. I was just glad the question came from Oscar.

I was scared that no one would look after me when I got sick or old. I wanted kids when I was still young. I wanted to be able to see them grow, have kids of their own and I didn't want them to be orphaned before they'd found their place in the world.

'I take it I'm sleeping in the shed,' Molly said, looking out of the window at the Cabin.

I nodded. 'Esther and Vince are in the guest room. Though you can share my bed if you want, there's plenty of space, and I don't snore because I'm not really sleeping.'

'As tempting as it is to share a room with a grieving insomniac, and to sleep on the side of the bed that was last occupied by her dead husband, I'll take my chances with the slugs.'

The Cabin had always been Oscar's domain. It was where he went when he needed some peace and quiet. It had heating and lighting and a pull-out sofa-bed. A kettle and a mini fridge. He didn't need anything else, not even me. After the argument he slept in there, and then on Saturday when he didn't come to bed, I'd assumed he was there again. I'd wondered about knocking on the door to say we should talk, but I didn't want another fight. In the morning there'd been no sign of Oscar or his car, and I thought he'd gone out as the dawn had crept over the house. It shames me to say that it didn't cross my mind that he could be in trouble, I only thought about how much trouble *I* was in. When he'd given me the silent treatment before, it had never lasted this long. Was he planning to leave me? He wouldn't tell me who he'd had an affair with but I had a feeling I knew. Of all the people he could have chosen ...

He said he needed a bit more time for this big international deal to come through and all his financial problems would go away. He said it wasn't his fault. He was stressed, unsure who to turn to. He seemed to think an affair was understandable under so much pressure. He told me to be patient. Said it would all blow over with time. So why was he dead twenty-four hours later?

CHAPTER EIGHT

Beth Lomas

I spoke to the vicar, chose the hymns, and cancelled Oscar's monthly subscription to the Real Ale Company. I did, however, keep the subscription to have a crate of wine delivered every three months. Certain things became essential items.

Once completed, each of these tasks seemed momentous. Every decision was a milestone. I'd always deferred to Oscar for important decisions and I still wanted to ask him whether he was happy with the hymns I'd chosen. Esther arranged flowers, cars, and readings. She and Vince were still living in the eaves like bats. It wasn't because of my hospitality, but rather so they could be where they could still feel their son, where his children were daily reminders that Oscar had lived and had lived well.

Esther had aged a decade since Oscar's death. Her normally perfect hair now fell flat past her ears. Her eyeliner smudged in the corner, her lipstick bleeding into the fine lines of her smoker's mouth. Today Esther was catching up with old friends over lunch while Vince helped Harvey at Lomas Lumber.

Molly kept opening her mouth to say something and then, shaking her head, she'd turn away. I appreciated that it wasn't easy to find the words for a bereaved person, but the fact that she'd flown back from Tuscany to be with me, was enough.

She was tidying the Cabin and organising the paperwork because I couldn't face seeing Oscar's handwriting on the notepad, or his jumper casually slung over the back of a chair like he'd only popped out for a minute. Esther had asked for Oscar's passport number so she could cancel everything at once. There was a website for such things, apparently, but it had been so long since we'd used them, I didn't even know where our passports were. I suspected the kids' ones would have expired by now. Oscar was the one who booked our holidays, paid our bills, kept an eye on the money and now, I realised, I didn't even know where he kept important documents. If he'd known he was going to leave me he would have left an instruction manual.

Gabe promised he would stay in school today. I wished I could get through to him, but he was secretive, impenetrable, and I rarely knew where he was, or who he was with. Honey was more open but just as hurt. She barely ate, barely slept, barely smiled anymore. I noticed that she'd started biting her nails until they bled. It was as if Oscar's death had cut the thin thread that bound us and we couldn't get to grips with being a threesome. We tottered and lost our balance.

I took advantage of a quiet moment to sit on the floor of the living room with a pile of condolence cards by my side. The postman pushed card after card through the letterbox. Envelopes in mauve and white from friends I'd half-forgotten, and friends I didn't remember at all. Some cards were religious, some plain, most had lilies on the front trumpeting their condolences. Some were hand-delivered by well-meaning neighbours who'd tiptoed up the path and quietly pushed open the letterbox before poking a card through, and slipping away again.

I'd hoped that the outpouring of love would soothe me and, for the first five or six cards, it did. But this one, with its blank envelope not even addressed to anyone in particular, caused my breath to catch. The front was white with silver embossed letters saying *Congratulations*.

At first, I thought it was a mistake, then wondered if it was a bad joke. I opened the card cautiously. I didn't recognise the handwriting inside. The words were all in capitals, the pen had been pushed so hard into the card that it had left deep grooves in the paper. I gasped and threw it to the floor, bringing my knees up under my chin and staring at the card as if it might start crawling towards me. Heat crept up my neck and into my hairline as if I'd been caught doing something wrong. I looked to the window, half-expecting someone to be watching. The bubble around me, of treating me softly, had burst. Not everyone was sympathetic.

'Hey,' Molly said, walking in carrying a box of papers. 'I think this is all rubbish. Do you want to have a quick look before I throw it?'

I wiped my cheeks quickly.

'Are the cards a bit much for you?' she asked, placing the box on the floor and coming to sit next to me.

I tried to laugh, but it sounded more like a grunt. 'You could say that.'

She put both arms around my shoulders and leaned her head against mine. 'Some douche-nozzle saying nice things again? How dare they?' I could hear the smile in her voice.

The congratulations card was face down, the price sticker of £1.99 still on the back. Someone in a rush. Someone who didn't care about looking cheap and who didn't care about anything but hurting me. I squeezed Molly's arm and then reached over to scoop up everything before she could see what had upset me.

'I don't want to read them, and I don't want to see them,' I said.

I dropped them all into the box of rubbish. 'Get rid of them would you, Molly?'

'Sure thing, boss. And then I'll put the kettle on.'

She stood up with the box in her arms and started walking towards the garden where we kept our bins.

'I tell you what,' she said with a grin. 'Standards are slipping. I remember a time when there'd always be cake in this house. That cup of tea is going to be a bit wet without a slice of Victoria sponge.'

I got to my feet. 'I get the hint. Christ, can't a woman be left alone to wallow?' I tried to smile.

'Wallowing is always done best with cake, babe. You know that.'

She went outside and I went into the kitchen. Looking at Molly's skinny frame, I didn't think she ate much cake. She was only getting me baking to give me something soothing and productive to do. I loved her in that moment. Loved her for knowing me better than I knew myself.

I put the butter, the sugar, and the eggs in front of me and stared. I wasn't sure I knew what to do anymore. Didn't know where to start. It used to bring me such joy – a sense of order in the chaos – but it was too frivolous now. Cakes were for birthdays, not for days when you felt the world was falling in on you.

'. . . the fuck?' shouted Molly.

I jumped and spun around. She was holding the discarded card in her hand.

'Oh God. Don't, Moll.'

54

'What kind of sick bastard sends a congratulations card? Do you know who it's from?'

I shook my head and she carried on shouting. 'When I find out who sent this card, I am personally going to ...'

'Moll, please.' I held my hands up in front of me to calm her down. 'It's someone's idea of a sick joke, that's all. I just want it to go away.'

'What does it even mean?' she asked shaking it at me.

I picked up a tea-towel and wiped my hands. 'I don't know. I suppose that, um, someone is saying I got what I deserved – a dead husband. And that it's my fault.'

'Utter crap,' exclaimed Molly. 'No, I'm not having that. I don't think that's what it means. I think someone is saying that *Oscar* got what he deserved. Maybe they're writing the card as if they were addressing Oscar.'

'Don't say that, Moll. No one could be happy he's dead. He was a wonderful man.'

'You know what else it could mean?'

I waited for her to elaborate.

'What if they know something? What if he didn't die by suicide? What if someone else was involved?'

I rubbed my temples. They felt tender.

'You don't believe he killed himself, right? What if this is *proof* that someone wanted him dead and this card is celebrating the fact that he's gone?'

'I don't know what to think anymore, but Esther thinks he was pushed,' I said.

'Never thought these words would ever leave my lips but, I think Esther's right.'

A noise in the hallway startled us and we heard Esther's voice say, 'Right about what?'

'You move like a bloody ninja, Esther,' Molly said with her hand on her heart. 'Here, look at this card, would you? Tell me what you think.'

I stepped between them and snatched the card from Molly. 'No,' I said.

'Who sent it?' Esther demanded.

I shrugged. 'I really don't want to talk about this.'

'She doesn't know,' said Molly. 'But it's not addressed to anyone.'

'What does it say?' Esther asked staring at the card in my hand.

Molly looked at me and I knew I'd have to say something because, if I didn't, she would.

'It says ...' I took a deep breath. 'It says "Congratulations. You got what you deserved. May you rot in hell."'

Esther's eyes widened. 'Goodness.'

Molly took the card back off me and said, 'We need to show this to the police.'

She handed it to Esther and said, 'I think you're right about Oscar being murdered.'

CHAPTER NINE

DC Lowry Endecott

'Do you still have the envelope in your possession?' Lowry asked Beth. She didn't think there was anything sinister intended, but she wanted Beth to think that she was taking her concerns seriously – before she rejected them as unfounded.

The card lay on the scrubbed wooden table between them.

'Sort of. I can ask Molly to get it out of the bin? I wasn't going to call you, because there's no harm done or anything but, looking at the wider picture of my husband's death ... I mean, you know, when you put it all together ...'

Lowry wasn't sure why she'd come. Uniform could have responded to the call but she genuinely liked Beth and felt sorry for her. Once you've told someone that their husband is dead – and they've thanked you for giving them the worst news of their life – it's very difficult to walk away. You wonder how they're getting on, whether they've pieced their lives back together yet, whether you could have delivered the news in a kinder way. Lowry's people skills might not be up to much but, despite appearances, she truly did care and want to make a difference.

'On its own, it's not ...' Lowry had to choose her words carefully. 'It doesn't suggest foul play. I can understand you wanting answers, Beth, and I wish I could give them to you, but all the signs, at this time, point towards Mr Lomas having taken his own life.'

'Yes, I know that, but isn't there someone investigating Oscar's death?'

'The coroner has ruled that an inquest isn't required. Mr Lomas died from his injuries caused by an accident or by his own actions. That's really the end of our involvement here unless you have other information that you deem pertinent to an investigation. But at this time, we are not seeking anyone else in relation to his death.'

Listening to herself talk, Lowry inwardly cringed. Who uses words like *deem* and *pertinent*? And why does she say 'at this time' so much. They were empty words that added nothing to a conversation. No wonder her boss, Finn, said she lacked the personal touch. If she got that job in London, she'd have to make more of an effort. She was a good detective, the only negative thing that ever came up at appraisals was the way she dealt with members of the public.

She watched Beth fidget with her mug. The two other women, mother-in-law and best friend, had made themselves scarce with assertions of, 'We'll be in the other room if you need us.' She could feel their presence burning through the walls as they strained to hear what was going on. Imagined ears on glasses on walls.

'*Is* there anything else you want to tell me, Beth?'

Beth shook her head. There was nothing more than a card that had been sent in poor taste.

'In that case ...'

'He had money problems,' Beth blurted out. 'Big ones. The company's in a mess.'

Lowry tried to nod sympathetically but this simply backed

58

up what they already knew – no one else had been involved in Oscar Lomas's death. He was a man unable to cope with the strains of life, and instead of seeking help he'd made the one decision he couldn't take back.

'He's being sued by three members of staff for unfair dismissal,' said Beth. 'It was the one time that his charm failed him. Oscar had been adamant that they wouldn't be getting a penny off him, though. He said it should be up to him who he hired and fired, and just because he didn't give them a written warning didn't mean they weren't bad at their jobs.'

'Have any of them threatened him?' Lowry asked.

She shook her head. 'Not that I know of, but Oscar didn't always tell me everything.'

'Names?'

'You'll have to ask Harvey. Or Miriam. She's HR, so she's been dealing with all of this. Oscar didn't like to talk to me about work. Said it would all go over my head.'

It wasn't the first time Lowry had spoken to a wife whose charming husband treated her like she was little more than a housekeeper. She wondered why they put up with it.

'Right. Okay then. I'll keep that in mind. Thank you for the additional information, and the coffee.'

Lowry had the impression that Beth would keep her talking for hours if she let her but she didn't want to give the woman false hope that they were treating her husband's death as anything other than what it was. She drained the rest of her coffee and put her hands on the edge of the table to push herself up.

'There were other things too,' Beth said.

'Such as?'

Beth pursed her lips, and after a moment or two she said,

'About a week before his death, Oscar came home with scrape marks on his cheek and a cut lip. He said he'd slipped on some gravel and showed me the red marks on his hands as proof, but he was shaken by it and didn't look me in the eye. I wish I'd asked more at the time because I didn't believe he'd tripped, I thought it was ... Look, I'm not trying to drop Harvey in it, but I thought they'd got into another fight.'

'*Another* fight?'

'Things had been strained between them. Recently, when they were in the same room, you could feel the atmosphere. And, when they were younger, they used to get into fist fights. There were a fair few black eyes and bloodied lips back then. I don't know. It's probably nothing. I don't think Harvey's capable of hurting Oscar. They drove each other mad sometimes but they adored each other really. But then ...' she lowered her voice. 'The day before he, you know, went missing. A man turned up here looking for Oscar.'

Lowry settled back into her chair. 'Okay. Go on.'

Beth got up and quietly closed the kitchen door. 'Esther and Molly don't know, and I don't want to tell them. Not yet because, well it's complicated, and Harvey asked me not to say anything in case it damaged the business or something. He's still hoping for a new contract that will save Lomas Lumber and, well I guess ...'

Beth sat back down at the table and picked up her empty cup.

Lowry studied Beth, whose eyes flitted to the window, the door, to the cup in her hand.

'Why don't you tell me what happened, Beth?'

'Okay, so ... It was probably nothing but if I don't say anything ... It was first thing in the morning. The kids hadn't long left for school. Oscar had already been out of the house an hour or so. I was surprised when the doorbell rang. And you could tell by the way they rang the bell that they were impatient. He held on to the doorbell for too long, you know? And I thought to myself, *here's someone in a hurry*. But then, when I opened the door, he stood there and didn't say a word. He kept looking over my shoulder into the house. For a moment I thought he was going to force his way inside, I even put my foot flat against the door so he couldn't push past me. He asked for Oscar and I said, "He's at work at the moment. Can I help you?" He said, "Give him a message from me". I asked his name, but he would only say that he was from a debt collection agency and it would be in Oscar's best interest to pay what he owed.'

Lowry raised an eyebrow. If nothing else, it was a clearer motive for suicide. But the question now was, did this man put undue pressure on Oscar Lomas that led to him taking his own life?

'And was Oscar planning to pay up?'

Beth put her cup down and pulled her shirt sleeves over her hands in a move that made her look more like a teenager being questioned about shoplifting. 'I don't know. I told him about it on Friday evening. Remember I told you we'd had an argument? Well, this was what started it. I just wanted to know how much financial trouble we were in. He was obviously keeping it from me but that was just . . . God, I really wish that was the worst of our problems, but I confronted him about the money and he thought I was talking about something else so it, sort of, turned out to be worse than I expected.'

'Worse how?' Lowry asked.

Beth's cheeks flushed with embarrassment. With her eyes

firmly on her cup, she said, 'Oscar thought I was referring to his adultery.'

'He was having an affair?'

'Well, he said it was one time, but I suppose they all say that when they're caught out, don't they?'

Lowry nodded in agreement. Didn't she know it.

'Who was he having an affair with?' she asked.

'I don't know. I asked, but he wouldn't say and I didn't want to give him the satisfaction of thinking that I cared. And, you know, I thought I'd have time to get to the bottom of it.'

'You must have your suspicions?' Lowry prompted.

Beth shook her head. 'No. Not me. Haven't you heard? I'm stupid. I never see what's under my nose.'

Lowry could see that Beth Lomas was one kind word away from bursting into tears, so she decided to leave it for now. But, from experience, she knew that there wasn't a woman alive who was content to accept that their partner had strayed and not want to know who with. She might not know what had driven Oscar Lomas to take his own life, but Lowry was sure of one thing – Beth knew more than she was letting on.

CHAPTER TEN

Molly Ingram

Holy mother of God, the state of some people.

Molly leaned against the side of the Cabin with a cigarette in her hand. It was a habit she'd long since broken but had been surprisingly easy to fall back into. She'd spent most of the morning making cups of tea and offering around boxes of tissues to people who should have known better than to put their grief on display like their best bone china. Why did people come to the dead person's house before the funeral? What was the point? And while she was on the subject, what was the purpose of funerals? She knew they were *meant* to offer closure, an opportunity for people to say goodbye, to pay their respects and, for those who had faith, comfort. But, really, why bother? She'd gone with Beth to the undertakers and her eyes had watered at the price of the cars and the coffin. She was going to have it written into her will that she should be put in a cardboard box and chucked on the bonfire. Set off a few fireworks. Job done. Enjoy the party. Free tequila shots for all.

Christ, she was tired. Something had woken her in the night, scrabbling around beneath the Cabin. Fur brushing against the wood. It made her skin crawl. Mice, rats, even rabbits, freaked her out. To be honest, there were plenty of small dogs that shouldn't be trusted either. When she'd mentioned the sounds to Beth, her friend had answered absentmindedly, 'Oh, that? Probably the rats.' As if it was perfectly normal to have a seething nest of vermin feet away from where you lay your head.

Today was going to be difficult. Molly laughed to herself. Well wasn't that the biggest understatement of the year? There was so much she wanted to say and exhaustion meant it was harder to keep it all in. She was having to bite her lip so much it was a wonder she hadn't drawn blood. She couldn't tell Beth everything that was on her mind. Certainly not about the last time she'd spoken to Oscar, nor that her business was going under and sixty people were about to be made redundant. But, last night, she did finally get round to telling Beth that Vijay had proposed.

'Oh my goodness. I'm so happy for you. Let's see the ring!'

'I didn't say *yes*.'

'What do you mean, you didn't say—'

'You called before I could give him an answer and then the moment passed and—'

'Molly Ingram! Don't you dare use me as an excuse. It only takes a second to say yes. See? Yes. I've said it again. What's really stopping you?'

'You're more important.'

'Moll.'

'Okay. I just didn't think he meant it. Who proposes after five months? I mean, he hardly knows anything about me.'

'Why should that matter?'

'Because if he really knew me, he wouldn't have asked.'

Molly kept picking up her phone to call Vijay and then throwing it down again. She hadn't switched on her phone since she arrived in Hellas Mill and she didn't want him to witness this part of her life. Molly in Hellas Mill was trash-Molly, poor-Molly, wrong-side-of-the-tracks-Molly. She would always be the girl who got free school meals. Though she'd only been in Hellas Mill for a week her vowels were already flattening and her accent getting stronger.

If Molly was good at anything, it was compartmentalising. Anything to do with the past, or Hellas Mill, was put in a virtual box to be opened cautiously a couple of times a year. Her life in London as a businesswoman, a high-flyer, was something that had only begun once she'd finally cut all ties with this place.

Molly didn't even like listening to music she'd once known every single word to. Anything from her past was to be shunned. She used to think she'd pay anything to erase the part of her brain that held teenage memories, but with age – and some might say wisdom – she realised that those incidents had shaped her. Her dad used to say that experience was better bought than taught but he hadn't told her how high the price was likely to be.

If it came down to the age-old choice between fight or flight, Molly would choose flight every time – first class wherever possible – but this was one day she couldn't flee from. It was time to put on her best thank-you-for-coming face and get back in there. All eyes would be on Beth, judging her, whispering about her, appraising the quality of the flowers, the food, and the grief.

Molly ground out her cigarette under her red-soled stiletto and began walking back to the house. The cars would be here in fifteen minutes. Esther had insisted on three cars for family and friends. They would traipse behind the hearse and try not to imagine what was in the flower-covered box. People in the street would stare as the black cars swept by. Old men would doff their hats. Women would pull their children closer to them.

Molly was going to be travelling in the first car with Beth and the children. Harvey and Miriam would be with Oscar's parents in car two. Distant relatives would be in the third. They could have squeezed in two cars, but Esther thought three made more of a statement. A statement of what though?

This would be the first funeral that either of the children had attended and their father's body would be the centrepiece. Molly was godmother to both of them, but her infrequent return to Hellas Mill, and their lack of desire to visit her, meant that they were almost strangers. Beth kept her updated as to how they were getting on at school, what they wanted for birthdays and Christmases but Molly didn't *know* them.

If anything good could come out of this, it was that it gave Molly the chance to reconnect with Beth and the kids. This tragedy had brought them together again when Molly had feared they'd drifted too far apart to ever find their way back to each other. The barrier that had been separating them had been removed when Oscar fell to his death. She wasn't sure Beth ever realised that Oscar was the reason Molly had been avoiding meeting up over the past year, but now she'd never have to know. Last night, though full of tears and tissues, had been ... well ... lovely. They had followed their memories – like breadcrumbs – back to a life that had been simpler.

With her hand on the patio door, she lifted her face towards the sun. *Come on vitamin D, do your magic.* She'd been so tired lately. Maybe she was ill? Or perhaps this is what it felt like when you got in touching distance of forty. She would have to come clean to Beth about the state of her finances, eventually. And the obvious question would be how she managed to get herself in such a mess, and Molly wouldn't be able to give her an honest answer. She'd almost told her last night, but it felt like a selfish thing to do, to bring her own worries to the forefront of a conversation when they were nothing compared to what Beth was going through.

Being away from work wasn't helping financially, nor putting the company back on track, but it was helping her state of mind to be physically away from London and from the faces of all those who were losing their jobs because of her. The directors knew the score, of course, and they were still hopeful for a merger, or a buy-out, but the bank was losing patience, and her best staff had already found alternative employment. No such thing as loyalty in this day and age. She was heading back home the day after the funeral for a meeting with the stakeholders. Though she was praying for a miracle, she didn't believe in them, and knew she'd be back in Hellas Mill living in her dad's spare room before long.

Her stay at Beth's was mostly free in lodgings and food, but she'd splurged on an expensive dress for the final farewell to a man she despised. She hoped she didn't spill anything on it today, as she'd have to take it back in the morning on the way to catch her train.

Inside the too-bright house, huddles of mourners gathered in the kitchen, a woman Molly didn't recognise was washing cups while another one dried. Around the table, Esther sat with Vince and some of their friends who looked far too pleased to be here.

Molly went into the hallway and paused at the open front door. There were people outside looking, in turn, sad and scandalised. They were here to gawp at the funeral cortege as if this was a daily soap opera instead of her best friend's life in tatters. She stepped back into the shadows before they saw her.

Voices floated in from the street.

'Was it true he killed himself?' a woman asked. Molly didn't hear the answer but she heard the resulting gasp.

'What was it?' came another voice. 'Money troubles? Marriage problems?'

'I heard he'd been having an affair.'

'Just the one?'

Laughter.

'It took her two days to report him missing. What does that tell you about the state of their marriage? If you ask me ...'

Molly turned at the sound of footsteps above her and saw Gabe on the landing wearing a navy blue suit and tie. He looked older than his years but still too young to be burying his father.

'Alright?' he said.

Molly nodded. 'Yeah, fine. Wish the bloody cars would hurry up, though. This waiting is ...' She wanted to say 'killing me' but the words died on her lips.

Gabe walked slowly down the stairs. Molly could no longer hear the voices outside but the sound of high-heeled shoes clipping up the path was both loud and rapid.

'I heard you playing guitar earlier,' she said. 'You're good. Really good.'

Gabe shrugged – universal teenage sign language for *whatever* – but Molly thought she saw the twitch of a smile on his cheeks.

Miriam rushed in, turned her red-rimmed eyes to Molly

and, deciding she wasn't important enough to bother with, flung open the living room door. 'Harvey. They're here,' she hissed. 'The cars are here.'

There was a collective intake of breath. People got to their feet. Grabbing bags and coats. Ties were straightened. There was the general air of a platoon readying for battle.

Molly looked at Gabe. 'You ready for this, kiddo?'

'No. You?'

'Not in the slightest. We'll get through it together, yeah?'

Harvey came out of the living room grasping Miriam's hand. She tried to shake it free. 'Harvey,' she said. 'You're hurting me.'

He looked confused for a moment then let go of her and stalked outside with his hands in his pockets. Miriam followed at a safe distance. Esther and Vince came and stood in the hallway. Beth followed, with her arm around Honey.

And then there was no other reason to delay going out and looking at the hearse.

The coffin.

The body of Oscar Lomas.

CHAPTER ELEVEN

Beth Lomas

A funeral was an event that didn't require an RSVP. I didn't get the last-minute dropouts because of childcare problems or emergency dental work. No one needed to inform me of dietary requirements. Dress code was obvious, start time was non-negotiable. There would be no turning up fashionably late, or embarrassingly early, and there was no gift registry. In some ways, it was the easiest party I'd ever organised, and yet it was the one party I dreaded the most.

The dress I'd let Molly talk me into buying was too flashy. Black lace over a pale satin slip, almost golden. Esther looked perfect, of course. Black trouser suit. Emerald-green scarf. Shoes that didn't court attention with every clip and every clop. I looked like I was trying too hard by her side. We felt Oscar's loss in different ways, but both of us had thought he'd be in our lives for ever. It wasn't meant to happen like this. Esther wasn't meant to bury her son and I wasn't meant to be a widow at thirty-nine.

Colleagues, friends and neighbours – the lines blurred as to which category was the best fit – were quite shameless in their curiosity. It was to be expected; I'd have done the same. I'd anticipated their sympathy, but not the low vibration caused by the hum of scandal. By their very nature funerals were muted occasions, but this one seemed quieter, as if shame was hiding under the pews. It was cold in the church and we buttoned our coats and our lips. And no one mentioned the word *suicide*. The readings didn't mention it, the vicar didn't allude to it, because no reason for death had yet been given. I had an interim death certificate, proof only of the fact he had died, not how. And still, I heard the hiss of the word like a dirty secret. And the less we spoke of it the more room it took up. Suicide.

'*What drove him to it?*' they wondered, with their eyes on my back. Miriam dabbed her eyes and tutted at me. She thinks I didn't notice her holding the order of service to her bosom and then sliding it into her handbag as a morbid keepsake.

I'd been aware of the congregation but had hardly distinguished one face from another as I made my way to the front row. The VIP seats. Oscar had been well-liked and well-respected. He'd given his time to charity and was the kind of man who stopped to speak to people in the street. A five-minute errand would turn into fifty as he chatted at length to the neighbours. Had his death changed the way they viewed him?

The hierarchy of death extended to how you met it. A noble death was right up there. Giving your life to save another got full marks, often a medal. Stoic acceptance was preferable. But a death that you'd brought on yourself ...? The best you could hope for was a sympathetic audience and, judging by the headshaking and the folded arms, Oscar was fresh out of luck.

I kept my eyes ahead, but not on the coffin, and moved my lips in time with the hymns. Music was usually such a joy, that the act of singing seemed forced and frivolous. The organist was a fraction too slow, so even the upbeat songs we'd chosen sounded like dirges. I longed for each song to end so I could sit down again.

The condolence train was the worst part of the day. They queued to touch their palms to mine. Some held on a fraction too long as if they were trying to convey thoughts through skin-to-skin contact. Others stumbled over their words as they tried to find different ways to say, '*sorry for your loss*'. I found myself comforting *them*, and pretending that I was doing fine, 'thank you for asking'. I'd not seen some of the people for years. Was it wrong to be just the slightest bit pleased to see them? My smiles were occasionally genuine until I reined them in and bowed my head.

Personal boundaries were left at home along with jokes and colourful clothes. I was embraced and touched by hundreds of hands, leaving me feeling dirty. Hattie Flint-Stanton was one of the worst. She kissed both cheeks and held me to her like we were long-lost friends united in grief. Her detective inspector fiancé, Finn Greenwood, tried to pull Hattie away by her elbow. She dabbed her dry eyes and clutched at her pearls. I wouldn't have been shocked if she'd thrown herself upon the coffin and wailed. Finn looked at me too hard and too long.

Hattie said, 'You know where I am if you need me. Anything. Anything at all, promise me you'll call. I know what it's like to lose someone. Do you remember Barnaby? Of course you do. All I'm saying is, I know about grief. Of course, Barnaby's death was an unfortunate accident. I gather it was the same with Oscar?'

I stared at her, but couldn't speak. Why did she have to

bring up Barnaby today of all days? Fiancé Finn didn't attempt to shake my hand. He nodded at me and moved Hattie on.

I'd told Gabe and Honey that Oscar's death was an accident. Preferable to believe he slipped rather than jumped, but I knew there was more to it than that. The more I thought about it, the more I became convinced that someone had pushed him. And the congratulations card meant that I wasn't the only one who knew.

I lowered my eyes and saw pair after pair of black shoes scurrying towards me like beetles. Someone here had sent me that card. I was sure of it. Would it be one of the quiet ones who was avoiding my gaze, or one of the showy grievers? They wouldn't be able to keep away, I knew that much. Either they were angry with me or they were angry with Oscar.

A man's hand slipped into mine and, as I raised my face to greet him, he spoke quietly. His voice was muffled by a bushy moustache straggling over his lips.

'Congratulations.'

'What? What did you say?' I looked around for Molly. Panic made me go limp and I took half a step backwards.

I tried to take my hand away but he closed both hands around mine and smiled softly. 'I said, "Commiserations". Oscar will be missed by so many.'

There was sympathy in his eyes. Had I misheard him?

'Who are you?' I breathed. But my voice was choked by the tightening in my throat and he slipped away to be replaced by another hand, another textbook display of mourning. I paid little attention to anyone else.

I tried to watch him as he slipped through the crowd but I blinked and he'd gone. I hardly knew what was real anymore. I just wanted the day to be over.

Stage Two of Grief

ANGER

CHAPTER TWELVE

Beth Lomas

I woke to a scream. My own. I'd dreamed that I was watching Oscar's coffin as flames clawed around it. Banging came from the heart of the blaze as Oscar burned. I tried to battle the fire to get to him but the heat drove me back. Every time I tried to reach him, the flames soared and grew stronger. I tried to call for help but my throat wouldn't work. No one could hear me. The ground became molten, my feet sank through the floor up to my ankles and I couldn't move.

I'd never been so relieved to find it was only a dream. I sat for a minute, waiting for my hammering heart to slow, and wiping my sweat-soaked hair off my face. I could still hear my scream reverberating off the walls but no one came running. No lights switched on. I looked at the clock and saw it was exactly three a.m. No matter how much I drank, or how many pills I took, three was the magic hour when I was wide awake. I'd suffered from insomnia on and off for most of my life and this was definitely an 'on' phase. I'd tried it all – meditation to medication – but nothing made a difference. Wine helped me fall asleep but it didn't compel me to stay there. I'd had too much to drink with Molly, after everyone else had gone home. Esther and Vince had gone to bed early and so had Honey. Gabe was staying at his friend Kit's house.

I'd told him I wouldn't let him go, but he looked at me as if I had no right to tell him anything and then he left anyway. Everyone deals with grief in different ways and I had to let him find his own path. I'd be waiting for him the moment he wanted to talk.

I needed a drink but someone was moving around downstairs and I didn't want anyone to see me – especially as I wanted another glass of wine. I wouldn't say I had a problem; it was only a short-term solution for getting through a difficult spell.

I staggered out of bed, one of Oscar's T-shirts clinging to me, the sheets damp with sweat. My head swam and I steadied myself against the wall waiting for the dizziness to pass. I opened the curtains and swung the window outwards. The night was still, without the slightest breeze. I sucked in the air. It tasted sweet and dewy in my dry mouth. Lit by the half-moon, a bat flitted past the window and I leaned out to watch its progress across the sky. I thought I detected movement in the garden. Though waking in the middle of the night wasn't ideal, I often saw foxes stealthily crossing our lawn and plundering our bins. Sometimes though, it was a rat. I couldn't stand them. Oscar had said he'd deal with them, but that was one task he didn't manage to cross off his list. I looked at the garden, tried to discern the shapes and the shadows.

But all I saw was a man standing by the pear tree. As my eyes struggled to focus, he took a step backwards into the shadows. I could have sworn he was looking straight at me.

CHAPTER THIRTEEN

Molly Ingram

'Shhhh. It's okay now. Hey, come on, you're safe.' Molly stroked Beth's damp hair and whispered calming words in her ear.

Beth's skin was clammy as if she was fighting a fever. They sat on the steps that led down to the grassed lawn. Beth's eyes were wide and wild, and she smelled of sleep and sweat. Molly hugged her, but her friend was rigid. This last week with Beth had sparked a reconnection of a decades' old friendship. A balm for her fractured soul.

'He was standing just there.' Beth pointed to the tree. 'Why doesn't anyone believe me?'

'Shush. Of course we believe you, but there's no one there now, is there? See? All gone.' Molly didn't think Beth was lying, but she also knew she *had* to be mistaken. The garden gate was still locked and there was no sign that anyone had been in the garden.

'It's not okay,' said Beth. 'I saw a man standing on my lawn. He killed Oscar. I know it. And now he's making sure I don't tell anyone. There was that man who spoke to me at the funeral. I'm sure he was watching me and . . .'

'Babe, everyone was watching you, it doesn't mean a thing.'

'He said "congratulations" like in the card.'

'You said yourself that you couldn't be sure what he said.'

When Beth had turned on the garden lights, the commotion had woken Molly. She'd found Beth almost hysterical and Vince trying to calm her down. For a moment Molly thought Vince was going to slap her, but instead he laid a hand on Beth's cheek. 'I see him too – all the time – out of the corner of my eye, but he's not there, love. I promise you, he's not there.'

Beth had shrugged him off, 'That's not what this is about. I'm not saying it was Oscar. It was someone wanting to scare me. To shut me up. They hurt Oscar and now they're warning me off.'

Vince had made a big performance of checking the corners of the garden and looking over fences. He patted Beth's head as if she were a startled dog and made his way back into the house. The kitchen door had been left unlocked in case Molly needed to use the bathroom in the night, but nothing was missing or out of place.

'Perhaps you were still half asleep?' Molly suggested. 'Dreaming, maybe?'

Beth was silent for a long time. 'Maybe. I don't know. I mean, yeah, I'd had a bad dream but I'd been standing at the window for a few minutes before I saw him. I think.'

'And we put away the best part of two bottles of wine, so ...'

Beth smiled a little. 'True. My head is still a bit ... fuzzy.'

'There you go then. Blame the Rioja, babe.'

'But just so you have the whole, you know ... picture. There's something I should tell you.' She curved her shoulders and bent her head towards the ground. Molly couldn't see her face.

'Okay,' Molly said. 'Let's hear it then.'

'I don't know why I didn't tell you before. Embarrassed, I suppose. Partly it's because Oscar isn't around to defend himself, and partly because Harvey asked me not to say anything.

He thinks that it could affect the business and . . . well, we're all relying on it not going under.'

Molly sat in silence waiting for Beth to continue.

'The reason I was so frightened by seeing someone in the garden is that, well, the day before Oscar died, a man came to the house. A big guy, six-foot tall. In his late thirties maybe? He said that Oscar owed someone a lot of money and that he was here to collect. I've been half-expecting him to come back. With Oscar dead, there's no way he can pay up, is there? And what if this guy thinks that I'm responsible for the debt?'

Molly let her arm slip from Beth's shoulder. 'What?' Despite the warm night, a chill ran up her back.

Here?

Frazer had told her . . . well, he'd not told her much and he hadn't responded to her text asking for a refund. She'd assumed he'd never made it to Hellas Mill to talk to Oscar. But what if he had? If the man at Beth's door was Frazer, if he *did* speak to Oscar . . . Had that been the reason that Oscar had killed himself? Had he been that scared? Of course, there was the chance that . . . no. Molly had to calm herself down. Not let her mind run away.

He was meant to apply a teensy bit of pressure to show Oscar that she was serious about getting her money back. Frazer was meant to scare him, not . . . what? Kill him? Was she honestly entertaining that idea?

'What happened after this man turned up at the house? Did he talk to Oscar?'

Beth shook her head. 'I don't know. Oscar was angry when he found out he'd been here, though. He said he'd sort it. Do you think he confronted him? Do you think that this man pushed Oscar?'

'No. Can't have been because ... well, no. Why would he? For a start, he wouldn't be able to get the money back if he killed Oscar, would he?' Molly was nodding as she spoke. She had to convince herself that was the case. 'And ... And if he hurt Oscar, why would he come back to the house tonight? No, he'd be long gone. Right?'

'Perhaps he still wants the money,' Beth said. 'What if the people he's working for want him to get the money out of me instead?'

'No. They wouldn't want that. Definitely not. Is it cold out here? Are you cold? I'm cold.' She rubbed her arms.

Molly needed to call Frazer. They'd agreed never to speak directly but this was worth breaking the rules for. Was this all her fault? Had Frazer hurt Oscar, or had Oscar seen no other way out but to jump?

Holy mother of God. What a mess.

'Now let's not leap to any conclusions. Okay?' Molly said. 'It might not have anything to do with that. If there was someone in the garden, it could have been anyone.'

'Or no one,' said Esther's voice behind them causing them both to jump. Molly looked at Esther who was standing backlit and monstrous. 'Now, who's going to put the kettle on and make us all a nice cup of tea? Molly? I'd like to have a private word with Beth.'

Molly jumped up, pleased to have an excuse to grab a moment on her own.

'Absolutely. Yes, no, that's a great idea.' She squeezed Beth's shoulder and jogged barefoot up the steps.

It was all she could do not to keep on running through the house and straight out the front door.

CHAPTER FOURTEEN

Beth Lomas

Once we were alone in the garden, Esther had placed a bony hand on my shoulder. To comfort me, I'd thought. But as she spoke, her grip tightened. Fingers dug into my flesh and I tried to arch away from her.

'You did this,' she hissed.

'What? I ...'

'I know you're hiding something. The truth will out, Beth. And if I find that you had something to do with my son's death ... God help you.'

The shock had rendered me speechless for a moment but I regained control of my mouth and knocked her hand away. 'How can you say that? I loved Oscar!'

'Yes, but he didn't love you, did he? And if you couldn't have him ...'

Every word out of her mouth was a slap around my face. I'd let her get away with talking to me like that for too long. It was hard to remember exactly what I'd said next, but I know that my words were yelled, hers were hissed. At the sound of my raised voice, Molly had rushed outside and stepped between us, dragging me into the house before I could say anything I might regret. But it was too late.

Molly spent the night in my bed. She said it was to

comfort me, but I could tell she was shaken too. Each time I looked over at her, her eyes were wide open and she was staring at the ceiling. We'd locked the windows and doors, made sure that no one was hiding in wardrobes, under beds, or behind the floor-length curtains. I checked on Honey a dozen times but she didn't stir as the light from the landing fanned out over her face. I'd wanted to wake her so I could hold her in my arms. I wanted to crawl into bed beside her like I used to do when she had bad dreams, but this time I was the one having the nightmares.

This morning I'd wanted to call the police but Vince had persuaded me it was a waste of everyone's time. Whatever I'd seen hadn't broken any laws. Nothing was missing, no one got hurt and, apparently, it wasn't against the law to scare me half to death.

And then they were gone.

Vince and Esther had got what they came for. Closure. Their son given the send-off he deserved. Molly made a last dash into town before heading back to London, and Gabe still hadn't come back from whichever floor he'd slept on. Apart from Honey asleep upstairs, I was alone in the house for the first time in a week. I walked through the kitchen and unlocked the patio door. I took a blanket and went out to sit on the bench, staring at the spot where I thought I'd seen a man looking up at the house. There wasn't even a mark on the grass. I'm not sure what I expected. A discarded cigarette? A perfect imprint of a size ten shoe? But all I had was my hazy memory and a distinct feeling of unease.

I rearranged the blanket on my knee. It was May, but the warmth of a couple of weeks ago had disappeared. Though cold, it was a beautiful day. Cloud-free with the faintest breeze. I wanted to be outdoors as much as possible at the moment. I couldn't stand the walls closing in on me and understood the pull of the Peaks now, more than ever before.

I heard the front door slam and footsteps into the kitchen. I hadn't realised, until then, that my shoulders had been up around my ears, I felt them release now that Gabe was home. I needed my children around me. I craved them, needed to hold them close, breathe them in, keep them safe. But I shouldn't feel this desperate for them.

'Gabe,' I called into the house through the open patio door. 'I'm out here.'

He hovered for a moment in the doorway. His guitar was slung over his shoulder, his hair was a mess and he looked like he'd hardly slept. He'd changed out of his funeral suit into jeans and my old Nirvana T-shirt. He called it vintage.

'Hi,' he said.

'Hi.'

How was it that we were so awkward around each other now? I used to know every thought that went through his mind and now he was an enigma to me.

'Y'okay?' I asked.

He scratched the back of his head and yawned. 'Tough night. Didn't sleep all that great.'

I nodded. He avoided looking at me. There was no point me shouting at him for staying out all night. I needed to bring him closer, not push him away.

'How's Kit?' I was struggling for conversation. Any minute now we'd start talking about the weather.

Gabe shrugged. This was the way he communicated nowadays, through a series of shrugs and grunts. Everything about his interactions with me suggested indifference.

He took his phone out of his pocket and I could sense I was losing him again.

'Come and sit with me for a minute.' I patted the bench.

He looked at the phone display. He had nothing more important to do, no one more interesting to communicate with, so he ambled outside and stood in front of me. He rounded his shoulders as if he was trying to make himself smaller. 'Yeah?'

'Sit down, sweetheart. I've hardly seen you this last couple of weeks. Talk to me.'

'Mum, I don't need a chat on coping with grief or whatever.' He kicked at a stone but it only moved an inch.

'Don't worry,' I said. 'I'm completely out of chat. I'm the last person to give you advice on how to cope with grief. I'm not exactly on top of it myself.'

He took his guitar bag from his shoulder and leaned it against the side of the bench. When he sat down, it creaked under his weight.

'Here.' I pulled the corner of the blanket out from under my knee and covered his lap with it.

'Where is everyone?' Gabe asked looking back at the house.

'Molly's visiting her dad and Honey's still asleep. Or, at least, she's still in her room. I'm worried about her. She's talking to you though, isn't she? And you will tell me if there's anything I need to know about or anything I can do?'

'I reckon as long as you don't fall off a cliff, you'd be doing better than fifty per cent of our parents.' I raised an eyebrow at him, but he didn't apologise. 'Where's Nan?' he asked.

I screwed up my face. 'Ah. Your grandparents have gone.'

'Nice of them to say goodbye,' he said.

'I'm afraid it's my fault. I mean, they were always going to go back after the funeral, but I thought they'd stay a while yet. But, there was an incident last night and I had words with your nan. I might have told her she wasn't welcome to stay.'

Gabe's mouth dropped open. 'You stood up to Nan?'

I grimaced. 'Sort of. I got angry. Not just with her, with everyone, with myself mostly.'

'What happened?'

'Well, I suppose I had a lot to drink with Molly.'

'She's a bad influence.'

'Hey! That's my line!' We smiled at each other and it occurred to me I hadn't seen his beautiful smile in so long. I wanted to see more of it, and I wanted to be the cause of it more often. I missed him. Even though he was here, in front of me, I missed him.

'So, what happened?'

'I woke up in the middle of the night, you know what I'm like. I looked out of the bedroom window and it was pretty dark, not much of a moon, but I thought I saw a man in the garden.' Though I'd been certain of what I'd seen last night, in the daylight I doubted myself.

'What?' Gabe turned to look at me. 'Who?'

I shook my head. 'Don't know. Might not've been anyone at all. There was no sign when I came downstairs. No one believed me. They said I was imagining things, that I'd had a bad dream but . . .'

'But?'

'It wasn't a dream. Someone, or something was moving around in the garden. Your nan suggested it was my conscience playing tricks on me. She said I'd had something to do with your dad's death and it was his ghost come back to haunt me, and she hoped I never had a good night's sleep ever again.'

'Wow,' Gabe nodded and laughed at the same time. 'Harsh.'

'Oh, it gets better,' I said. 'She said I drove him to his death and I ... well, I snapped. I don't remember exactly what I said, but I remember using the words "interfering old witch" and saying that if she wasn't going to be helpful, she should get the hell out of my house.'

Gabe whistled. 'I wish I'd seen her face.'

'Trust me, you don't. It immediately sobered me up. That woman's glare can wither a person at forty paces. Grandad hugged me this morning but your nan waited in the car, didn't say a word. She's finding this whole thing difficult. I get it. God, if I were to lose one of you two ...'

'Well, I'm glad you said something. I could see it was driving you mad having her in the house. I'm pleased you put your foot down. You should do it more often.'

'What? Like, stop letting you sleep at your friends' houses and go to parties. Less time on the Xbox?'

He smiled that lazy smile of his I'd missed so much. 'No need to go crazy,' he said. 'Only, don't lose yourself trying to keep everyone else happy.'

I lay my head on his shoulder. 'You know, those are wise words, Gabriel Lomas. There's hope for you yet.' And what I really meant was that there was hope for *us* yet. This was the first time we'd spoken properly in weeks. Finally, I seemed to have done something he approved of.

We sat in silence watching a robin hop on the lawn, fix us with a beady eye, and flutter onto the table. We watched it hop closer, unfazed by us. No fear. A car drove by too fast up the lane behind the house, and the robin took flight.

'Gabe?'

'Hmm?'

'Are you angry with me?'

I heard him take a deep breath and my head rose with his shoulders. 'No. Yes. Maybe. I'm angry with everyone but, actually, not so much with you.'

'But you blame me for what happened to your dad.'

'No. I blame Dad for that. Do you believe he committed suicide?'

I sat up straight so I could look him in the eye. I suppose I knew this would come, but I'd not prepared for it.

'Oh, Gabe. Well, we don't use that phrase anymore. It's better to say died by suicide. You know, to, I guess, highlight the fact that people don't really have a choice. It's an illness driving them, and "committed" suicide makes it sound like a crime, like "committed murder" or something.'

'Nicely side-stepped,' he said. 'But you didn't answer my question.'

I looked at the ground.

'I don't know. Honestly, I don't. But, yes, that's what the police are saying.'

'But he could have fallen?' There was something like hope in Gabe's voice.

As a parent, you carry many burdens. The heaviest one is knowing how much information is appropriate to share with your children. I wanted to answer their questions honestly. I wanted them to know they could trust me, rely on me to tell them the truth. But I also wanted to protect them from anything that could drag them into adulthood too soon.

'Yes, I suppose he could've fallen. But when they found your dad's car, he'd left his wedding ring there. The police think that it's not the kind of thing he'd do if he was planning to come back.'

'Well, they're wrong,' he said. 'There's plenty of reasons why he might have done that. Millions.'

I put my hand on his and smiled. 'I don't know about millions of reasons, but . . .'

The fact that Oscar had left his wedding ring in the car felt like a message meant just for me. As if he knew he was in danger when he went up to Cloud Drop.

Gabe slipped his hand from mine and sat forward with his elbows on his knees. 'What if he was meeting someone,' said Gabe.

It was so close to my own thoughts that, for a moment, I thought I'd spoken aloud. 'What do you mean?'

'Nothing. Forget it.' He leaned forward, about to stand, but I held his arm.

'Gabe, no. Please talk to me. If you know something . . .'

He angled his body away from me, looking at the ground, weighing up his options.

'Gabe,' I said. 'I need to know.'

'But what if it's bad?'

'Anything that might explain what happened to your dad can't be bad, Gabe. Just tell me.'

I wanted to shake it out of him but had to remain calm or he'd clam up.

'Okay. I saw him, once. Me and . . . Look you've got to

promise not to overreact, right?' He looked straight at me then. I nodded and tried to give an encouraging smile. My chest tightened.

'Go on.'

'This one day ... It was a while back. Me and Kit, we bunked off school and well, I wasn't going to say anything because, you know, I knew that it would mess everything up. I didn't know what to do.'

I waited. Hardly breathing.

'We saw Dad,' he said. 'With a woman.'

'Oh.'

I slouched into the bench and pulled the blanket up around me. The other woman. I'd hoped that Oscar had the sense to keep that part of his life a secret. Now I wondered who else knew, and whether I'd ever be able to move on from it if I didn't confront her about it.

'I wouldn't have said anything, but when he left his ring in the car, well, men take their wedding rings off when they're having affairs, don't they? That is, you know, I've seen it in films and stuff. So he might have been meeting her up there?'

I nodded. It explained why Gabe had been so angry with his dad recently. He'd let him down and ceased to be the man that Gabe had always looked up to.

'Where were you when you saw Dad and this woman?' I asked.

'We were having a smoke behind the swimming pool and they were sitting in Dad's car.'

'Just sitting?'

He shook his head. 'They kissed when she got out.'

'Right. And when was this?'

'A couple of months ago? I dunno. It was just after my birthday. Sorry.'

'Don't be.' I put my hand on top of his. 'I already knew. It's what we argued about the night before he disappeared.'

In another life I would have lectured Gabe about smoking, about bunking off school. By rights, he should have been grounded, but why did it matter anymore? It only mattered that he was opening up to me.

'What did Dad tell you?' he asked.

'That it was a one-off. That it was already over. A mistake.'

We sat in silence, listening to the birds. Both smarting from the way Oscar had disappointed us.

Gabe shuffled around so he was facing me on the bench. 'Did you believe him?'

'I don't know. I wanted to but, I was angry and hurt. I didn't think it would be the last conversation we'd ever have. If I'd known ... Even with what he'd done, I still loved him and I just don't know whether he knew that at the end.'

'So you hadn't said you were leaving him or anything?'

'God, no. I wouldn't have ... I could never ...'

'So he had no reason to jump then, did he? There has to be more to it, right?'

I shrugged, looked away. 'Well, *I* think so but, unless we can convince the police to look into it, it's going to be recorded as death by suicide.'

His face darkened. A frown deepened between his brows. 'And what are you going to do about *her*?' he said.

'Nothing yet,' I said. 'But don't worry. I will.'

Gabe's face relaxed, relieved that he hadn't dropped the bombshell he'd feared, that I already knew what Oscar was capable of, but then his face crumpled as if he'd felt a stabbing pain. 'What if we're wrong, Mum? What if it all got too much for him and he felt bad, about the affair and stuff? I've been reading up on it, and suicide is more common than you'd think in men his age.'

And that was what we were all afraid of. No one wanted to believe they were left behind through choice, that we missed the signs, that we weren't enough to make him want to wake up one more day.

CHAPTER FIFTEEN

Molly Ingram

A year before Oscar's death

Oscar had called her up in the middle of a slow afternoon. He was in London having negotiated an exciting deal and needed someone to celebrate with. He had a little time before his train, could she meet him for champagne? *Please?*

Had she ever heard Oscar Lomas say *please* before? It must be one huge deal. Never one to turn down the chance of mid-afternoon Moët, Molly sent emails from her mobile as the taxi crawled down Gower Street. One of the perks of being her own boss was never asking anyone's permission to leave early or arrive late. Truth be told, she never really switched off from work. She would often draft job adverts for *The Times* or read through CVs at the weekend because she was passionate about her work.

Oscar was already at the bar when Molly got there, two tall glasses of rising bubbles waiting on the table. 'Either I'm especially honoured,' she said, 'or you know absolutely no one else in London.'

He laughed and kissed her on both cheeks. 'It's a bit of both. I don't want the guys I work with to see what a big deal this is to me. Playing it cool until the paperwork's signed.'

'But you don't mind acting like a big kid in front of me, is that it?'

'You've known me too long to think I have any maturity. Besides, you run your own business. You know how much these wins mean when it's your name above the door.'

They clinked glasses. 'Cheers to that!' Molly said.

They ordered food, a sharing platter of meats and cheeses, and chatted easily. Oscar's excitement for this new deal was infectious. He'd been trying to break into the international market for years. Harvey had warned him against it, said they were better off concentrating on the domestic market. Harvey was a *big fish, small pond* kind of guy.

'What does Beth think?'

'She literally couldn't care less,' said Oscar. Molly thought she noticed a hint of sadness in his voice, but he pointed to his empty glass, said, 'Shall we get a bottle? This is going down rather well.'

Oscar was one of those men who got better looking with age. The grey at his temples suited him. His eyes were bright blue against his tanned skin. She'd never known what Beth saw in him, aside from those conventional good looks. Molly had grown wary of men who wore their charm like a badge. Oscar was arrogant, opinionated, and often rude, and Molly hadn't expected him and Beth to last. It goes to show that opposites really do attract.

As they upended the bottle in the ice bucket, Molly couldn't have said what they'd talked about, but it had all seemed hilarious. A second bottle seemed like a great idea at the time. Friday-morning-Molly would view this as the start of the slippery slope. Thursday-night-Molly was a fool.

Oscar looked at his watch and swore. Then he started to laugh.

'I missed my bloody train! And the next one too. It's nearly ten o'clock!'

Molly laughed with her hand over her mouth. 'Won't Beth worry?'

'Beth? Hah!' The laughter had disappeared and he splayed his fingers and looked down at his wedding ring. 'She won't have even noticed I'm not there. Still, I should call her and let her know. You know, keep up the pretence.'

As Oscar pulled his phone out of his coat pocket Molly excused herself and went to the bathroom. It was only when she began to walk that she realised how much the alcohol was affecting her. She sat in the toilet stall with her head in her hands and considered a micro-nap, a rejuvenating doze. She couldn't remember last time she'd been this drunk.

She swayed as she came out of the cubicle and caught sight of herself in the mirror. Her face was flushed and her hair a mess. A button on her blouse had come undone without her knowing it. She'd been flashing Oscar all evening and hadn't once noticed his gaze stray. He was a good man, she'd thought. A true gent. She leaned closer to the mirror and checked her make-up. Holy mother ... what a state.

When she returned to the table Oscar had already paid the bill and was putting his coat on. A generous tip was folded under his empty glass.

'It's been a lovely evening, Oscar. We should do this again next time you're down in London.'

He looked at her in that way of his which made the rest of the room melt away.

'I've told Beth that the meeting overran and I'm staying in London tonight.'

'Oh,' Molly said. 'Do you have somewhere to stay?'

He stood close to her and stroked her hair with the back of his hand. 'I certainly hope so.'

CHAPTER SIXTEEN

Beth Lomas

I woke up thinking I could smell Oscar in the bedroom. That particular musky scent of sweat and citrus lingered but the more I breathed it in, the quicker it dissipated. It was three a.m. Then three ten. Three twenty. Four. There was no point trying to get back to sleep. Molly had gone back to London, the children were asleep, and I was alone. This is what life would look like from now on. This was my normal.

And I hated it.

How could he do this to us? He didn't die by suicide, so that left two options – either he slipped, or he was pushed. If he hadn't gone up to Cloud Drop that day neither of those things could have happened. He was an idiot and I wished I could tell him to his face.

Even if Oscar hadn't died, I might still have found myself on my own tonight. He never said he'd leave me, but no matter how you spun it, he slept with someone else. And if he wasn't planning on leaving me, would I have taken him back? I was generally a silently seething partner in any disagreement we had but I wouldn't stand for this kind of betrayal. My anger went back further than his death, it was anger about the affair, and the lies about the money. It was fury that he wasn't the man I thought he was.

He'd been more preoccupied of late, but it wasn't as if I hadn't asked him what was going on. I knew there'd been problems at work but he said it was no one's business but his. Perhaps I should have made him talk about it, but he always said that I didn't have a head for business. He called me his little bird brain.

If he'd been upfront with me about his financial issues perhaps all of this could have been avoided, but he'd hidden everything from me until it had blown up in his face. And now I'd never know if, given the chance, we would have worked out our issues and emerged the other side stronger for it. He'd robbed me of the chance to make it right.

I think I knew about the affair before Oscar admitted to it. I'd felt something shift between us, could see that the more I tried to please him, the more I annoyed him. I started calling him at work, looking for reassurance that everything was okay. I hated myself for being so needy but couldn't seem to stop myself.

This . . . mistake, this affair, it was nothing compared to the years of love that we had shared. When faced with the woman who'd had an affair with Oscar, I'd said nothing. I didn't want her to know that I knew. Part of me couldn't stand the idea of the confrontation, but part of me enjoyed the fact that I knew enough to ruin her. Would she still get marriage proposals if people knew what she was like?

There was no chance of getting back to sleep now. The light was beginning to spill under the curtains and I may as well do something useful while the kids slept on. I wanted to look at what Oscar had left behind in the Cabin. I needed our bank statements. Perhaps he'd left a secret fortune and the kids and I could close up the house and go abroad. I'd always fancied a trip to Canada.

I slipped out of bed and pulled on the clothes that I'd discarded on the floor the night before. As I tiptoed downstairs, I played that game of, 'If money wasn't an issue, and you knew you couldn't fail, what would you do?'

I pictured myself as a businesswoman like Molly. Sharp suits, heels that didn't rub or pinch, knowing that every penny I spent I had earned. I imagined people doing what I told them, because God knows, having children means I don't get to experience it often. I imagined falling into bed at the end of a long day, proud of myself. Sleeping soundly knowing I'd done my best. I'd always fancied the idea of having a catering company, after all, I loved to bake. And then that wicked confidence sapper – reality – whispered in my ear that I was too disorganised to run a company. Terrible with money. And if I couldn't get my children to listen to me, why would anyone else?

I always encouraged the children to pursue their dreams, and used to ask them, 'What do you want to be when you grow up?' And I would tell them, yes you can be a marine biologist and a professional rugby player and a rock star. All at the same time. I never expected them to be any of those things but I wanted them to always ask themselves what made them happy and – more than that – what excited them?

I didn't have a dream as a child. I enjoyed looking after people, thought I'd be a doctor or a nurse or a therapist. But then there was that incident with Barnaby Flint-Stanton and all I wanted to do was hide away. I worried that we'd be caught and so I kept my head down and stayed quiet. Apart from Molly, Oscar was the only one who knew what happened at the party that night. I told him when we were first married, back when our love felt bomb-proof. It was the last part of me that I was yet to share. My darkest secret. I'd hoped he could absolve me, that he'd tell me I had no choice and that he understood. I saw a flicker behind his eyes, just before he pulled me in for a hug, which said that he didn't know his wife as well as he thought he did.

He never threatened me, but he did once say with a laugh, 'You're stuck with me now because I know all your secrets. If you ever left me, I could destroy you.' I kissed him and said I'd never leave him anyway. But it stuck in my mind.

I rotated my shoulders and heard my neck crunch. I really could do with a holiday. Molly had already found the passports for me and brought them into the house. 'Use them or lose them,' she said. A family holiday was just what we needed. I didn't know how much longer Gabe would want to come with me. I wasn't his favourite person to spend time with. It felt like I was losing everybody too quickly, as if my usefulness was coming to an end. I was now a widow. Gabe was gearing up to flee the nest. What was my role, if I was no longer a wife or mother? Thank goodness, Honey was still too young to be thinking of leaving home. If I could keep her as my baby for ever, I would do. She used to say that she would never move out. That, if she got married, they would live on the top floor with her husband and sleep in bunk beds. I still remember the days when Gabe used to say he'd marry me when he grew up. Where had that sweet child gone, and would I ever get him back? He was now the same age as I was when Hattie threw that birthday party that would change all of our lives. I knew better than most that it only took a single event to change the course of your life for ever.

I made myself a hot chocolate using up the last of the milk. It wasn't like me to put myself first. I'd tried to be the perfect wife and mother even though, as far as I knew, I wasn't being graded for my efforts. I made a loaf of bread in the bread maker most days, had homemade granola in Kilner jars in the pantry, and I made pancakes every Sunday. Homemade cakes every week. I was first in line to help the PTA by donating cupcakes and cookies. But since Oscar had died, I hadn't been able to bake at all. The children had lived off kind donations from neighbours and takeaway pizza. Since Oscar's death, I'd lost weight. Oscar would've been pleased. He was always quick to point out when I'd gained a few pounds because he worried about my health, that's all. How could I argue with that?

I took the key to the Cabin from a hook by the door and slid open the patio door. A bird's shrill cry overhead was answered by one in the neighbouring garden. The walls between us were high and we rarely spoke, but I felt I knew more about my neighbours than was entirely comfortable. My house was in the middle of a grand terrace and there were certain points in the house, especially the landing, where the walls bled sound. On one side was a B&B, on the other an older couple whose children had flown the nest years ago. I popped round to check on them from time to time. Took cakes.

I'd fallen in love with our narrow three-storey house as soon as I'd seen it. Roses grew around the porch in thick braids obscuring the door from the road. There were iron railings around a sloping front lawn and an old-fashioned lamp-post by the gate which hadn't changed since it was powered by gas. There was a small park opposite, a river that split it in half, and we were in walking distance from the bandstand where I'd spent a large portion of my childhood. It was the house of my dreams and all Oscar could say was that parking would be a nightmare. Despite his initial misgivings, he borrowed money from his parents to secure the house. I couldn't imagine ever moving. Even when the kids left and I would be on my own, I wouldn't budge. I'd turn the top floor into a studio and take up painting. Perhaps I'd turn the house into a B&B like Marsha and Phil next door, but I couldn't see myself living anywhere else.

There was a faint light in the sky, telling me that morning was on its way. I couldn't stand in the cold, reminiscing the day away, so I wrapped my arms around me and crossed the damp lawn. I'd never mowed the grass, it had always been Oscar's domain. I glanced around as if I could find someone to do it for me then and there. I'd not noticed how much Oscar did until he was gone. Did that make me a bad wife? Was that why he had an affair, because I didn't value him? I'd give anything to rewind time and make sure he knew how loved he was. I'd show him that the only reason I was so angry with his betrayal was because I loved him so much and I was hurt by his actions.

The headache behind my eyes came back, as it always did when I tried to make sense of what had happened to us. I reached out for the Cabin door and stopped with my fingers inches from the handle. The wood was splintered around the lock. Through the window I could see that there were papers everywhere, and drawers gaped open.

I thought back to the night when I'd seen someone in the garden. It wasn't a figment of my imagination. He was going to break into the Cabin but found Molly sleeping there. And so he carried on watching us, waiting for her to go home. But what had he come back for?

CHAPTER SEVENTEEN

DC Lowry Endecott

'I'm so glad it's you, DC Endecott,' Beth said as she opened the front door. Her face was pale and there were dark shadows under her eyes.

'Please, call me Lowry. How are you, Beth?'

'I'd offer you tea but we're out of milk. I might have some fruit teas in the cupboard. Honey went through this phase ...' Beth walked away down the echoing hallway, leaving Lowry to close the door and follow. She noticed that Beth didn't answer her question. But then, it wasn't the best thing to ask a grieving widow.

'I meant to go to the shops first thing but when, well ... everything got away from me and then, when I called the station, they said someone would come round first thing, I didn't want to miss you, so ...'

It had been a week since Lowry had last been to the house, but already it had changed. It was messier. Chaotic. Shoes were piled in a corner instead of on parade in the shoe rack. Unopened mail addressed to Mr O Lomas lay in a shallow dish on the table. Cards addressed to Beth, ignored by their side. There were piles of books and clothes on the stairs hoping, with futility, that someone might pick them up next time they walked by.

Dying flowers in cloudy vases gave the air the smell of fetid undergrowth. Rosebuds had withered but hung on to stems above crisp leaves that were turning brown.

Beth filled the kettle from the kitchen tap despite having said she couldn't offer Lowry a drink. She was absent-mindedly looking out of the window. Her hands relying on muscle memory to carry out the tasks expected of her. Lowry looked around the room, taking in the dirty cups in the sink, the washing machine full of wet clothes.

'I haven't touched anything,' Beth said. 'I used a broom handle to open the door so I could have a quick look inside. Did I do the right thing?'

'Yes. Thank you.'

'From what I can tell, they've taken Oscar's laptop and gone through his files and drawers, but I can't be certain. Molly – that's my friend – did you meet her? Well, she tidied up in there and brought some important documents into the house, but I never thought about the laptop.'

'When did you notice the lock had been forced?' Lowry asked.

'About half four? I'm not sleeping well at the moment. I wondered whether the sound of them breaking into the Cabin was the thing that woke me, in which case the break-in happened more like three o'clock.'

She left the kettle in the middle of the draining board, instead of putting it back on its base, and unlocked the patio doors, sliding them open.

'I don't normally keep these locked during the day but it's made me feel a bit, I don't know, vulnerable I suppose. I don't like the thought that someone was so close to where we were sleeping.'

'When was the last time you went in the ...'

Lowry indicated the building at the bottom of the garden. It seemed wrong to call it a shed. It was an expensive glass and wood construction which would have cost most of her annual salary. It looked incongruous here where everything else was antique, historic.

'We call it the Cabin. It's a home office really. Oscar's haven away from the damp, old house. He wanted something modern and new in his life.' She paused and said quietly, 'In more ways than one.'

'When did you last go into the Cabin?'

'Oh, I don't know. I rarely go in there unless it's to tell Oscar it's time for dinner or to collect dirty cups. I was only going in there today to see if I could find something about our bank accounts. Everything is electronic nowadays isn't it? Can't remember the last time I saw a bank statement. I'm embarrassed to say that I have no idea how much money we've got. Oscar gave me an allowance for things like food shopping.' As if sensing Lowry's judgement she quickly said, 'I know that sounds old-fashioned, but I'm not good with money. Really. It's shocking just how bad I am. Oscar was only looking after us. We had a joint account, but I know he also had a personal account that the mortgage payments came out of, so I was going to look for the details when I saw the lock had been broken.'

'Right. Everything was in his name? The bills and what have you?'

'Yes, Oscar spoiled me, really. God knows how I'm going to manage now. Especially seeing as the codes and login details for pretty much everything were on that laptop.'

'Right.' Lowry was trying hard not to judge, but some

people made it difficult. Why was Beth defending a man who'd been sleeping with another woman and had lied to her about his financial problems? 'And you don't work,' she said.

Beth lowered her head. 'No. I mean, I've been thinking about setting up my own company for a while to sell the cakes I bake – maybe do party food – but I've not cooked a thing since Oscar died, and I'm not sure I'd be able to handle the business side of it anyway.'

Lowry had noticed two locks and a bolt on the front door, and a burglar alarm on the house, so why would anyone keep a laptop and important documents in a glorified shed? They walked side by side down the garden. Lowry noted the high walls either side of the long, narrow garden and a worn wooden fence behind the Cabin. There was a gate in the fence where a bolt and padlock lay undisturbed. Lowry's guess was that they'd come in over the fence. It wasn't that high. All they'd need to do is give a friend a leg up or, if they were acting alone, climb onto a bin.

Lowry walked to the fence and looked over it. There was an alley behind the house, just wide enough for a car to fit down it, and she could see another fence and then the gardens of the houses behind them, a mirror image of this terrace. At the end of the row of houses, there were three garages.

'Your garage?' she asked pointing towards them.

'Yes. The one with the black door.'

'But that's not been broken into?'

'Thankfully, no.'

'Okay,' Lowry said. 'There's been a spate of thefts in the area in the last couple of months. Mostly bikes out of sheds and loose change out of cars.'

'Yeah, my sister-in-law has had her car broken into and the paintwork scratched three times in as many months.'

Petty crime was on the increase in Hellas Mill, an area which, until recently, had benefitted from the low insurance prices of a relatively crime-free area. The laptop would be sold on for a tenth of its value. If Beth was lucky, they'd only be interested in what they could sell for a quick pound instead of planning to commit fraud from any personal information they could find on it.

She sighed and wondered whether she'd have time to go horse riding with Hattie later. It was difficult to care about the job when all this would lead to was paperwork, not an arrest. She'd seen a dozen similar crimes in the last two months, but no one expected to see their things again, all they wanted was a reference number for the insurance claim.

This wasn't the job she signed up for, though it had served its purpose at first. A messy breakup left her needing to get away from everything she thought she knew and wanting a slower pace while she put herself back together. But now she was getting bored. And annoyed that she wasn't making as much of a difference as she needed to. The police here were under-resourced and treated with a lack of respect that used to be reserved for people who broke the law.

'They didn't attempt to break into the garage or the house, just the Cabin?'

'That's right.'

She was pinning her hopes on a new job, in London, where the work would be more rewarding. She'd spoken to her old boss, Greta, about making the move, but she had to concentrate on the job she already had right up until the new job was confirmed. Not everyone got to do a job that excited them each day. Sometimes bills just had to be paid.

She'd been feeling dissatisfied with her life recently. It was any number of things that contributed to her mood but it was the invitation to Hattie's third wedding – Finn's first – which triggered it. It was going to be an even bigger event than her previous two and seeing as Lowry had given up on the idea of even having one wedding, it seemed greedy to her.

Finn was Lowry's boss, but it was Hattie who'd become her best friend in Hellas Mill. Everyone seemed to be moving into new stages of their lives. Exciting stages. Hattie was already talking about what the future held. Friends that Lowry had left behind in London were settling down, moving on, some relocating to the commuter belt for gardens and country pubs. Girls she'd known from school were posting pictures of their children on social media, of new cars, of new houses, new jobs. But what did Lowry have to look forward to? She'd always lived day to day until she realised that every day was the same.

Beth cleared her throat, expecting something more from Lowry.

'Yes, right, well . . . You did right to leave everything as it was. I imagine it was just kids, chancing their luck.'

She stepped inside, the room smelled of warm wood and sawdust. It wasn't as messy as it looked from the outside, it hadn't been a frenzied emptying of drawers and smashing pictures. This had been methodical. They knew what they were looking for.

'I'd like you to have a good look around and make note of everything that's missing,' Lowry said. 'And if you have any serial numbers, that would be helpful too. Was the laptop valuable?'

'Not really. It was old. Five maybe six years? Oscar's been saying for a while that he wanted to get a new one.'

'And was there anything else of value in here that's obviously missing?'

'Like I say, it was Oscar's office. I hardly came in here. As far as I know the only thing he kept in here was the usual household paperwork like house insurance and car insurance. You know. When the road tax is due, and stuff like that. I keep trying to make sense of why someone would break into the Cabin instead of our garage which is away from the house and has expensive bikes in it. It feels ... significant.'

Lowry had been to plenty of shed break-ins and none of them had been significant as anything other than bored teens looking to cause chaos. She stepped closer to a circular object on a shelf above the desk, and saw it was made by Bang & Olufsen. A speaker which she would have expected to be worth more than the laptop. Easier to carry too. Wireless headphones lay on the desk with the matching logo. There was the sound of scratching coming from beneath her feet. Lowry paused and looked down.

'Rats,' said Beth. 'I need to deal with them before they eat through the floor. I just can't ... I just don't know where to start. There's too much going on.'

It seemed to Lowry that the statement could have applied to much more than just rodents. Beth looked like a woman overwhelmed by life right now.

'You know, I think I saw him,' Beth said.

Lowry clenched and unclenched her hands. 'Sorry? You *saw* the person who broke in?'

'Maybe. I mean, I saw someone in the garden, but I didn't actually see them waving a crowbar about, so I can't be completely sure.' She turned and walked slowly back towards the house and Lowry had no choice but to follow her if she wanted more information. She took one last look around the Cabin. The expensive furniture, the mini kitchen. She opened the small fridge, but it was empty.

The man had an entire factory, a business, why did he need an expensive office at home? Perhaps his life hadn't been that different to Lowry's. Some jobs you just couldn't leave at the door. You were never really off duty.

She stepped out into the fresh morning and began walking up the gently sloping garden. Lowry didn't know what to make of Beth Lomas. When she reported her husband missing, she'd noticed that Beth was distant, in a constant daydream, dropping little hints and phrases and then not elaborating when asked. Even now, with the break-in, it was as if she knew more than she was saying.

As Lowry stepped into the kitchen she asked her again, 'You saw who did it?'

Beth nodded. 'I saw him on Monday night.'

Lowry leaned against the wall and looked to the ceiling. 'You told me the break-in was last night.'

'It was. I think he came here the night before and found Molly sleeping in there. It was around three a.m. that time too. I woke up and went to stand at the bedroom window. There wasn't much to see.'

She folded her arms and looked out at the garden.

'Anyway, I looked outside and there was a man in the garden. By the time I got downstairs he'd disappeared and there was no sign of him. I think he came back last night to finish the job.'

Lowry pushed herself off the wall and reached for her notebook from her pocket. 'Did you get a good look at him?'

'Not really. I saw enough to know he was tallish and had a medium build. It was dark. I couldn't tell you what clothes he was wearing or the colour of his hair. All I can tell you with absolute certainty is, he was there. Molly and Esther tried to tell me I was imagining it, but I know what I saw.'

'Any ideas?'

'My first thought was the debt-collector who came to the house the day before Oscar died. And if the computer is missing, perhaps he's trying to track down his money? I don't know, but it's the only thing that makes sense to me.'

'And he was on his own?' Lowry asked.

Beth shrugged. 'I didn't see anyone else.'

Lowry's mind started whirring as it often did when she got a sniff of a proper case. What if it wasn't the computer itself that was of value but the information on it? What if there was something on there that someone didn't want anyone to see?

'You say that Oscar was having financial problems. Is there anyone you can think of that would be implicated in this – other than the debt-collector – that might have wanted to dispose of the information?'

'Not that I know of, but you'll have to talk to Harvey – Oscar's brother and business partner. It turns out I knew very little about Oscar's life either inside or outside of work.'

Lowry studied Beth. She was a strong looking woman, shorter than Lowry by several inches. Could she have overpowered Oscar and pushed him over the edge? If she'd killed him elsewhere and taken his body up there, she would've needed help.

She couldn't believe she was considering the possibility that this was a murder, but she had to admit that this wasn't as simple as it first appeared. If it wasn't suicide then the question was – who killed Oscar Lomas?

CHAPTER EIGHTEEN

Beth Lomas

I closed Gabe's laptop and picked up my cup. I'd been staring at the screen so long, my tea had gone cold, but I drank it anyway.

I felt bad for snooping. And worse that I hadn't been able to learn anything from my pathetic attempt to pry.

He knew I was using his laptop to try and access my bank account, perhaps he'd deliberately cleared his search history. His passwords had changed since the time when he used to share them with me, in the days before he had anything to hide. What happened to the good old days when kids kept diaries under their mattresses for parents to sneak a look at? At least he was talking to me a little more now, but I still hadn't seen him cry. I feared he was bottling up his emotions. Was he talking to his friends about how he felt? A teacher perhaps?

Honey was at least showing her emotions and letting me comfort her. I didn't want her to feel that she had to keep her hurt hidden in case it upset me. She'd been asking a lot about what happens after death.

'Do you believe in heaven, Mum?'

'I'd like to,' I said.

She'd looked at me like I was a puzzle. 'So why don't you?'

'It sounds too good to be true. I think it might be something we tell ourselves to lessen the pain of loss. If we can convince ourselves that we'll see our loved ones again then it won't hurt as much.'

'You're funny,' she said. 'Why wouldn't you take advantage of believing something that stops the pain?'

According to the internet, I've already sailed through the shock and denial stage. I'm now in the anger phase of grief. But anger doesn't even come close to describing the fury that is fizzing through my veins right now.

Would it be socially acceptable to shout, kick and scream, then blame it on a phase? Don't blame me if I ram your car when you cut me up in traffic, it's just the grief. Did I steal your parking space? Grief. Did I walk away when you were in the middle of telling me how your son was getting on at university? I can't be held to account because of, you know, the grief.

But I'd never do that because it's not who I am. Or, at least, it's not how I like to portray myself. Inside, I'm churning with anger, seething with rage, and yet I smile and I nod. I managed to convince myself that anger was the real weakness, but I'd gone so far the other way, that I'd turned into an automaton. While putting out anger's flames I'd doused my passion too. In protecting myself from the hurt, I'd stopped taking risks or experiencing new things. To stop the feelings that scared me, I'd stopped myself feeling anything.

Oscar's death had awoken feelings in me that I couldn't control. The anger, the fear, the grief, the ... relief. I put my hand over my mouth, shocked at my own admission. No, that couldn't be right. I didn't want him to be dead. I didn't want to spend every waking moment wondering how he died and who'd killed him. Life was more complicated without him. Finances were tight, my children were distressed, I didn't know what was going to happen from one day to the next, but ... I felt something that reminded me of freedom.

I was distraught about Oscar, of course I was, but the reality of not having him around wasn't much different. Sure, the bins didn't get taken out, but there had to be more to a marriage. I'd lost the status of being his wife, and as it turned out that wasn't worth as much as I thought it was.

I no longer had to cook curry on a Friday night. I never had to bake a peanut butter cake ever again. I could wear whatever I wanted, go wherever I chose, let the dishes pile up in the sink and leave the ironing for another day – if I wanted. And that was the key; I might *choose* to make a curry on Friday, I might not, and no one would be angry with me for my decision.

I'd spent most of my life trying to keep Oscar happy, but I never stopped to wonder how happy he made me. I told Lowry that I didn't know who he was having an affair with but that wasn't true. I've worked it out now. The texts, the glances. I should have known.

I don't know why I've not already confronted her. I hate arguments, like most people I suppose, but that's not it. I'm embarrassed. She isn't someone who holds her tongue. She might point out how Oscar wasn't getting what he needed at home and I'd look at her slim waist and her plump lips and I'd feel inadequate. I was an idiot to think that I could hold Oscar's attention. She's the same age as me but looks younger. She's livelier, more fun. Successful, desirable. Compare her to me and, well, I don't come out looking good.

As much as I told myself that it wasn't my fault, I couldn't help but feel that Oscar's affair reflected worse on me than it did on him. He was still attractive to members of the opposite sex, but I couldn't remember the last time someone looked twice at me. No flirting, no wolf whistles, it was as if I'd ceased to exist sexually.

I tried to imagine how she'd been feeling since Oscar's death. Was she upset or did she never love him?

When people sympathised with me, I wanted to shout that my marriage wasn't everything it looked like from the outside. I didn't lose Oscar on the day he died. I lost him long before that.

CHAPTER NINETEEN

Molly Ingram

Everything Molly had worked hard for had disappeared and she had no one to blame but herself. She had ruined her own life and the lives of people she loved. She was a waste of space. An embarrassment.

It was lunchtime but, apart from the position of hands on a clock face, there was no reason for her to get out of bed. A talk show panel of perpetually angry women was on the television. Molly wanted to change channels but she'd lost the controls under a mass of blankets and didn't have the energy to hunt for them.

Her bladder ached. She needed the bathroom but couldn't be bothered to move. She wondered how it would feel if she wet the bed like a child. Wondered if adult nappies worked. Her landline was ringing again. Last time, it had woken her from a pleasant dream but there was no one she wanted to talk to. She'd hoped that yesterday's meeting would have presented her with options to save her business. Or at the very least give her additional time to turn the company around.

'We've been trying to contact you for the past week,' they'd said. 'There is no other choice.'

And so she'd filed for bankruptcy. Farewell to a good credit score. Adios to solvency. People had lost their jobs, thanks to her, and they'd be lucky to see any redundancy pay thanks to Oscar Lomas. And that wasn't even the worst thing to have happened to her this week.

Frazer wasn't returning her calls or messages. If he had something to do with Oscar's death, he'd probably got rid of the phone by now. The sensible thing to do would be to go to the police and let them track him down. It was important for Beth to know that Oscar didn't die by suicide or, if he did, that Frazer had encouraged him along that path. But it wouldn't bring him back, and if Frazer had killed Oscar, then Molly would be guilty too because she was the one who set Frazer on Oscar's path. With no paper trail and no contract, how could she prove that she hadn't asked him to kill Oscar? And then she would also have to come clean about, well, about *everything*.

She'd lent him £200,000. And then another £50,000. *Not for much longer*, he'd said.

'You know I'm good for it and I'll pay you back with interest within a matter of weeks.'

Molly was relying on Oscar to be a decent person. However, he was the kind of man who slept with his wife's best friend, so it should have been obvious that his morals were questionable. Molly wouldn't go as far as to say he'd black-mailed her, but the result was the same. She was aware of how thin the ice was beneath her feet as she transferred the money to him. He hadn't threatened her and yet she was compelled to keep him happy. The request for money had come a week after their night together, and she hadn't agreed because he'd seen her naked, she'd agreed because he made a good argument about how he needed a bridging loan, and the banks weren't keen to support him. She'd agreed because she believed it was a good deal and she knew how close to the line it got when it was your own business sometimes. And she wanted him to succeed for his sake and for Beth's. Of course, it had crossed her mind, briefly, that if she said *no* he could make things difficult for her, but mostly she wanted to show him how mature she was about what had happened between them. She was showing how there was no awkwardness, even though she was dying inside.

Molly groaned. She was dehydrated, hadn't had her morning coffee and she could feel her pulse in her temples. It was times like this – not that there had been any times *quite* like this – when she hated being alone. Oh, to have someone who would bring her a cup of tea in bed. Someone who would make her a slice of toast. She'd give anything for a bacon butty right now and she hadn't eaten bacon since 2015.

After three months with no word from him, she'd called Oscar at work and said, 'So, this is difficult, but I need that money back by the end of the month. Bills to pay. You know how it is.'

'No can do,' he'd said.

'Oscar, this isn't funny. You said I'd have the money back by now and I have serious overheads. At the moment we're keeping it between ourselves. If I have to get external help with this there'll be things coming out that you'd rather keep between us.'

'Are you threatening me?' he asked with laughter in his voice.

'Now why would you say that? I'm simply reminding you that—'

'You have far more to lose than I do.'

'How do you work that one out?' she asked, though she'd broken out in a cold sweat.

'If Beth found out about us, she'd forgive me. She loves me and she loves our life, there's no way she'd give that up. I'm the father of her children. We're a unit. You? She'd drop you and never see you again. Who are you anyway? A hanger-on from childhood days? A drunk embarrassment of a friend?'

She was glad he couldn't see her face and how his words wounded. 'What makes you think I care?' she'd said. 'Right now, my priority is that money. I want it back by the end of the month otherwise everyone will find out what you're like. Not only Beth, but your kids, your parents, your staff. You won't be such a big man then, will you?'

He'd been silent for a moment and then he'd started to chuckle.

'Oh, Molly. It's a dangerous game you're playing and I know that you care too much about Beth to hurt her like this.'

'She'd get over it, find someone better than you. Better than me, too. You're right, I've not been a good enough friend to her. She'd move on, have a far better life without either of us in it.'

'In prison?' he asked.

'Sorry?'

He lowered his voice, but it seemed louder in her ear. 'Oh yes, Beth told me everything.'

Molly shook her head and sighed. 'I literally do not have a clue what you're talking about. Look, get that money in my account in the next two weeks or—'

'I know what happened,' he said. 'Beth told me about you and that toff. Barnaby, wasn't it?'

Molly felt like someone was pouring cold water over her scalp. She placed the phone in her other hand and wiped her sweaty palm on the arm of her chair.

'Did Beth forget to mention that she'd told me?' Oscar asked, with a smile in his voice. 'Hattie Flint-Stanton's brother wasn't it? I know the woman quite well. In fact, I'm seeing her later today. Do you think she'd like to know what happened to her brother?'

Goosebumps erupted up and down Molly's arms. They'd sworn never to tell a soul. How could Beth have been so stupid?

'She was protecting you, wasn't she?' Oscar continued. 'Are you willing to let her go to prison because you've always been a slut? Must Beth always clean up your mess?'

'You wouldn't.'

'Wouldn't I? Let's say that I plan on taking your secrets to the grave with me, but if anything were to change . . .'

Molly squeezed the phone and hissed into the mouthpiece, 'Unless you pay me back by the end of the month, Oscar, you'll be seeing that grave sooner than you expected.'

CHAPTER TWENTY

Beth Lomas

I'd taken a sleeping tablet to stop the nightmares. I wanted to close my eyes and wake up eight hours later without remembering a single dream.

I'd been asleep for a couple of hours when I heard ringing. For a moment I couldn't work out where the sound was coming from. It took an age for me to open my eyes and scramble for the phone.

'Yes?' I cleared my throat.

There was no sound from the other end. I was about to hang up when I heard someone take a breath.

I struggled to sit up against the pillows. 'Who is this?'

A sigh. A woman's sigh. Light and soft.

'Who's calling?' I asked.

Silence.

'If you're after Oscar,' I said. 'He's dead.'

There was a click and the line went silent. I clutched my nightshirt and took a deep breath. I pulled the sheets up to my neck, made myself smaller. Sometimes it felt like Oscar had been gone for years, and sometimes it was as if he'd only just left the room. If that call had been for him, Oscar was Schrödinger's cat; in that person's world Oscar had still been alive until a moment ago. I envied a world where I didn't have to deal with his death every single day. Every time I had to explain to someone that Oscar had died, it was a punch to the stomach.

I placed the phone back on its base, my hand shaking. I thought of Oscar's affair, wondered if more than one woman was pining for him.

'No, Oscar, don't you dare do this to me. Don't you dare.'

I didn't want to share him with anyone else, even in death. Couldn't I be allowed to be the only woman missing him like this? It had been almost two weeks since his body had been found but I still hadn't found peace because there was still so much I didn't know, and so much I would never know.

Oscar and I hadn't been intimate for some months before ... the accident. Well, not with each other anyway. I thought it was a phase. All couples had them. We'd been together for almost two decades; it was understandable if we went through periods of not being crazy about each other. I'd thought it would be a storm we'd weather together. Our marriage was something we'd concentrate on again once Gabe and Honey had flown the nest. But we never got the chance.

I pulled my dressing gown off the back of the door and went down the stairs passing pictures charting our family growth. Wedding photos of when we were a two. The day we brought Gabe home from hospital. Honey in Gabe's arms the first time he met his little sister. At the bottom of the stairs a photo of the four of us together on a boat. Tanned skin, white smiles. Looking like the perfect family.

My whole body tensed and I wanted to hit something. Lash out. Scream. Oscar's face, smiling for the camera, looked smug. His arm was around me yet there was enough space between our bodies for sunlight to stream through and illuminate Honey's hair like a halo. I tore it from the wall, the nail coming with it, a piece of plaster falling to the carpet.

I wondered whether I'd ever know the truth about my husband. And then I thought I *had* to know. It came at me like a torrent, a gale. I needed to understand what had taken him to the top of Cloud Drop that day and I could only do that by bringing all our secrets out in the open.

I marched into the kitchen, dropping the picture into the bin and picking up my mobile. It took seconds to find the number I was looking for. I pressed the dial button and waited for a sleepy voice to pick up the phone. My heart was beating so loudly I thought I wouldn't be able to hear her voice.

'Hello?' she croaked.

'Hi, it's Beth. We need to talk about you and my husband.'

CHAPTER TWENTY-ONE

Molly Ingram

'And then I said to her, "well don't eat it then", but she did and my word, if she weren't up all night being sick. I mean, who buys sushi from a garage?'

Molly was on her way back to Hellas Mill next to a well-meaning woman who could have sat in any one of the seats in the near-empty carriage but had chosen to sit in the seat she'd reserved. Molly adopted her very best don't-talk-to-me face, which worked on London buses and tubes, but was no barrier to the woman next to her.

'Oh dear,' Molly said.

'And now she can't eat fish at all. She had a prawn sandwich the other day and it went straight through her.'

'Goodness, that's ...'

'I said she should try a nice piece of cod from the chippy but she said, "Mum, I don't think I can," and I said, "well, what are we going to have on a Tuesday night now then?" And she said, "Sausage." Sausage! I mean, it's a fish and chip shop, not a sausage and chip shop!' She laughed and nudged Molly's arm with her elbow.

Molly smiled along with her but, when the woman's phone rang and she started rummaging through her bag, Molly was relieved to be able to turn back to the window.

There was something fascinating about watching the backs of houses as the train sped by. All these lives, all with their own secrets and their own lies. Trampolines, greenhouses, and discarded fridge-freezers gave Molly just enough of a picture of those lives to make a snap judgement, but she'd never know if she was wrong.

There was nothing to keep her in London now. She'd sent Vijay a message to say goodbye then turned off her phone in case he tried to call her. She didn't tell anyone she was leaving because there was no one who cared. She had no work. She didn't even have a goldfish that needed feeding. There were no meetings to cancel nor social engagements to rearrange. She simply locked up her flat and got on the next train, leaving the life she'd worked so hard for, yet had destroyed so easily.

'No, I'm on the train,' the woman said into the phone. 'Yeah. No, Colin's going to pick us up.'

Molly would have to get used to other people. Her money had served as a barrier for a long time. A safety one, and an emotional one. It kept her cosseted and protected and, now that it was gone, she was having to take a good look at herself. Frankly, she didn't like what she saw.

Every time the train went through a tunnel, she studied her own reflection. When had those lines appeared under her eyes? Last time she had her legs waxed, the beautician waxed her big toe. Her big toe! When – and why – did hair start sprouting in unnecessary places like toes and chins? She knew she wasn't a classic beauty, but she had always worked hard on her appearance. There was so much you could hide with concealer.

She could have stayed on in London, hiding out for a little

longer but it was time to face up to the mistakes she'd made. Never had Molly expected to be coming back to Hellas Mill again so soon. This time, though … this time she was going to stay awhile. Her dad had said she could live with him for as long as she liked and, as painful as returning home was, it felt right, poetic somehow that she would face her past from her childhood bedroom.

She'd gone to see her dad before heading back to London and was surprised at how nice it was to spend time with him. Molly told him what she'd been unable to tell Beth. That she'd lost everything and she didn't know what to do next.

'Come home then,' he'd said. 'Come home. I wouldn't mind the company.'

It struck her that the reason she'd put up a barrier between them wasn't because of anything Dad had done, but because she was pretending to be someone she wasn't and that was far easier to do if you didn't have to look your past in the eye. There was no hiding from it now, though. Molly was nothing but trouble. She'd ruined her life, and Beth's too. Her past had caught up with her and she couldn't keep running.

CHAPTER TWENTY-TWO

Beth Lomas

I showered, shaved my legs and blow-dried my hair. Of course, it didn't matter how I looked, that wasn't what this was about, but I wanted to feel good about myself today. Why shouldn't I hold my head up high? I wasn't ashamed and, judging by her voice on the phone last night, *she* wasn't either.

We'd agreed to meet at the band-stand in the park at three p.m., the earliest she could get there. It had the added bonus of only being an hour before Honey needed taking to her piano lesson, so I couldn't let it drag on. The public setting would help us be civil and keep our voices down.

For a change, I was early and she was late. It was an in-between day, the sky was part clouded and the sun dipped in and out, playing hide-and-seek with the children. I rarely came here anymore, not now the kids were at an age where they could come without me. Oscar and I used to love coming here on warm evenings, our arms around each other's waists and each of our steps matching the other as if we were part of the same being.

A family with two young children, twins, sat on a blanket on the grass and rolled a ball to each other. I envied those precious pre-school years, though I hadn't realised their value when they'd been mine. An ice-cream van pulled up, ready to catch the kids as they came out of school. A dog ran past, its lead streaming behind it, seemingly without an owner. I was watching its progress, wondering whether I should try to catch it, when I heard footsteps and a voice behind me.

'Hello, Beth.'

For a moment I didn't turn. Across the park, a man appeared and whistled. The dog loped in a circle and bounded back to him. I tried to put off the inevitable moment of confrontation and was struck with the realisation that this had been a terrible idea. I couldn't remember what I'd hoped to achieve by confronting her.

I turned slowly. Her chin was jutting out, she looked defiant, a little angry. Would it have killed her to look even a little bit embarrassed? Instead it was me who was struggling to keep eye contact.

'Hello, Hattie. Thank you for coming.'

She adjusted the strap of her handbag which was slung across her chest. Her handsome features, which had been too angular when we were teenagers, gave her a sculpted look now. Even if you were meeting her for the first time, you'd know she was rich. It was the knee-high brown leather boots, the tailored jacket over slim-fitting jeans. It was family money. Horses and racing. She had taken over Wesley Manor, where she grew up, and her parents had moved into a converted barn out the back. She looked a lot like her brother, Barnaby, but now wasn't the time to think about him. Today was about what Hattie had done to *me* and my family.

'Hello, Beth,' she said, glancing at her watch. 'What did you want to talk to me about?'

'I think you already know.'

'Come out with it,' she said. 'I've got problems with the wedding caterers and I need to get over there by four.'

The wedding was big news in the village. Everyone was welcome, even Oscar and I had been invited. Brazen of her to have her lover at her nuptials. It suited her that he couldn't attend now.

'For obvious reasons Oscar and I won't be coming. Him because ... well, he's dead, and me because I have an issue with the fact you were sleeping with my husband.'

My heart trembled in my chest. I hadn't expected to come out with it like that.

She glanced over her shoulder as if concerned that some-one would hear us, but no one was anywhere nearby. She moved closer and narrowed her eyes at me. 'Look, I don't know what he told you, but it was nothing more than a teensy bit of fun that got out of hand.'

'That's a strange apology,' I said.

She raised a single eyebrow. 'Is that what you were expect-ing? Look, I wish it hadn't happened because I love Finn more than anything in the world, but I don't owe you an apology. You must have known that he was going to ask for a divorce as soon as the children left home so don't play the victim with me, Eliza*beth*.'

I gripped the handrail until my knuckles whitened and I felt the gold band of my wedding ring dig into my finger. The life that Oscar had described to her was different from the one I had been living. Either that, or Hattie was manipulating the facts to suit herself.

'You seem to be mistaken, *Harriet*.' She winced at the sound of her full name. 'I'm afraid Oscar might not have been one hundred per cent honest with you. But then you knew he wasn't an honest man, didn't you? It looks like you fell for his lies. But don't feel bad about it,' I touched her arm. 'He wasn't after your brains.'

She stepped away from me. 'I don't know why you're over-reacting. You're not the first woman whose husband strayed and you won't be the last. In this day and age, it's to be expected.'

I couldn't help but smile because she was still as I remembered her. She was without shame or humility. The whole family were bad news. Over the last few years we'd seen each other at events, bumped into each other in town. We were always civil to each other. But then, I was civil to everyone.

'Wow. You sound like Oscar,' I said. 'He told me that it didn't mean anything, but at least he knew what he'd done was wrong. If you honestly think that all husbands stray, Hattie, then I feel sorry for you. Why marry again if you don't expect Finn to stay faithful?'

She shook her head as if she pitied me. 'There's more to a successful relationship than monogamy,' she said.

I walked around the band-stand, touching each supporting strut. I wondered how many hands had touched this wood and how many of them had been adulterous.

'When did the affair start?' I asked.

'It wasn't an affair. We slept together once, that's all.'

'My son saw you kissing in Oscar's car.'

'Me? In his car?' She looked horrified at the thought. 'God, no. I'd never do anything so sordid as be seen in public.'

'I don't believe you,' I said. But my conviction wasn't as strong as my words.

'To be frank, Beth, I don't care if you do. I have nothing to hide. You can believe me or not, it's entirely up to you, but I am not wasting another moment of my time trying to convince you.'

'Why did the affair stop?' I asked her.

'I've told you, it wasn't an affair. I wanted one last fling before I got remarried but Oscar had ulterior motives.'

'What do you mean?' My breath caught in my chest. Had he been in love with her? Planning to leave me?

'Your dear husband was only after my money. It happens a lot more than you'd expect. Well, a lot more than I'd expected anyway. When I refused to lend him any, he tried to blackmail me. I had to tell Finn everything. He went crazy and confronted Oscar, but Finn still wanted to marry me. He's a better man than I deserve and I'll spend the rest of my life making it up to him. Listen, is that everything?' asked Hattie, 'because I really should get going.'

She hesitated, looked for a moment like she was sorry. 'I know it doesn't feel like it right now, but it meant nothing to either of us. We used to flirt all the time, but it was just a bit of fun. I was flattered by the attention, to be honest. We'd been drinking. He was celebrating a big deal at work, and then we were kissing and . . .'

She suddenly pushed her shoulders back, as if she'd said too much. 'Anyway. What's done is done.'

She blew out her cheeks and turned to go, but I needed more from her. This might be the only chance we'd get to speak openly about this.

'Hattie, wait.'

She paused at the edge of the band-stand, her hand still on the wood, but only turned her head slightly.

'I'm trying to understand – to make sense of what

happened to Oscar. Not just you and him, but everything that was going on in his life in the last few weeks. The police think it was suicide, but they're wrong. They must be. If there's anything that you know … If he confided in you about anything? Please. Oscar was the last person in the world who'd end his life like this and I owe it to my family to find out the truth.'

Hattie's shoulders shook like she was laughing but there was no smile on her face when she turned back to me. 'Oscar? God, I know. I thought there had to be some sort of mistake when Finn told me it was suicide. Oscar always gave the impression he thought the world was a better place with him in it. Hard to imagine anything that would make him think otherwise.'

'His mother thinks he was murdered,' I said.

Her hands tightened around the strap of her handbag but she didn't say anything.

'And you've told me that Finn knew you'd slept with Oscar. And that the two of them fought. I remember the night Oscar came home with a bloody lip and grazed hands. I knew he was lying when he said he'd fallen. Was that Finn? Oscar was lying about so much by then. I suppose the question is, how certain are you that Finn didn't go back to finish the job?'

CHAPTER TWENTY-THREE

DC Lowry Endecott

'So, talk me through what happened,' Lowry said to the older man seated across the table.

His name was Randall Curtis and, from what she'd been told by Miriam Lomas, he was the most outspoken of the three men pushing for a ruling of unfair dismissal. The ringleader. It wasn't just the loss of his job which had made him vocal. He was the one to complain about overtime, working conditions, unpaid leave. An unofficial shop steward if you like.

'When?' he asked.

'The day you were sacked.'

Lowry had to shout over the cacophony of voices in various states of inebriation. Friday night in The Rose and Crown was never quiet, and so it was the perfect place to get information from people whose lips were loosened by booze.

'Not much to tell,' Randall said, wiping beer foam off his bushy moustache. 'I was coming to the end of my shift when Oscar Lomas called me into his office and told me not to bother coming in on Monday.'

'When was this?'

'Six months ago, give or take. Not long before Christmas, as it happens. He wouldn't let a little thing like that get in the way of his plans. I used to work for his old man, Vince. He were a decent bloke. Shame when the brothers took over.'

Lowry closed her hands around her glass of lime and soda. 'You worked there a long time, then?'

Someone pushed by Lowry, knocking her chair. She pulled it closer to the table and leaned in to catch Randall's answer.

'Going on forty years. Got a job there as soon as I left school. Never worked anywhere else.'

Lowry did a quick mental calculation and was surprised that Randall was only in his late fifties. As her gran used to say, 'must've been an uphill paper round'. He was a neat man, a strong-looking man. Carried a bit too much beer-weight around his middle, but he wasn't in bad shape. It was the lines on his face and the seen-it-all-before eyes that made him look ten years older than he was.

'Must've hit you hard. After all those years of loyalty, just to be let go like that?'

Randall picked up his pint and drank. Lowry watched his Adam's apple pulsate. He was tense, she could see it in the way he gripped the glass, his fingers white with exertion. When he placed his glass back on the table, it was almost empty.

If there was more to Oscar's death, and she was beginning to think Beth was right about that, then the most likely candidates were the sacked men, the person Oscar owed money to, and the partner of the woman Lomas was having an affair with. Because she was the one pushing for a murder investigation, Lowry had ruled out Beth as a suspect though she knew, better than most, that a woman whose partner had been unfaithful had the perfect motive.

Her boss, Finn, didn't know that she was here tonight, digging around without anything more than a hunch. She needed more information, and she needed to prove to herself that she wasn't taking an interest in this case because she felt a kinship with Beth, one wronged woman to another.

Even when she told Finn about the laptop being stolen and the possibility that there could be files on there that someone didn't want coming to light, he'd looked annoyed with her. 'Let it drop,' he'd said. 'If you want to look into the petty theft in the area, then be my guest. But we have no reason to believe there's a link between Oscar's death and the break-in.'

No one had seen the debt-collector, nor the man in the garden, except Beth. There was no evidence of foul play, nothing suspicious, but there was a niggle in the back of Lowry's mind. A thought just out of reach that stopped her from falling asleep at night, that nothing about Oscar's death was as it seemed.

The Rose and Crown was even busier now, lines of pints being carried through to the beer garden. The occasional thud of a dart hitting dartboard. For a man who was known for being vocal, Randall was being remarkably quiet so Lowry tried again.

'Can you tell me what happened after Oscar Lomas asked you to leave?'

Randall smoothed down his moustache and said, 'I did what I always do on a Friday. I came here. Had a couple of pints. Only this time I didn't go into work on Monday. Just like he told me.' He folded his arms as if that was the end of the story.

'What reason did he give for sacking you?'

'Every reason under the sun. Said I was too slow. Said there'd been complaints about me. Some rubbish about

137

restructuring. None of it meant anything. He said if I went quietly, he'd sort me out with a decent payoff, but if I caused trouble, he'd make sure I never saw a penny.'

'Had there been complaints about you?' Lowry asked.

'None that I know of.'

'Why do *you* think he let you go?'

'Got himself in a bit of trouble money-wise, didn't he? Needed to make cuts and thought that getting rid of those of us that were older would do the trick, I suppose.'

'But he'd offered you money to go quietly?' Lowry said. 'You mustn't have thought money was a problem at the time.'

'Aye, but that were bollocks – pardon me French. I didn't know about the rumours back then. As far as we were concerned it was business as usual. There was some big deal in the offing. When I asked how much I were getting, he told me to wait until the new year, that he didn't know how much he could spare right then. New year came and went and me and a couple of others got ourselves a solicitor.'

'The other two . . . that'd be Ken Phillips and Brad Poole?'

'That's them.'

'What did your solicitor think the chances were of successfully suing Lomas Lumber?'

'Well, it's one of them no win, no fee places so I'm guessing she thought it were pretty good or she wouldn't have taken us on.'

'But you didn't get anywhere with the claim?'

'Not finished yet. We're suing the company, not him, so I guess there's still some chance, even though he's dead. P'raps our chances got better now he's not in the way but we're not the only ones, are we? They're saying that he owed money all over the place and that's why he did himself in.'

'Are they?'

Lowry tapped her fingernails on her glass. The story of suicide due to financial problems had spread far and wide, it was going to be a push for her to convince Finn there was something else that they hadn't spotted.

'Have you managed to get another job yet?' she asked.

He shook his head. 'Not much about nowadays for a bloke my age. I volunteer at the animal shelter three days a week. Keeps me out of trouble.'

Despite trying to keep a neutral face, Lowry's eyebrows shot up. Randall didn't look the type to look after cats and dogs, though she could understand why he needed to do something to ward off the beast of boredom.

'What do you do with the rest of your time?'

'I go for walks.'

'You're a keen walker?'

He nodded.

'In the Peaks?'

He nodded again.

'The place where we found Oscar Lomas's body – Cloud Drop – do you ever go up there?'

He was silent for a moment. Lowry thought she saw something in his eyes harden as if he understood what she was getting at.

'Not at my age, love. My knees can't take it. No, I like something a bit gentler.'

'Did you do any walking in the Peaks on the weekend that Oscar Lomas went missing?'

'I was helping my daughter decorate her new home all weekend.'

Lowry could sense Randall start to close down.

'And what about Ken and Brad. Have they found work?'

He nodded. 'They're younger than me and have what you'd call transferable skills. Both of them got taken on by Toyota.'

'That must be tough for you.'

'Nope. I'm glad some bugger round here has a decent job. I don't need much. I got no mortgage, the kids have left home. As long as I've got money for a few beers, I'm okay.'

Lowry looked at his glass and said, 'Talking of which, can I get you another one of those?'

He studied her. Really studied her. Randall stared for long enough that Lowry raised her fingers to her cheek, thinking she must have something on her face.

'You don't think he killed himself,' he said at last, a slow smile spreading across his face.

'I'm making sure we've not missed anything,' Lowry said. 'And that Mrs Lomas gets the answers she deserves.'

'Now, if you're looking for someone who wanted him dead, you should be looking at the wife.' Randall lifted his glass. 'She's a mysterious one. There's some who thought she knew something about what happened to a lad that died. Years back, mind.'

'What lad?'

'You know the Flint-Stantons? Yeah? Their boy. Terrible shame.'

He drained the rest of his beer and said, 'It's always the quiet ones you have to watch.'

CHAPTER TWENTY-FOUR

Molly Ingram

Molly sat in the park opposite Beth's house. It was the other side of town to where they'd grown up. This was the polished side, the side that you aspired to live in. She used to walk by these houses as a child and think they were beautiful. So grand and clean. A three-storey house always seemed elegant to her. Her parents had lived in a bungalow so anything with stairs was exotic. Having an upstairs floor was posh. Having two was downright decadent.

In London, she lived in a flat. Again, no stairs. She lived life on one level. No way up, no way down. And now she was taking the escape route.

She wasn't sure how much to tell Beth. It would be a relief to unburden her conscience, but it would only succeed in making Beth feel worse. It wasn't the one-night stand with Oscar or the folding of her business. Those things were bad enough, but they were nothing compared to the fact that it was her fault Oscar was dead. For the first time, she was glad that she and Oscar didn't have a formal deal over the money. This way there was nothing to lead the police to her, but she would always know what she'd done. There was no getting away from the fact that she set the ball in motion. She caused Oscar's death.

Molly and Oscar weren't all that different. Both ran their own companies, both were ruthless. Both were, ultimately, selfish. And both of them failed to appreciate the one woman who had always been unwaveringly loyal to them.

Sleeping with Oscar had been her first mistake but not her last. Lending him money, letting him manipulate her . . .

When clients had been slow to pay her, she'd employed someone to chase payments, send threatening letters, and enforce interest on late payments. But she'd occasionally considered another route when she couldn't get all she was owed. Not seriously. Well, a little. She'd heard about a man who had a talent for getting money out of those who were reluctant to pay up. He was a bit of a loner, lived in a cottage on Bodmin Moor and was occasionally seen shooting magpies off telephone wires with an air rifle.

She'd kept the number in the just-in-case section of her desk drawer. Eventually, after half a bottle of wine, she sent him a text message asking about availability and fee. Putting out feelers, she'd said. Only for when she was without any other options. His name was Frazer, though she'd initially misheard and thought his name was Razor, which gave him an entirely different kind of vibe. As her options ran out Frazer's ran in. She sent him money via PayPal, a 'delivery address' in the notes. The rest was up to him. He was to *deliver* whatever he saw fit to make Oscar cough up what he owed.

He took the money and six days later Beth called Molly to say that Oscar was dead. It didn't take a genius to put the two things together, so why had it taken her so long to realise what she'd done?

What would be better for Beth? That Oscar was murdered, or that he jumped? Because it didn't matter anymore what was best for Oscar. Should she confess that she paid a stranger the last of her savings to scare a man into paying her back? If she ended up in prison, at least she'd have a roof over her head.

She stood up and walked towards Beth's house as if she was approaching the edge of a high diving board. Three boys on bikes sped past laughing and she waited for them to disappear before she rang the doorbell. She hoped that Beth would be out so that she could say, 'Well, I tried . . .' but she could hear movement on the other side of the door.

She was trembling as the door opened.

'Molly? Oh, Molly. I'm so glad to see you. What are you doing here?'

Beth had been crying. Her hair was sticking up on one side and there was a coffee stain on her pink shirt. She smoothed her wild hair away from her face.

'I needed to see you. I've got something to tell you and I wanted to do it in person,' Molly said.

Beth pulled her into a hug and burst into tears. Molly felt Beth's weight as she crumpled against her and Molly had to hold her upright.

'Hey, what's wrong? Let's get you inside.'

Molly guided Beth back into the house and kicked the door closed as Beth sank onto the stairs.

Molly stroked Beth's hair and crouched down beside her. 'Oh babe, not a good day, huh?'

'I try not to cry in front of the children, but when they're at school I seem to do nothing but sob all day long. Everything is such a mess, Moll, and I don't know how to unravel it. I didn't know him. My own husband and I didn't know him at all. The business was failing and I knew nothing about it.

There's no money in savings. He was bailing out the business with our own money. And now I find out about the affairs. How could I have been so blind?'

'Affairs?' Molly felt the blood drain from her face. 'What do you mean?'

'It's all my fault.'

'None of this is your fault, okay?' Molly swallowed hard. 'Who was he having an affair with?'

Beth hid her face in her hands. 'Hattie.'

Molly sat down on the floor with a thud. 'Barnaby's sister?'

'Yep.'

'Shit.'

'And I think there's someone else too because Gabe saw them together and Hattie swears it wasn't her.'

Molly stared at a grey smudge on the cream wall. Hattie Flint-Stanton. Though she had no right to, Molly felt betrayed by Oscar.

'How did you find out?' she asked.

'I saw a text from Hattie about a month ago and I'd noticed a couple of missed calls on his phone. I thought it was odd that she was messaging him but forgot all about it until Oscar said he'd been seeing someone. At the funeral, she was acting strange. And then it all fell into place, but I didn't know what to say to her. I confronted her yesterday and she said Oscar was only after her money. He was trying to get her to invest in the business and, when she refused, it all cooled off.'

'Arsehole!' said Molly getting to her feet. 'So, what, he slept with women so he could get them to part with their money? The bastard!'

It shouldn't have surprised her to find out that he was a serial philanderer but, somehow, that stung.

'The Flint-Stantons are the richest family in the area,' Beth said. 'I suppose it makes sense. He would have been desperate to save the business.'

'Don't you dare make excuses for him,' Molly said. 'Most people would go to the bank for a loan. They'd turn to banking before bonking.'

Beth looked at her sharply and pinched her lips together.

'What?' asked Molly.

Beth smiled. 'Did you really just say, "banking before bonking"?' She started laughing.

'Well, yeah.' Molly's shoulders relaxed a little. 'It's a good slogan. Someone should use it.' She smiled too. It was good to hear Beth laugh again.

Molly tapped her fingernails on the wooden bannister, wondering whether she should say anything about why she'd come. It would be a shame to ruin the mood which had unexpectedly lightened.

Beth got to her feet and wiped her eyes with the back of her hand. 'Sorry, Molly, you've not even taken your jacket off and I've already cried and dropped this on you. What are you doing here? Shouldn't you be at work?'

'There is no work,' Molly sighed. 'The business has gone under and I am officially unemployed.'

'What? Oh Molly, no. You've worked so hard.' She placed a hand on Molly's arm, her eyes wide with concern. Molly placed a hand on top of Beth's. With everything she was going through, it was astounding that Beth still had the capacity to worry about other people.

'Yes, I've worked hard, but I've also made some ridiculous mistakes. And I mean, *colossal*. I'll tell you about them sometime, but not today. I didn't look after the money side of things very well. It was completely my own fault and I'm sorry that some lovely people have lost their jobs. They should get what they're owed eventually, but it's a bit shit.'

'Is there nothing you can do? Take out a loan or something?'

'No. I've had financial advisors all over this. We're screwed.'

'I am sorry Molly. What happens now?'

Molly noticed a penny on the floor by the skirting board and bent to pick it up. Beth put out a hand to stop her and then changed her mind. 'Go on,' she said. 'You need it more than I do.'

Molly stood up straight, wondering whether to be offended. 'I wasn't taking your money. I was only picking it up. It'll take more than one penny to sort my life out.'

'No, no. That's not what I mean. It's for luck. I've been leaving pennies all over the house and garden for the days when I'm struggling and need a bit of extra help.'

'What?'

'Find a penny, pick it up. All day long you'll have good luck,' said Beth.

And, like that, the opportunity to tell Beth about the affair passed.

After Barnaby died Beth had been ill for six months and then was never the same again. She'd become fearful and superstitious, never venturing outside if she could only see a single magpie. She never stepped on cracks in the pavement and would scream if someone opened an umbrella in the house. Molly had gone along with it, anything to help her through the toughest of days. They'd spend hours in the park looking for a four-leaf clover.

'Do you have any red wine? I could murder a drink,' said Molly putting her arm around Beth's shoulder.

'It's only eleven o'clock!' Beth said.

'Fine. Have it your way. We'll drink white.'

CHAPTER TWENTY-FIVE

DC Lowry Endecott

Lowry slipped off her shoes and squinted against the morning sun streaming through the windows. Hattie handed her a glass of water, sat on the opposite sofa, and exhaled as if she'd already had a long day.

'This is an unexpected and most welcome pleasure,' Hattie said. 'How *are* you?'

Lowry sipped her water and then placed the glass on the low coffee table. 'I'm fine, thanks.'

'Fine? You don't sound it.'

'Yeah, fine. How are things with you? All sorted for the wedding?' asked Lowry.

'God, no. Didn't Finn say anything? The caterers have gone bust – let us down at the last minute. Are they allowed to do that? They've refunded the deposit, but that's hardly the point, is it? Finn says he can't arrest them for poor business skills, but there must be something we can do.'

Lowry managed to stop herself from smiling. It wasn't that she didn't care about her friend's problems, but it was nice to have issues that didn't revolve around the death of a local businessman. Hattie would solve the problem – she always did – because things frequently went Hattie's way in the end. She could be brutal in pursuit of what was in her best interest, so it was unlikely she was going to let the loss of caterers, a week before her wedding, cause too many bad nights' sleep.

'I'm desperately calling around different places but they're all booked up. How can they all be booked? I mean, for goodness' sake! Take on extra staff, stay up later to bake another bloody cake. How difficult is it? You'd think these people didn't want to make money. At this rate, I'll be making cheese sandwiches and buying a cake from M&S. Urgh! My first wedding was a silver service five-course meal. The second one was a barbecue on a beach in the Maldives. I am not having my third one remembered as the one where people had to bring their own sandwiches.' She sat upright, suddenly. 'Oh, hold on!'

She snatched up her mobile saying, 'Sorry. I'll just be a sec,' as she tapped on her phone. Lowry watched as Hattie screwed up her face in concentration, paused, looked up to the ceiling, muttered something under her breath and then started typing again.

'Lowry,' she said, throwing her phone onto the seat beside her. 'You are a genius. I'll see what Finn says, but it could work. What do you think?'

'I have no idea what we're talking about,' Lowry said. 'Enlighten me.'

'A picnic of course! But more, I don't know, *glamorous*, upmarket. Swap the white linen tablecloths for gingham and get those traditional wicker picnic hampers for each table. Bottles of champagne, smoked salmon, baguette, cheeses. Oh, we could go all retro with quiche and pork pies but, instead of cheese and pineapple on sticks, we could have Manchego and quince jelly. It could be so much fun.' She clapped her hands together.

'Of course, I'd need to source about fifty hampers at short notice, but if I don't find a caterer, I could at least order a buffet from Waitrose. I won't let it go wrong, Lowry. I just won't. I want the day to be perfect. And it's not about how much money I spend – my first two weddings proved that. I want it to be a great big party. I'm inviting pretty much everybody in the village to the evening do. But if I can't feed them ... Argh!'

'Do you know Beth Lomas?' Lowry asked.

Hattie raised an eyebrow, her lips pursed.

'Silly question,' said Lowry. 'Everyone knows everyone around here. Anyway, she's quite the baker by all accounts, and might be able to help you out? She was telling me she was thinking of setting up some sort of catering company, so ...'

Hattie bunched up the sides of her hair in her fists. 'I'm not *that* desperate. Right. That's it. No more wedding talk. I need a wedding-free space or I'll go mad.'

She shook her arms and twisted her head from side to side as if she was literally shaking herself free of stress.

'Right, my dear friend,' Hattie said. 'Distract me. It's not like you to pop by unless you've got something on your mind or want to go riding. Seeing as you are not dressed for riding it must be the former so, if you value my sanity at all, spill those beans.'

To casual observers, Lowry and Hattie were unlikely friends. There was an age difference, a class difference, and a major difference in the amount of money in their bank accounts. Their paths wouldn't have crossed if Finn hadn't started dating Hattie, and Finn and Hattie's paths would never have crossed if Hattie hadn't abused the Prime Minister when he visited a local town when the dam was threatening to burst. But, despite it all, they shared a love of horses, of laughing at absurd situations, and a fondness for Finn.

'Between us,' Lowry said, 'I'm working on a case that isn't really a case. On the face of it, there's no crime, but I can't shake the feeling that I'm missing something and, you know me, I'm not usually a gut-feeling kind of copper.'

'Do go on,' said Hattie with a salacious glint in her eye.

'I ... well, I was hoping you might be able to help me. I think there's more to Oscar Lomas's death.'

Hattie nodded and leaned over to check her phone. 'Right. Okay. And, um, what does Finn say?'

'Finn doesn't know I'm looking into it, and I'd appreciate it if you didn't mention anything to him until I've had a chance to lay out all the facts. He thinks it's a straightforward suicide. The coroner agrees.'

'Well, that's that then. You can close the case and move on. Are you sure I can't get you something more exciting than water? Iced tea?' She sat forwards with her hands clasped too tightly on her lap. 'Are you bringing anyone to the wedding? What about the one with the nice teeth? Mark, was it?'

Lowry looked at Hattie's too-bright smile, her white knuckles. 'Is everything okay? You shut me down a bit quickly there. What aren't you telling me? Has Finn said something?'

'Oh, come on. What would I know? I'm only thinking that it doesn't really matter how that man died,' Hattie said. 'I mean, he's still dead, no matter how it happened. Who cares? Now back to Mark. Is he a dentist, or am I imagining that?'

Lowry jerked backwards in her seat. 'Hattie! I can't believe you just said that. Oscar had a lot of secrets and,' Lowry sat up straight to mirror Hattie's posture. 'And now you've got me thinking that you know more than you're letting on.'

Hattie stood up. 'For goodness' sake.' She stalked around to stand behind the sofa. 'Are you accusing me of something? You think I know something about Oscar's death? I don't need to put up with this in my own house. I could ask you to leave, you know.'

Lowry didn't know how the mood had changed so quickly. She touched her fingers to her temples and blinked hard. 'Hattie, what just happened? Why so defensive? I was only asking if—'

'Finn can't have approved of this little visit,' Hattie said with her hands on her hips. 'He promised me that none of this would come to light. I can't believe he said something. He was the one who was adamant that no one find out about it.' She folded her arms and walked up and down in front of the window.

Lowry got to her feet slowly, like she was dealing with a wild animal. 'Hattie, I promise you, I have absolutely no idea what you're talking about. Finn hasn't told me anything.'

Hattie stopped pacing and looked at Lowry, her mouth ajar, eyes wide. 'It wasn't Finn?'

Lowry shrugged. She still didn't know what they were talking about but her mind was in overdrive. Oscar, Hattie and Finn. What could they have in common?

'Oh, Lord,' said Hattie clamping her hand over her mouth. Some of her anger faded, and with it the colour drained from her face. She let her arms drop limply to her sides and said, 'It was *her*, wasn't it? Beth. I should've known that she wouldn't keep her mouth shut.'

She put her hands on the back of the sofa and let her chin drop to her chest. 'Look, Finn knows all about it and we've worked through our issues, okay? There's really not much else to say.'

As Lowry began to piece it all together she shook her head. 'You and Oscar Lomas? Tell me you didn't.'

'You didn't know?' asked Hattie looking up at Lowry. 'But I thought you ...'

'Beth Lomas told me she didn't know who Oscar was having an affair with.'

'Oh, she knew. She requested a little tête-à-tête yesterday in the park. It was like being summoned to the headmaster's office. I thought she was going to slap me across the face, but she just wanted me to know that she knew all about it. She wanted to humiliate me and I suppose I deserved it so I stood there and took it like a big girl.'

Hattie pinched the bridge of her nose then shook her hair and stood up straight. 'She asked me if I thought Oscar had killed himself and I'll tell you the same thing I told her. He didn't seem the type but, given what I know about his business and the state of his marriage, it seems clear he took the easy way out.'

Lowry was momentarily lost for words. Infidelity was one thing that she couldn't stand, and Hattie knew that. If there was one failing of the law, it was that people couldn't be arrested for breaking your heart.

'I've got to say,' began Lowry, 'I wasn't expecting that. You might need to give me a minute to take this all in.' She took a deep breath and concentrated on the pattern on the carpet.

'It only happened once,' Hattie said. 'That's all. There's your bombshell. Hattie Flint-Stanton isn't a saint. But you already knew that or you wouldn't be here.'

'Actually,' said Lowry, 'the reason I came here this morning was to ask you what Beth Lomas had to do with your brother's death.'

★

Hattie swirled the amber liquid around her glass. The ice cubes clinked together, releasing the aroma of brandy into the air.

'Barney died on my fifteenth birthday,' she said.

'I'm so sorry.'

Hattie flicked her hand by her ear as if she were swatting at a fly. 'It's just another day. No reason why shitty things can't happen on your birthday, but it's always made me think that it's cursed. I've never celebrated a birthday since. It's hard for my parents. I mean, how do you throw a birthday party for one child on the anniversary of your other child's death? I don't remember it ever being a conscious decision, but birthdays just didn't happen after that.'

She sipped her brandy and winced.

'I had a little soirée and invited the whole class. There were maybe fifty people there. I wasn't that popular, but having a large house with a pool and a hot tub makes people want to party with you. Barney was eighteen months older than me and pretty much all the girls in my class had a crush on him. Some of the boys too. He wasn't that good looking but, you know what teens are like, older boys with money are like catnip.

'Despite my parents' orders, there was alcohol at the party, and drugs. My dad was keeping an eye on things, and we were forbidden to go in the pool. That was the only rule. Of course, there were a few idiots who jumped in anyway. My parents were terrified that someone would end up drunk at the bottom of the pool. It was a huge responsibility – fifty drunk teens and so many ways for them to get into trouble. It turns out they were right to be worried, but not in the way they expected.'

Hattie took another drink and shook her head. 'But of course, I couldn't see that, and we ended up having a huge row. I wanted everyone to think I was fun, but my parents wouldn't let anyone relax for even a second. My dad shut down the whole party, pulled the plug on the music, and said he was calling the police who'd be very interested in the underage drinking and the drugs. Everyone left pretty quickly after that.

'Barney was laughing at me, saying that my party would go down in history as the lamest party of all time and I'd be lucky if I had any friends left by Monday morning. It was humiliating. I ran and locked myself in my room swearing I'd never talk to any of them again. Usual teen stuff about them ruining my life.

'We can only guess what happened next, but Barney must've decided to sit in the hot tub, take drugs and drink what was left of the beer. When my father went downstairs the next morning, he found Barney in the hot tub. Dead. There were drugs in his system and he must've fallen asleep.'

Lowry rubbed Hattie's arm. 'I had no idea. I knew he'd died young but ... I'm so sorry. That must have been terrible for you. Were you close?'

'Why? Would it make it easier for you if I told you I hated him?'

'Sorry, no. I shouldn't have ...'

Hattie covered her mouth with one hand and she swallowed. Her face softened and when she looked back at Lowry she smiled sadly.

'No, it's me who should apologise. I'm a little sensitive when it comes to my brother's death.' She took a deep breath before continuing. 'No, we weren't close. Argued most of the time, if I'm honest, but he was still my brother and there've been many times in my life I wished he was still here.'

'Can I ask,' Lowry said, 'and if you'd rather not talk about it, that's fine but, I don't understand what Beth Lomas has to do with your brother's death?'

Hattie rubbed a hand over her eyes, smudging her mascara. 'Who told you she was involved?'

'I was talking to Randall Curtis last night. He said there was more to Beth than meets the eye and that she had something to do with it.'

Hattie rolled her eyes. 'Honestly, the gossip in Hellas Mill . . . It was something and nothing. What happened was, Beth was at the party with her friend Molly – I've told you, *everyone* was at the party. We were in the same school year, but never close. Anyway, the morning after the party her bed was empty. Her parents thought she'd been abducted, run away or something. They called the police who found her an hour or two later on the band-stand in the park, completely unharmed but she wasn't making much sense. She had no idea how she'd got there and couldn't remember anything that happened after the party. She probably took something, if you know what I mean. They took her to hospital and well, the rumours were that she lost her mind for a while. She didn't come back to school for the rest of the term. Everyone was convinced something weird had happened, what with Barney drowning and the police were looking for her at the same time as we found my brother's body, well, people thought there had to be a link between the two things.'

'But there wasn't,' said Lowry.

'No. How could there be? You've met Beth. She's so unassuming. I don't like her, but she had nothing to do with

Barney's death. And, aside from smothering Oscar, she didn't have anything to do with his death either.'

They sat side by side in silence while Hattie finished her drink.

'Why didn't you tell me about you and Oscar?' Lowry asked.

'I didn't want you to think badly of me,' Hattie said. 'I never planned on Finn finding out but Oscar tried to blackmail me and so I had to say something.'

'He was blackmailing you?'

'He didn't get the chance, did he? I immediately told Finn so Oscar lost his leverage. He was lucky that's all he lost. Finn was furious. He went to see Oscar and have it out with him. Finn says there was a bit of pushing and shoving but not much of a fight. Oscar got the message to leave us alone anyway.'

Lowry bent over, head in hands.

'What? What's wrong?' asked Hattie.

'You've just told me that both you and my boss had a motive to kill Oscar Lomas.'

'What do you want me to say? Lie? If I'd seen him standing on the edge of a cliff, I'd have given him a good old shove. But I didn't. And neither did Finn. If you keep looking into this, Lowry, you'll find plenty of people who wanted Oscar Lomas dead, but that doesn't mean he didn't kill himself.'

Stage Three of Grief

BARGAINING

CHAPTER TWENTY-SIX

Beth Lomas

Molly drove us to the undertakers.

I negotiated with God, my guardian angels, and anyone or anything that might be listening. If I could get to the end of the week without drinking, could Oscar come back to us? If I held my breath until I'd got up the stairs, could we chalk it up to a bad dream? If I gave my life, would He swap it for Oscar's?

The undertakers telephoned me yesterday. 'Mr Lomas's ashes are ready,' they said. I wanted him home, even in this form. Though it was only a pile of dust where my husband used to be, I'd take anything they offered.

The undertakers was a new brick building. Small and bland, it could have easily been a dentist's or an estate agents. I'd passed this building hundreds of times and never taken any notice of it before.

Molly helped me into the office as if I were an infirm woman of advanced years. The walls of the waiting room were lilac and the chairs a deep purple. It was the colour I'd associate with grief from now on. Heartbreak was purple, like a bruise.

Esther had brought in one of Oscar's expensive suits with the brightly coloured lining for his funeral. I had no interest when she tried to show me what she'd chosen. What did it matter? Who even saw it? How could we trust that the undertakers would do what they said and not take the suit home to sell on eBay?

The funeral director had smile lines around his eyes and mouth, and a good-humoured glint in his eye. It was hard for me to equate this face with the job that he did. His day-to-day business was corpses and coffins, how did he motivate himself to come to work?

'Sorry to keep you waiting, Mrs Lomas.'

I seemed unable to speak.

'Not at all,' Molly said. 'We've only just arrived.'

Had we? We could have been here for five minutes or five hours. Time moved in a different way now. It had stagnant stretches and then, suddenly, lurched forwards and forty-five minutes were misplaced.

'Can I ask you to sign here, Mrs Lomas?'

I moved the pen over the pale blue paper but the signature didn't look like mine.

'This is Mr Lomas's watch,' he said. He held a small paper bag out towards me and I physically recoiled. I couldn't stand to touch something that Oscar had been wearing when he died, as if death was contagious. I moved away from it and Molly stepped forward.

'Shall I take that?' she asked.

'And these,' the man said, 'are the particulars he was wearing when he arrived. Your mother-in-law, the other Mrs Lomas, said you'd want them.'

I turned my face away. Why would I want to keep the clothes he'd died in? Were they blood-stained? Torn? Who in their right mind would want to see that? Sickness rose in my chest. Bile burned my throat.

I heard the rustling of plastic as Molly took the bag from him with a polite, 'Thank you.'

'And finally,' he said.

I turned back to him then. There was only one thing it could be. Oscar. Or what was left of him. My husband, so tall and strong, full of laughter and stories, all reduced to dust in a cylinder with his name on. The genie in the lamp, but no number of wishes would bring him back.

How could he be so small when everything he'd done had been so big?

Who did this to you, Oscar? Who was it?

And at once, I forgave him. No matter what he'd done, he didn't deserve this. My husband was a flawed man, a man who made mistakes, but he deserved people to know that he hadn't taken his own life. I would find out who was responsible, even if I didn't like the answer.

CHAPTER TWENTY-SEVEN

DC Lowry Endecott

Lowry asked Harvey to show her where he'd found Oscar's body. He agreed, but the hunched shoulders and the deficit of conversation suggested a certain reticence to engage with her.

Heads bowed against the drizzle, they marched up the ridge with their eyes on the uneven ground beneath them. As the path narrowed, Harvey moved in front of Lowry batting aside the low hanging branches and tendrils of bramble swiping at their faces. Though everyone had told Lowry that the younger Lomas brother was the kinder of the two, she was yet to be convinced. Her questions were met with gruff answers. Her attempts at polite conversation ignored. Not that she minded. Chit-chat wasn't her speciality either.

She'd heard that the brothers had a close bond, but that wasn't the impression she was getting from Harvey this morning. It had only been two weeks since he'd found his brother's body. The grief and the anger would still be raw, but Harvey Lomas kept his emotions contained. He was helpful, without volunteering any information; sad but not heartbroken. When he spoke, he appeared to be more concerned about his business than his brother. Lowry had said that he didn't have to take her to Cloud Drop if it was too difficult for him. That she would understand if he'd rather not go there yet.

'It's no bother,' he'd said. 'It's good of you, but there are other people there to hold the fort.'

It had taken her a moment or two to realise that he was talking about Lomas Lumber, while she was talking about the trauma of revisiting the spot where he'd discovered his brother's battered body.

By his own admission, Harvey was a facts and figures man. And the fact was, the figures weren't good. His speech was clipped, terse, whenever he spoke about the business. His annoyance wasn't in itself suspicious but, in front of the detective who was trying to ascertain whether there'd been anyone else involved in his brother's death, she'd been anticipating a barrage of reasons why he loved his brother and could never have hurt him. Even the most law-abiding citizen often felt guilty.

Lowry knew that Harvey was a community-minded man. He gave his time voluntarily to Peak Rescue because he was practical enough to be able to help people without getting sentimental. He had all the skills and the training but it seemed he had none of the empathy. He appeared to be the sort of man who got the job done.

'The rain's changed everything,' Harvey called.

'Sorry?' Lowry had heard him perfectly well but wanted him to slow down a moment.

He waited for her to get closer and then said, 'The rain has changed the landscape. It wasn't like this at the weekend.'

'Changed how?'

'These rocks and stones weren't on the path, and the bushes were at least a foot shorter.'

Lowry was a fit person. Boxercise, horse riding and Barre had strengthened her muscles, but the climb to Cloud Drop was causing her legs to cramp. She turned to see how far she'd come. The valley bowed before her and she placed her hands on her hips, trying to catch her breath. Her hair was sticking to her face, whether by sweat or rain she couldn't tell.

'Not far now,' Harvey said.

'Admiring the view,' she called.

He waited for her at the base of a steeper climb.

'Is this the only way to get to Cloud Drop?' Lowry asked as she approached.

Harvey looked about him. 'For someone like Oscar, yes.'

'Meaning?'

'Wilders Pass is pretty much a straight line from the road to the waterfall. You could approach it from the other direction, but Oscar left his car down there in the lay-by.' He nodded towards the road which was now the width of a piece of string. 'He wouldn't have walked ten miles round to the other side to climb from that direction. You could climb up alongside the waterfall, but you'd need proper gear. Oscar wasn't that kind of climber.'

'What do you mean, "that kind"?' Lowry asked.

The frown line between Harvey's brows deepened. He wasn't old, but his face showed the tell-tale signs of a man who spent a lot of time outdoors.

'Oscar knows these hills about as well as anyone. If you want a guide to take you to the most beautiful views and the off-the-track places of interest, Oscar's your man. He's been coming up here since we were children. But he can't climb a sheer rock face, or even abseil down it. He's more likely to take the easy route.'

There was something about the curl of his lip that made Lowry think he wasn't only talking about climbing. Rusted iron railings ran along the base of the rock. A sign warned them to keep out. There were flowers resting against the railing. Lowry bent to look at them but there was no note.

'Any idea who these are from?' she asked.

Harvey shook his head.

He put his hands on the top of the metal fence and pivoted over it. Lowry took a step backwards so she could see the top of the rocks. It was the height of a house but not particularly steep. Still, she could see that it would take serious physical effort. Almost certainly Lomas would have gone up there under his own steam. There was no way Beth could have thrown him over her shoulder and climbed up there.

'Ready?' Harvey asked, motioning behind him.

Lowry pushed herself up and over, landing lightly on the other side of the railings. 'After you.'

Harvey climbed the hill like a mountain goat and was at the top before Lowry had pulled herself halfway. She could hear the waterfall now, though it sounded more like the low hum of a distant motorway and the rumble of lorries. Lowry's foot slipped and she fell back a little. She readjusted her grip and pulled herself onto the next rock.

As she reached the top, her eyes level with Harvey's boots, he stooped and offered her his hand. Lowry ignored it and heaved herself up to the ledge.

'How many people walk this route in an average week?' she asked between shallow breaths.

'No one should come up here. There are enough warning signs,' he said.

'That's not what I asked.'

There was a pause before Harvey answered. 'Not many. We don't tend to see anyone up Wilders Pass from October to May. And of those, I'd be surprised if any came up to Cloud Drop. There are other, more popular, walks around here that have a tearoom or what have you. And it's too challenging for people only wanting somewhere to stop for a picnic. No, most of them stick to the disused train tracks and the well-trodden routes that end by an ice cream van.'

Lowry got to her feet and swayed a little.

'Through here,' Harvey said pointing to thick trees behind them. He bent to get under the boughs. He pushed branches aside but let them spring back towards Lowry's head.

'The climb isn't as straightforward as I was expecting,' Lowry said.

'That's why no one discovered the body for a while. You can't see this spot from anywhere else on the trail. If we weren't specifically out here looking for Oscar, we wouldn't have found him.'

'Strange though that no one questioned why his car was there all weekend,' she said.

Harvey tilted his head to one side, considering this for a moment. 'It's not a busy road and there are often cars parked there while people walk their dogs down by the river. I suppose it's not so odd. Besides, people don't like to get involved if they can help it. It's human nature.'

Lowry followed Harvey as the path dipped down towards the thundering sound of the waterfall. It was dark here. The tree canopy was almost impenetrable and it focused your eyes on the view. There was a bench of sorts. An old hunk of wood. Lowry sat down. She needed to give herself a moment before she approached the edge.

'This is it?' she asked.

Harvey nodded. 'Yes. Cloud Drop. Named because it's in the clouds and there is quite the drop, I suppose. I always thought it was quite a poetic name. Better than some of the names you get round here, like Devil's Arse and what have you.'

The corners of Lowry's mouth curled. 'I've not heard of that one.'

'It's over in Castleton. Good for caving.'

Harvey rested his hand on a tree trunk and stared out over the valley made soft focus by the mizzle.

'Can I ask you something?' Lowry asked. 'If you wanted to kill yourself, would you do it here?'

Harvey seemed to consider this for a moment. 'Here?' he asked. 'I suppose it's as good a place as any.' He went and stood far too close to the edge for Lowry's liking.

'What I'm trying to understand is, why here? Why not take an overdose? Why not hang himself? Was this a particular favourite spot of his?'

Harvey shrugged. 'For one thing, there'd be no passers-by,' Harvey said. 'No one to stop you once you've made up your mind. Chances of bumping into anyone here, especially the weather being what it was at the time, were very slim indeed.'

'Okay. Anything else?'

'You'd die – no chance of ending up with life-limiting injuries. I suppose that'd be something I'd consider before choosing how to do it. This kind of drop, it'd take you less than three seconds to hit the rocks or the water. Not long enough to wonder whether you're doing the right thing.'

'But does it make sense, doing it here? Climbing all this way? He could have swallowed pills in the comfort of his own home.'

'He wasn't the most considerate of men, but my brother wouldn't have wanted Honey and Gabe to see his body.'

'And Beth?'

'Of course.'

'But doing it here ... there was always going to be the chance that you would be the one to find him.'

'The pools at the bottom of here are deep. They flow into underground caves. If he'd fallen right, his body might never have been found.'

Lowry nodded. Maybe Harvey was right. 'I suppose I'm just finding it difficult to understand the motivation. And not just for your brother's death, but for suicide in general. It takes a lot of conviction to go through with it. It's so ... purposeful. He must have felt like he had no other option and yet no one around him noticed how desperate he was. I just don't understand it.'

She looked towards the horizon at the last view Oscar Lomas had ever seen.

'That's where you're going wrong – trying to understand Oscar. This is the kind of place people might come to contemplate life. There's a bench, a view, and very little chance of seeing another soul. When there are no other distractions, you're left with nothing other than yourself. I guess he got to thinking and decided he didn't like what was in his head. It happens.'

'Have there been any deaths here before?' she asked.

'Not for a while,' he said. 'But, yes, it used to be a notorious suicide spot when my parents were growing up.'

'You told me that Oscar gave no indication that he was thinking of taking his own life. So why did you come up here when you were looking for him?'

He rubbed his brow and lowered his eyes.

'We'd heard that Oscar's car was in the lay-by at the bottom there. There's a warren of caves where people like to go potholing. My guess was he'd fallen into one of them. We were going to turn back before the weather hit. I wasn't that worried about him. Even injured, he could look after himself. I'd have put money on a broken ankle and him having hunkered down in one of the caves.' He pointed at a narrow path that carried on into the trees, 'Along here there's a hermit's cave. Every now and again you find beer cans and cigarette butts in there. Not much more than kids I'd guess. I was going to check there before we headed back.'

'You get kids all the way up here?'

'You'd be surprised at the lengths they'll go to, to get away from prying eyes.'

Lowry stood up and took a couple of steps towards the edge of the cliff.

'What are the chances he could have tripped?' she asked.

'It's a possibility,' Harvey mused. 'He could've leaned over to get a good view of the waterfall. When the sun's at the right angle the spray comes off in rainbows. It's quite beautiful.'

Lowry had never met Oscar Lomas, but he didn't sound like the kind of man who went looking for rainbows.

'You were the last person to speak to Oscar,' she said.

Harvey nodded. 'He called me late on Friday night.'

'What did he say?'

'Well, he didn't say he was going to throw himself off a cliff, if that's what you were wondering.' Harvey sighed, put his hands into his pockets, and stared out to the horizon. 'I'd popped by the house and he wasn't in. He was calling to see what I'd wanted.'

'Did you argue?'

'No. But he was pissed off. He'd argued with his wife and was annoyed that we were having problems at work. We both were. When you're running your own company it's not just about paying your bills. It's about pride and status, and the hundreds of people who work for you. In a town like this, if the company goes under it has an impact on everyone. The guys who get laid off don't get milk delivered by the local farmer anymore because they can get it cheaper at the supermarkets. They stop being able to afford the local pub on a Friday night. There's a knock-on effect. I suppose I shouldn't blame Oscar for wanting to run away from it all but . . .'

'But?'

'But it's what Oscar does. He does whatever suits him without thinking of the consequences. He's done it before, but this time he really fucked up. Big time. And I'm the one left to clear up the mess, as usual. Does that sound like I'm a heartless bastard, because I'm not, you know? I'm going to miss him. He's my big brother. We did everything together and now he's gone. And I can't tell you how much I want to scream and shout at him for being such a selfish idiot. Bloody hell,' he wiped his face with the palm of his hand. 'Sorry. I can't say that kind of thing around the family. We're all being terribly *correct* about the whole thing and making sure we use the right phrases and pretend like he had no fucking choice.

'Beth and Mother shouldn't be putting ideas in your head about anyone else being involved. My brother found, for the first time in his life, that he couldn't get away with doing what he wanted, so he had the world's biggest tantrum. That was him through and through. Even as kids, if he was losing a game, he'd say it was "lame" and quit; turn over the board

172

or pick up his ball and go home. Whatever it was, if he wasn't winning, he didn't want to know. But the more we keep talking about this, and the more we try to find anyone else to blame, he's still winning. If you listen to Mother, you'll find that nothing was ever Oscar's fault. But I refuse to make excuses for him anymore. We need to put this all behind us and move forward as a family.'

Lowry had never heard him speak so much or for so long. She moved towards the edge, making sure that Harvey was to her side rather than directly behind her. 'Where exactly was the body?' she asked.

'Can you see a ledge about a hundred feet down on your left? It was there.'

Lowry peered over but she was nervous about getting too close to the drop.

'How did he get there? Wouldn't he fall straight down?'

'Could have hit the rocks and spun there, the force of the water might have pushed him out.'

Lowry wasn't convinced. She got down on to her knees and leaned forward. The water thundered onto rocks below and into a seemingly endless hole.

She looked up at Harvey. 'You said you were on your way to check the hermit's cave.'

He nodded.

'But you wouldn't have noticed Oscar's body unless you stood at the edge and peered over. What made you look for him there?'

Harvey stared ahead of him. His face hardened.

'Wishful thinking,' he said.

CHAPTER TWENTY-EIGHT

DC Lowry Endecott

Finn was waiting by Lowry's desk when she got to work.

'A word?' he said before striding into his office and leaving the door wide open.

'Shit,' she muttered as she dropped her bag and jacket on her desk. PC Claire Sackler looked up from her computer and raised her eyebrows.

'He's in a foul mood,' she warned.

'Any idea why?'

She shook her head. 'Search me.'

Lowry had worked with Finn for three years. He was promoted and became her boss two years ago and she'd still not adapted to the fact that she had to report to him. She hated that there was always a barrier between them now, a sense that she couldn't let her guard down in front of him.

She crossed the office and closed Finn's office door behind her. She folded her arms and remained standing as she waited for him to finish typing on his computer. His office was a mess. There were biscuit crumbs on his desk, grease spots on his paperwork. His bin was full of food wrappers and screwed up sheets of paper. Lowry regretted not taking her sergeant's exam when Finn did. It could have been her at that desk now, calling the shots. She didn't doubt that she could do the job, but exams tended to trip her up. Against a clock, her mind went blank. And she didn't think she could bear the humiliation of failing.

'Is this going to take long?' she asked.

'Somewhere better to be?'

'Always.'

'Are you going to sit down, or what?'

'I don't know. Are you going to tell me why you're in a mood?' Lowry asked.

Finn stopped typing and swivelled his chair to face her. He sighed and said, 'Oscar Lomas.'

. Lowry uncrossed her arms and sat down in the seat across the table from Finn.

'Yeah,' she said. 'Maybe I should have told you I was going to the crime scene.'

'There *is* no crime.'

'Says you. It doesn't feel right to me. Everyone I've spoken to says that Oscar Lomas would never kill himself.'

'What did you want him to do? Take out an ad in the *Telegraph*?'

'You're being facetious,' Lowry said. 'And I don't think that's helpful.'

'You do remember that I'm your boss, don't you?'

'And you do remember that I'm required to look into all avenues surrounding—'

'Yes, but that's it,' Finn shouted. 'You're not are you? You've got it into your head that someone bumped him off and now you're trying to find evidence to back that up. It's called confirmation bias, Lowry. I expected better from you.'

'I didn't think it could hurt to check everything was as it appears to be,' she said.

'He left a suicide note,' Finn barked. 'He left his car unlocked with his valuables in it and then he went to the top of Cloud Drop and jumped. There's nothing more to it than that. We've looked into his financial records, he had debts up to his arsehole. Marriage problems. Mid-life crisis. Or maybe he couldn't stand the constant fucking drizzle. Pick any reason you like.'

'What about the debt-collector? What about the break-in. We don't have the full picture and you know it. I've a gut feeling there's more to this than meets the eye.'

'Gut feeling doesn't carry much weight with the CPS,' Finn said with a sneer. 'I've twenty unsolved burglaries from this year alone and I'd bet that none of them were to cover up anything. Sometimes the most obvious explanation is the right one.'

'And sometimes it isn't.'

'Leave it, Lowry. The guy is dead. Whatever his reasons for jumping are, they're none of our business.'

'Especially as he was having an affair with your fiancée, right?'

It was as if all the oxygen had been sucked out of the room. They stared at each other but Finn was the first to look away. He glanced at the door as if to check that it was closed. 'That has absolutely nothing to do with this case.'

'I spoke to Hattie.'

Finn picked up a pencil and rolled it between his thumb and forefinger. 'I know.'

'And she told me how Lomas tried to blackmail her.'

Finn kept his eyes on the tip of the pencil.

'She also said that, when she told you about it, you went after Lomas and got into a fight.'

Finn made a sound between a grunt and a laugh and looked over his shoulder at the grey skies beyond his window. 'Hardly call it a fight. He saw me get out of the car and he started to leg it. Idiot slipped off the kerb, fell, and hit his face on the pavement. It was karma that kicked his ass, not me.'

'Do you have any witnesses that could—'

'Don't start! If this tells us anything, it's that he had financial problems and was so desperate that he seduced Hattie to try and get his hands on her money. If he didn't fancy seeing my face around every day, that's fine by me. Perhaps he couldn't live with the fact that he was such a fucking lowlife.'

Lowry stood and put her hands in her trouser pockets.

'You're probably right,' she said. 'But you don't need me to tell you how this looks. Yes, everything points to suicide but that doesn't take anything away from the fact that there were people who had it in for Lomas – including you. His wife doesn't believe he killed himself.'

'Families never do. It's hard for them to admit that they had no idea what was going through the mind of a husband, son, brother. They always feel like there must've been something they could've done. For some of them it gives them another focus rather than dealing with their own grief. You know all this, Lowry. What's this really about?'

'What d'you mean? Why can't it be about Lomas?'

'You've got itchy feet. I can tell. You're bored and when you're bored, you're dangerous. You start looking for things that aren't there and you get obsessed.'

'Not me,' she said, folding her arms.

'Then explain to me why you've been talking to Greta French at the Met?'

Lowry was wrong-footed for a moment and couldn't think

of anything to say. She should have spoken to Finn first but, while she was still making up her mind, she thought she'd see whether it was even a possibility.

'Look, it's nothing,' she said. 'Keeping my options open. If I'm going to progress through the force I need to move on. And if I have to move, it should be to somewhere where something happens apart from land disputes and car accidents. I'm not adding value here, Finn, but that's not the reason I'm looking into Lomas's death,' she added. 'I honestly think there's something we're missing. Why would he take his wedding ring off and leave it in the car? When have you ever heard of someone doing that?'

'I don't know. Perhaps he wanted to make sure that it got back to his wife. There was no guarantee that his body would be found or identified. He could've been carried down the river for miles. Or his body might never have made it out of the underwater cave system down there.'

'You think it was premeditated then?'

'Of course. There was a note.'

'It was one word! A word that could've meant anything. What if we're seeing what we expected to see? A note and an abandoned car, so of course we're thinking suicide but ...'

'But nothing, Lowry. He had money troubles and he was sleeping with women who weren't his wife.'

'And what are the two biggest motives for murder?' Lowry asked, leaning over Finn's desk. 'Sex and money. We have a motive, Finn.'

'A motive for suicide, because there is nothing else it could be. Listen closely, Lowry, because this is an order. Back off from the Lomas case. Because if you want me to put in a good word with Greta French, you'd better start doing what you're told.'

'And that's the deal is it? Back off or you'll ruin my career?'

'I want you to stop wasting resources and you want a new job in London. This way we both win. Now get out my office and be thankful you've still got a job in this backwater that you hate so much.'

CHAPTER TWENTY-NINE

Beth Lomas

With Oscar home where he belonged, I felt a huge sense of relief. Even in this reduced form, it felt right that he was here with me. Molly was staying at her dad's house hoping to rebuild her relationship with him. She said it was just until she could find a job, and that she'd go wherever work took her, but I was hoping that she could be persuaded to make a life here in Hellas Mill once she saw how lovely it could be. And how much I needed her.

Only now that Oscar was dead did I realise that my entire life had revolved around him, his family and his friends. He had been my best friend and we had done everything together, leaving me little time for other friendships. Since Esther and Vince had gone home I'd not heard from them. Harvey hadn't called. Miriam was silent. I wondered whether I was considered part of the Lomas family anymore. For the sake of the children, I hoped so. But, in case we were being set adrift I had to start looking to the future.

I stood in front of Oscar's open wardrobe with a stack of cardboard boxes, and a handful of black bin-liners. It was a high diving-board moment; something I was dreading but would ultimately be worth it. Today I felt strong enough to tackle it, but who knew what tomorrow would bring. I slipped

Oscar's shirts from their hangers and held them to my face. I touched his cuffs and thought of the times I'd helped him as he'd struggled to get his cufflinks in and remembered how I'd watch his reflection in the mirror as he tied a Windsor knot. Strangely intimate moments that I hadn't realised I'd miss.

I folded the shirts carefully, as if Oscar might wear them again one day, and laid them in the bottom of a cardboard box. The ties I lay flat, and then I changed my mind and wound them into tight balls like a tray of Danish pastries. He owned about thirty ties but only wore four of them regularly. All were Christmas presents from the children or me. I wished I'd been more inventive in my gift-buying, but Oscar decided that Christmas presents and birthday presents for each other were a waste of money. We struggled to find something the other wanted and would inevitably spend money that wasn't necessary. 'Commercialism gone mad,' he'd say.

'Remember the reason for the season,' Esther used to say, as if to celebrate Christmas with gaiety was an affront to God himself. I always thought that any reason to show people how much they were loved was a good thing. However, Hallmark's profit margin around Valentine's day was enough for my husband to declare he would never celebrate such a thing. Cards? Waste of money. Restaurants? Overpriced, to take advantage of romantic sops. He said he didn't need a specific day to tell me he loved me. Now I looked back at our life together I couldn't remember the last time he told me he loved me and wholeheartedly meant it.

We used the words to punctuate our sentences with abandon.

'Drive safe. Love you. Oh, can you pick up some milk on your way back?'

'*Sorry, Beth, meeting overran and I've missed my train. Going to have to find somewhere to stay in London tonight. Love you.*'

But when was the last time we looked at each other and felt the pull of our hearts? When was the last time we longed for each other? I yearned for him now as I'd never craved him before. I was trying to find my way back to him through broken memories but I was already forgetting how he laughed and how he walked.

The only time he showed his romantic side was our wedding anniversary. That was our day, and ours alone. He would always have a bouquet of pink and white peonies delivered to the house. My favourite flower and the one I'd had in my bridal bouquet. I took a deep breath. It would be our anniversary in a week. How was I meant to approach a day so full of happy memories, knowing that the person who made the memory so perfect was no longer here to share it with me?

I was hoping for a note from beyond the grave. A forgotten gift or a token. Something to tell me he still loved me at the end. I'd been reading about grief. Some people thought that white feathers were a gift from a deceased loved one, while others thought those who had died came back as birds to say a final goodbye but I had nothing.

I was desperate to believe that he could still reach out. Where was my moment? My awakening. My connection to the other side. I screwed up my eyes and prayed without words. I opened my heart, begged to feel something, but all I got for my troubles was the beginnings of cramp in my toes. I adjusted position. Perhaps I was trying too hard and wanting too much.

I took one of his suits out of the wardrobe and laid it on the bed. I couldn't throw it out because it must have cost hundreds of pounds. I wondered about keeping it for Gabe's future job interviews, but how would he feel wearing a dead man's clothes? I decided to pack it away until I knew what to do with it.

I folded the jacket first and placed it on top of the shirts. The trousers were creased where he'd been sitting down, a handspan of lines at the top of the thigh. I ran my fingers through the pockets and felt something in there. I pulled it out and placed it on my hand. It was a receipt. I smoothed it open and saw it was a fancy restaurant in London. Well, I couldn't be sure of the fanciness, it wasn't a restaurant I'd ever heard of, but the fact a meal for two had cost him over one hundred pounds made me think it was a considerable step up from a fast food restaurant. I wondered who he was dining with because it certainly wasn't me.

I heard the front door slam and was about to call out '*I'm up here, Oscar,*' when I remembered that it wouldn't be him. It couldn't be him. If I didn't concentrate, I slipped back into thinking that Oscar could walk in at any minute. It was cruel for my careless mind to give me hope.

I sank to the floor. Not dramatically. I simply folded myself down to the carpet and, when my knees were under my chin, I listed to one side until my cheek was on the knotted rug. I lay there with my eyes open, hugging myself. The energy from mere minutes earlier had drained from me as reality swiped at me. I was wrong to think I wasn't ready to do this. I wasn't ready to erase Oscar from the house.

It was the receipt in the pocket. The reminder that I didn't know everything about him, even though I had shared every last ounce of myself with him. Who was I even grieving for? Did I know him at all? I didn't want to hate my husband, but it was difficult to remember the good times. Perhaps there weren't any good times after all. I'd give anything to take away this feeling of helplessness. I needed a focus and for now, all I could think to do was concentrate on finding out who killed Oscar. It was the project I needed, the quest that would get me out of bed in the morning. If I found out the truth perhaps I'd be able to move on with my life.

I heard footsteps on the stairs. I knew that the slow, heavy tread was Gabe's.

'Mum?'

'In here,' I called from the floor.

The door opened and Gabe's face appeared. 'What're you doing?' he asked. 'Are you hurt?'

'No. I'm getting a different perspective, that's all.'

To his credit, he didn't question me, just accepted that sometimes I needed to lie on the floor.

'Oh. Okay then. Is there anything to eat?' Gabe asked.

'Give me ten minutes and I'll start dinner.'

'No cake?'

'No cake.'

'Oh.'

There always used to be cake in the house but, since Oscar's death, I hadn't felt able to do the little things that brought me joy. It felt frivolous to cook anything that wasn't strictly functional. My mother always said you needed a light heart to bake a light sponge. I was only fit for rock cakes.

'Gabe?'

His face had disappeared behind the door but he came back again.

'Can I ask you something? You don't have to answer straight away.'

Gabe looked wary. 'Okay.'

'What would you prefer I did? Spoke kindly of your dad and preserved your memory of him? Make him into a saint, if you like. Or would you rather know the whole truth, warts and all, even if it coloured your memories?'

Gabe walked into the room and sat on the bed. I didn't look at him. I was focusing on the chipped paint on the deep skirting-board, wondering about redecorating.

'You've found something out, haven't you?' Gabe asked.

'Not really. Just, I don't know, confirmation of what I already knew. One minute I think your dad was my soulmate, a perfect man, and I can't live another moment without him, and the next I hate him for what he's done to us and then I feel guilty. I wonder whether it's easier to love him or hate him.'

I still had the receipt balled up in my hand, a vague notion about tracking down the restaurant, seeing if I could work out who he'd met with, but scared that I wouldn't like the answer. It could be a business expense, an investor, a colleague. Or it could be another woman. Someone other than Hattie.

'Sorry, darling, I shouldn't ask you questions like that. It's my job to protect you.'

I sat up and smoothed the hair away from my face.

Gabe frowned at me. 'I hate this crap. I'm not a kid, Mum. The more you keep from me the more ...' He took a deep breath and appeared to start again. 'Look, me and Dad, we didn't talk much or hang out together, right? Most of the time I was pissed off at him for grounding me, or getting on my back about my grades, you know? He never said what was going on with him, and now he's dead. If he'd, like, talked to us more we'd have seen what was going on with him but I just thought he was a dick. Do you know what I'm saying?'

'So what you're saying,' I paused, 'is that I shouldn't be a dick.'

He smiled. God, I loved that smile. I reached out and touched his face. He no longer flinched away from me.

'Okay,' I said. 'Here goes.' I pushed my shoulders back and nodded as if to give myself permission to speak.

'The woman you told me about – the one you saw your dad with – I thought I knew who it was and I went and spoke to her in the park a few days ago. She said it wasn't her with your dad in the car. She swears they only ever met at her house. I assumed she was lying but it's just struck me that she might have been telling the truth. And, if that's the case then there was someone else your dad was seeing so, I was wondering, if you recognised the woman you saw with him.'

Gabe didn't look shocked, not even a little surprised. 'Who did you think it was?' he asked.

'Hattie Flint-Stanton.'

He shook his head. 'It wasn't her.' Gabe wrinkled his nose and looked towards the window. Looked at his nails. Looked anywhere but at me.

I felt cold. 'It's okay,' I said. 'I don't expect you to remember what she looked like, or anything. I don't know why I brought it up.'

I started to get to my feet. The pain in Gabe's eyes stopped me from wanting to pry.

'I thought you knew,' Gabe said. 'You said Dad had told you about it.'

'He did. Well, he said there had been someone. I assumed it was Hattie because of the missed calls and messages I'd seen on his phone, but to be honest, he never said who it was. I made an assumption. Look, let's not talk about it anymore. Okay?'

Gabe's reticence to say anything meant that I knew her. It meant that Gabe knew I'd be hurt when I found out. I wasn't ready for that today.

'I thought you knew,' he repeated.

He began pulling on his fingers, a childish tell of anxiety from when he was small.

'It's okay,' I said, taking his hand to stop him fidgeting. 'It doesn't matter. It doesn't change anything. He could sleep with a hundred women and he would still be your dad and love you more than anything in the world. I'm going to find out why and *how* this happened to him. Trust me.'

Gabe looked at the floor. Shook his head.

'I can't trust anyone,' he whispered. 'No one.'

'Don't be silly. You can trust your family.'

Gabe sneered and said, 'Even Aunty Miriam?'

CHAPTER THIRTY

Molly Ingram

It was nice, thought Molly.

And what an underrated word *nice* was. Being back home with her dad was like putting on slippers after a day spent in heels. Her old room, the way that the mugs were in the same cupboard they'd always been in. Her favourite yellow mug with the chipped handle, still lurking behind Mum's bone china. It had been years since she'd stayed the night here, and yet it felt like no time at all. The shower head was still too low, but was now being held on with an adjustable clamp. The back door was still coming away from its hinges and you had to lift it upwards in order to lock it. There was comfort in the never-changing rhythm of her childhood home.

Perhaps her upbringing hadn't been as bad as she remembered. Her parents had loved her in their own way. She'd never gone hungry, even though there'd never been any money to spare. If she'd never met Barnaby, she might've been able to finish her teenage years without anything to single her out from every other girl of her age. It was as if everything she'd done since the night of Hattie's party had been tainted by guilt.

'What do you want in your sandwich?' she called.

'Eh?'

'Your sandwich. What d'you want in it?'

The bungalow was small, and if it hadn't been for the canned laughter coming from the television there'd be no need for Molly to raise her voice to be heard.

'Ham.'

Molly had become increasingly distant from her father over the years, barely speaking to him except on his birthday and at Christmas. It was uncomfortable holding a conversation when she was the only one able to string more than one sentence together. Now she was here, though, they could sit in silence for hours and never feel the need to speak up. It was easier face-to-face. She wondered how many of the things she'd been putting off would have been better if she'd confronted them head on. If she'd spoken to Vijay about what was going on instead of ghosting him, she might be planning a wedding by now. If she hadn't buried her head in the sand when the business started losing money she might have been able to save it. She couldn't blame it all on Oscar, though he had been the mistake that brought it all crashing down. The truth was her business failed because the market had turned and she didn't do what she needed to do to remain competitive. She was being undercut at every turn and, instead of coming up with a plan, she crossed her fingers and hoped for the best. And because she ran away from her financial problems, in the same way as she ran from everything else, she didn't have much of a relationship with her dad, had lost her boyfriend, and her business was gone. And most of all, she'd destroyed what was left of her self-respect.

Molly wondered if her old doctor was still at the practice in town. She'd run out of the anti-depressants her London GP had prescribed her. Not that she believed herself to have depression. No, she was just going through a rough spot that's all. No number of pills could take away the guilt of what she'd done, but she'd been glad of the help to control the creeping anxiety that had surfaced for the first time in years. She hadn't thought they'd been helping but now she was without them, she felt restless and fearful. She'd come back to Hellas Mill to hide out from the real world for a while but was starting to think that the whole of her adult life had been spent in hiding, and it was only now that she could begin to look at her life and make things right. Given half a chance she could be a better daughter and a better friend. Beth had suggested Molly stay with her for a while, but Molly's conscience was starting to eat her up and she couldn't work out how to make things right with Beth while she was standing right there in front of her.

There was no reason why Beth would ever have to know about Molly and Oscar. It wouldn't change anything, except leave her with one friend less. She'd do anything for Beth to stay in the dark. She'd stay here as her dad's carer until she was old and grey if that's what it took to make amends.

She wiped the crumbs off the kitchen side and took the sandwich in to the sitting room.

'Here you go,' she said.

Dad looked up from the television long enough to take the plate from her. 'You not having anything?'

'Not hungry.' Her stomach was knotted, and she hadn't been able to keep anything down since she'd been back in Hellas Mill.

Couldn't eat, couldn't sleep.

It was Oscar's death that kept her awake at night. She'd

tried to stand up to a bully but had made everything worse. When would she learn? It was Barnaby Flint-Stanton all over again. Her desire to defend herself had resulted in the deaths of two people. She'd never meant for it to happen but, because of her bad decisions, countless lives had been ruined.

CHAPTER THIRTY-ONE

Beth Lomas

'What do you think?' asked Hattie.

I took my mobile away from my ear for a moment and looked at the display. Yes, Hattie had called me, and yes, she was asking me to cater her wedding. I cleared my throat and put the phone to my ear again.

'I'm sorry, but I don't think I—'

'Is it the money? Because, if it is, you can name your price. I'm desperate. The wedding is a week away and I've tried everyone else. You're my last hope. This would benefit both of us.'

I didn't know whether to be offended that she'd tried everyone else before me, or flattered she'd asked at all. Either way, I couldn't accept.

'No. It's not the money. I'm not in the right head space to be taking on work like this. I only buried my husband ten days ago.'

'God, I know. And I feel like an absolute heel asking you at a time like this, but it could take your mind off things. Lowry Endecott said you were considering setting up a catering business. There'll never be the right time, just the right opportunity and this is it. And I know I'm not your favourite person at the moment. You'll have lots of reasons to say "no" but I'm begging you to put the past behind us. I think ...'

She went quiet as if she was struggling to find the right words. 'I think that we have a history that predates Oscar, and you know what I've been through. You were there the night that Barnaby died and I hope that—'

'I'll do it.'

'You will?'

I'd have said anything to stop her talking about Barnaby. 'The cake. I'll definitely bake the wedding cake.'

'That's marvellous. Oh, I can't thank you enough. I don't mind what you do. Honestly, as long as it has at least three tiers and matches the rose gold theme I'll leave it entirely up to you. Won't you at least consider doing part of the buffet?'

The money would come in handy. Taking a step towards having my own catering company would serve me well for the future but, more than anything, I'd do it just as long as I didn't have to address what happened to Barnaby Flint-Stanton.

'I'll need to look into what I can source at such late notice and whether I can get some help. Can you leave it with me and I'll let you know for sure in the morning?'

'Oh, you star. I don't know what I'd have done if you'd have said no.'

Hattie was talking as if I'd already agreed to it.

'Does this mean that things are okay between us?' she asked.

'I don't know. I think maybe it could be. We're adult enough to keep it civil and, besides, I don't have any ill-feelings towards you. Really I don't.' Until I said it, I hadn't realised that it was true. 'And as you say,' I continued, 'this is beneficial for both of us.'

Now I knew about Miriam and Oscar, Hattie's indiscretion seemed minor. She hadn't been in my house, hadn't cradled my children when they were young, hadn't been on holiday with us, laughed with us. All my anger was directed at Miriam now, I just hadn't worked out how to handle it. Surely Harvey didn't know or he wouldn't still be with her and he would have confronted Oscar at some point. But, oh, what if he did? What if he was angry enough to push his brother to his death?

'Sorry? What was that?' I asked. Hattie had started speaking again but my mind was occupied elsewhere.

'I was saying that there's no budget, just spend what you need to spend and then give me an invoice.'

'I'll ... I'll need paying immediately. Not when you get back off honeymoon. I can't afford to be out of pocket by hundreds of pounds.'

'No, of course not. I'll pay before the wedding if you like. Just let me know how much I owe you. We'll talk tomorrow then, yeah?'

'Yes.'

'And Beth, I can't tell you how much I appreciate this. Thank you.'

I hung up and realised my palms were sweating. I'd not considered how Oscar's infidelity would affect Harvey. I'd not seen him or Miriam since the funeral, but they would be at Hattie's wedding along with everyone else who'd been caught up in Oscar's lies.

And I knew then that it was never in doubt that I would agree to cater for Hattie and Finn's wedding because I might finally get answers about who was responsible for Oscar's death. But more than that, Hattie's house, where the reception would be, had a house of horrors feel to it. I'd had countless nightmares where that house had featured. Bad things had happened there, but it was now time to address them and put it behind me. For Molly too. She didn't know it yet, but I planned to bring her in on this because I couldn't do this on my own. Not only did she need the money but she needed to revisit Wesley Manor too. Hattie's fifteenth birthday party had set us both on paths that had led to unhappiness. I'd hidden myself away. Scared of my true nature, scared of everything, I hid behind Oscar and let him control every aspect of my life – and thanked him for it. People thought he was domineering but I honestly hadn't seen it that way. I'd been a willing follower, until he steered us into debt, and started an affair. And now that he was gone, it turned out that I was capable of more than I knew. For both Molly and I, it didn't matter which route we pursued, it was always going to bring us back to where it all began, stripped of our armour, and having to start all over again. But this time I'd be the one in control.

CHAPTER THIRTY-TWO

DC Lowry Endecott

Lowry took a sip from her beer bottle and skimmed the webpage for flats to rent in South London. She'd be lucky to get a flat half the size of her house for less than treble the mortgage. She didn't have many belongings so it didn't make sense for her to have spare rooms and second bathrooms anyway.

Greta had sent her the information for the new task force she was setting up, but hadn't officially offered Lowry the job yet. She knew a couple of people in the Met and had spent the evening sending messages to them, 'to catch up', but Lowry's eyes kept being pulled back to the notebook by her side. Even though Finn had been clear she should let the Lomas case go, she wasn't prepared to give up yet. If Finn had been open about his run-in with Oscar, and encouraged her to explore all avenues, she might have been more inclined to move on. But it was usually the ones with something to hide who tried to silence you. Her relationship with Finn was important to her but not as important as discovering the truth about Oscar Lomas's death.

At the top of one column, she'd written *Indications OL was killed by suicide.* And underneath she'd written:

- *Money problems (Unable to pay debts. Factory closing? Being sued for unfair dismissal).*
- *Marriage problems (Affair with H.F-S. Angry wife. Local police DS angry with him).*

At the head of the other column, she'd written *Indication OL was killed by someone else.* The list was almost identical.

- *Money problems (who did he owe money to? Factory workers losing jobs. Unfairly dismissed employees Randall, Ken and Brad).*
- *Marriage problems (Wife angry enough to kill? Jilted lovers? Furious partners? Started affair with the wrong woman).*
- *Womaniser.*
- *No obvious signs of depression/mental health issues.*

Out of those reasons she liked the womaniser one most. Not that she liked it – bad turn of phrase – what she meant was, that one seemed the most likely. Lowry had once wanted to kill a partner who was unfaithful to her. She'd thrown kitchen utensils at him, including a toaster and a kettle, though he was out of the door before she started on the knives. And that was nothing compared to what she wanted to do to the tart he moved in with and eventually married. Her name was Natasha but Lowry always thought of her as Na-*trash*-a. She'd spent far too many months trying to catch her speeding, or find anything that could be used against her in court. Lowry was lucky she hadn't been suspended. The move to Hellas Mill had been forced upon her but it turned out to be just the change she needed.

She wrote in capitals THEFT OF LAPTOP. Could it have contained something that would confirm Beth's suspicions that someone killed Oscar? A sound from her phone let her know that she'd received a message. It was from an old colleague. Hey, you! Long time no see. How's tricks? Bored of arresting sheep yet? Drop me a line next time you're down. Beers on me. Tom.

Tom was definitely going on the 'pros' column of her 'move to London' list. Lowry loved a list. For and against. A pro and a con. Disappointing Finn would be on the 'con' side but she couldn't think of anyone else who would care if she left town. Hattie would be sad, momentarily, but social media meant that everybody felt closer nowadays anyway. She'd always known she wouldn't stay here for ever, yet she felt a tinge of sadness at the thought of leaving the first house she'd owned.

There was a timid knock on her door. Lowry nearly didn't answer it. It would probably be a charity guilting her into saving the children, the elderly, or the whales. But there was something about the hesitant nature of the knock which made her curious. She placed her beer bottle down and was at the front door in three steps. She opened it a crack and was surprised to see Beth Lomas standing there fidgeting, smiling, grimacing.

'Beth? What are you doing here?'

'Sorry to bother you. Can I come in? Just for a minute?'

Lowry hesitated, then opened the door wider.

'Sure. Why not?'

She should have said, 'Let's talk at the station tomorrow.' Or 'why don't I come and see you in the morning?' But Beth looked so vulnerable at that moment and Lowry couldn't imagine her coming over if she didn't have a very good reason.

'How do you know where I live?' Lowry asked as she closed the door.

'This is Hellas Mill,' Beth shrugged.

Lowry saw the other woman take in the sparse surroundings, the half-empty beer bottle, the open notebook, the plate on the floor with the remnants of toast.

'How can I help?' Lowry asked before Beth could read what was on the pages of the lined paper. She hurried to the sofa and closed the book.

'When I called Harvey at work earlier in the week, his assistant said he was showing you Cloud Drop,' Beth said.

'That's right.'

'Why?'

Yes, indeed, why? She didn't want to give Beth false hope but wouldn't keep things from her either. The question was how much she should say. Should she tell her that she agreed there was a chance someone had murdered Oscar? That Beth, herself, was one of the suspects? That her boss – whose fiancée was having an affair with the deceased – had told her not to investigate further despite there being no evidence that Oscar Lomas was in the state of mind to end his own life?

'I like to be thorough,' Lowry said. 'I needed to see for myself. It was all routine, I can assure you.'

'It wasn't,' Beth was shaking her head. 'Nothing is routine. They all have their secrets.' She laughed and put her fingers to her temples.

'Are you okay, Beth?'

Beth was pale and there was a thin covering of sweat on her top lip. Lowry directed her to an armchair and she sat.

'I'm always the last to know. God, what an idiot. Do you

suppose they're all laughing at me? Even my son knew before I did. Ha! Christ, you must think I'm so stupid.'

'What are you talking about, Beth?' Lowry sat on the edge of the sofa. 'What did your son know?'

'He knew who it was – the affair.'

'Are you talking about Hattie Flint-Stanton?' asked Lowry.

'You knew about that?' Beth's eyes widened and she opened and closed her mouth twice. She shook her head slowly. 'No,' she said. 'I mean, yes, her, but she wasn't the only one. Do you want to know something about my husband? No loyalty. None. Not to me, not to his children, not to his brother. I wouldn't take anything Harvey says at face value because he had a lot to gain from Oscar's death.'

'Like?'

'Well, for a start, Oscar was having an affair with his wife, Miriam.'

Lowry took in the news silently. It would explain a few things about Harvey's behaviour when they went to Cloud Drop. The comment he'd made about looking over the edge to search for his brother's body being 'wishful thinking'.

'Have you spoken to either of them about it?'

'No. I thought Miriam and I were … well, okay, so we're not best friends. I mean, if it wasn't for Oscar and Harvey, we'd never have anything to do with each other, but I've known her for nine years. You'd think that'd count for something. We're family. Harvey's been avoiding me and I thought it was because he was struggling to come to terms with his brother's death. I was actually worried about how he was coping, which is why I called him at work.'

'Do you know for certain that they were having an affair, or that Harvey knew about it?'

'Oh, I *know*. Gabe was certain it was Miriam he saw his dad kissing. So now you know what Harvey's hiding, perhaps you could talk to him. He's more likely to tell you the truth. He doesn't have to spare your feelings.'

'Me?' said Lowry. 'You'd be surprised at how little truth I encounter. Rarely happens in my job.'

Beth sighed and folded her hands in her lap. 'Something I've realised over the past few weeks is how little I knew about my husband. I don't know whether I'm particularly stupid or whether Oscar was particularly clever at hiding things. We have no savings, you know. Nothing. He cleared us out completely, and I had no clue. I left all the financial stuff to him. I'm like a cliché of a fifties' housewife. I stayed home and baked cakes while he worked and took care of the finances. I'm not an idiot, you know, though it must look like it to you. I thought that by keeping things calm and ordered at home it enabled him to run the business and that would benefit the whole family.'

'For what it's worth,' said Lowry, 'I don't think you're an idiot. But just because your husband was having affairs doesn't mean that he didn't die by suicide, or that he didn't fall.'

'No. I know that, but it does mean that there are people who would have been glad to see him dead. You've thought it too, haven't you? If Harvey has something to cover up, he'd make sure to paint it in such a way that would leave you in no doubt that Oscar jumped. He knows those hills better than anyone, and his wife was having an affair with my husband. If anyone could do it and make it look like an accident it's Harvey.'

'The problem I have, Beth, is that all the signs point to your husband taking his own life. He had debts building up, his company was in trouble. Unless I have a good reason to investigate this as a potential murder, my boss isn't going to let me look into this.'

'The same boss who has a reason to want Oscar dead for sleeping with his fiancée?' Beth asked.

Lowry bowed her head a moment. There was no denying the fact that Finn had motive, but she was as certain as she could be that Finn couldn't commit murder, no matter how jealous he was. But was she in the same position as Beth – unable to see what was under her nose because she was too close to the situation? To go against Finn's orders, when she had no evidence to go on, would be career-limiting at best.

'There's something else,' Beth said. 'Well, not something else, more of the same I suppose.'

Lowry sighed. She should never have let her in. She should have done this the right way, at the station. She wasn't sure she wanted to know what else Beth Lomas had to tell her but also knew she couldn't resist asking. 'What is it?'

'When I saw Harvey after Oscar's death, he had bloodied knuckles. It could have been from climbing down the rock face but there's no getting away from the fact that, with Oscar gone, Harvey is head of Lomas Lumber and number one son.'

CHAPTER THIRTY-THREE

Beth Lomas

Though people could see Wesley Manor from the road, playing peek-a-boo over the hedge, it wasn't until they came up the driveway that the grandeur became apparent. Undoubtedly the largest house in the area, Finn Greenwood had done well marrying into such a dynasty. There couldn't be many detective sergeants in the police force who could also call themselves lord of the manor. I wondered how far he'd go to keep that title.

The sun had shone all day, as it had always shone on Hattie. The huge white marquee had glowed in the sunshine, while guests milled about with tall flutes of champagne in their hands. Waiters with drink-topped trays had slipped amongst revellers with the stealth of assassins, while a string quartet played popular classical music that I recognised but couldn't name.

The day had been a success, and not just for the newly-weds. Molly and I had worked flat out for days making the food. I'd been icing the cake until the early hours of the morning and was pleased with how it looked. People had taken business cards I'd left in piles on the tables and it seemed I had a plan to make money while doing something I enjoyed. It was also a venture that Molly and I could grow together.

She had the business brains and I had the cookery skills and knowledge. It was a match made in heaven – or in desperation.

Though I was ready to go home and fall into bed, I still had one more thing to do. I still had to confront Harvey and Miriam. They couldn't avoid me for ever. I'd been too busy during the day, but I'd seen them sitting side by side, steadfastly not speaking to each other, checking their watches.

In Hattie Flint-Stanton's overtly floral bathroom I reapplied my lipstick. It was a wedding-appropriate shade of red, and one that I'd bought especially for the occasion. My hand shook and painted over my lip-line, making my mouth look grotesque. I was a child caught playing with her mother's make-up. I often felt that I was playing dress-up, pretending I was an adult when I should still be in knee-high socks. Against my protestations that I couldn't afford it, I'd gone shopping with Molly and bought a green silk dress which made my eyes shine. The skirt was full and danced about me as I walked. There was nothing else in my wardrobe quite like it.

Was it too soon after my husband's death to be wearing such a bright colour? The etiquette of Victorian mourning would have a widow wearing black for two years. Queen Victoria was known for her top-level mourning. She'd even give Esther a run for her money.

I feared people whispering behind my back and thinking that I wasn't looking nearly upset enough. Every smile or laugh would make them think that I didn't care about Oscar. What they didn't know was that I was sick of my own sorrow and couldn't stand the thought of talking to another person about how much Oscar would be missed. My grief was no longer on public display, and I wouldn't apologise for trying to get my life back on track. Oscar hadn't considered my feelings when he was alive and I wouldn't consider his now he was dead.

Hattie had offered me a lifeline that I couldn't ignore, and it had brought me somewhere I'd sworn I'd never revisit. Though we were each doing the other a favour, the cost was significantly higher for me. It cost her money – of which she had plenty – and a smidge of dignity. For me, it re-opened wounds that had never fully healed. I was taking money from a woman who had slept with my husband. A woman whose family had almost destroyed my life. She was the reason that the last words I'd said to Oscar were cruel and laced with hate. She was the reason that DS Finn Greenwood wouldn't let Lowry investigate Oscar's death as murder. But I needed that money, and today was also a chance to get closer to those who had cause to want my husband dead. Finn and Harvey, the wronged men. Hattie, Miriam and I, the lovelorn women. What a joke.

It was worse for Molly, being back where her childhood had ended. It was here that I had betrayed her, while thinking I was helping. It was here she lost her first love. She said she never thought about it anymore, but I saw that haunted look in her eyes and I recognised the smell of brandy on her breath as we passed in the kitchen. Maybe I'd been wrong to ask her to help me today, but I'd thought it was something we both needed. Neither of us could put our past behind us until we'd confronted it. It was somewhat of a mantra to me nowadays.

I stepped outside and saw Molly waiting for me with a cocktail in each hand.

'I hope one of those is for me,' I said.

She'd let her hair down but it kinked where the hair band

had held it away from her face. She'd changed into a dove-grey jumpsuit with wide legs that swayed when she walked. It seemed to hang straight down from thin straps on her shoulders. If it wasn't for her belt, you'd hardly know where her waist was.

'You alright?' I asked as she passed me a glass.

She scratched her nose. 'I guess.' Her make-up, normally so perfect, was smudged.

'We shouldn't be here,' I said.

'Yes, we should. We both need the money. Neither Oscar nor Barnaby are going to stop us getting on with our lives.'

Molly had seemed outraged, *offended* even, by Oscar's affairs with Hattie and Miriam as if he had slighted her instead of me. But that was best friends for you, they felt your pain, they got offended on your behalf and they would do anything to protect you. I loved Molly's loyalty. I knew that she was the one person I could always count on.

'Ready babe?' Molly asked as we walked across the lawn.

'I suppose so.'

'Say the word and I'll steal a bottle of Bolly and we'll go sit on the band-stand in our finery and get pissed for old time's sake.'

'I know I said I was going to confront Miriam,' I said stopping suddenly and grabbing Molly's arm. 'But I don't know anymore. Perhaps we should just pay our respects to the bride and then go home. I haven't got the energy for confrontation.'

I expected Molly to argue with me but she took hold of my hand and squeezed it. 'Whatever you need,' she said. 'I meant what I said about the Bolly.'

A sudden burst of laughter caught our attention and we both looked towards the marquee. Hattie was easy to spot; she was the centre of everything and the reason half the town was there. Finn had his hand on her waist and everything anyone said appeared to be hilarious. Hattie's floor-length gown was the same rose gold that had been on the invitations, and it clung to her curves. Looking at her now, it was impossible to believe that Oscar had only been after her money.

I finished the drink in my hand and shook my head as the bubbles tickled my nose. 'I'm going to need another drink.'

As Molly steered me towards the open bar, neither of us were smiling. It was obvious we were both seeing a different party. One from twenty-five years before. It was a warm day, much like today but there had been a breeze back then.

I looked towards the place where the swimming pool used to be. It was a tennis court now.

'It was an accident, Beth,' Molly said quietly.

I looked at her and she didn't seem to have aged since she was fifteen. Maybe it was the vulnerability in her eyes, which I hadn't seen in so long.

'Was it?' I asked.

It had haunted me all my life – not so much that I was responsible for Barnaby's death, no, he was responsible for that. The thing that bothered me the most was that I didn't feel bad enough about it and, if I had to, I'd do it all again.

CHAPTER THIRTY-FOUR

Beth Lomas

The night that Barnaby Flint-Stanton died

Everyone had left by the time Beth returned to Wesley Manor. The evidence of the party was in black bin-liners, stationed like sentries up the driveway. The smell of beer and greasy pizza boxes soured the air as she passed. She'd taken Molly home while the party had been in full swing, calling her parents from the phone in the house, begging a lift. Her dad didn't ask questions, probably thinking Molly's tears nothing more than a bruised heart.

Molly was asleep on the blow-up bed on Beth's bedroom floor. They'd cried and said they'd make Barnaby pay for what he'd done. Beth stole brandy from the kitchen cabinet and made Molly drink it even though she said it burned. Beth had told her she'd make it okay, and here she was, wanting to make it okay, but with no idea how.

Beth expected there'd still be a few people at the party, sitting around the pool, laughing at in-jokes and outcasts. She was disappointed that she'd lost her chance to confront him in front of everyone and expose him as a rapist. Though the house was in darkness, there were lights on in the garden as she made her way, silently, towards the back. If Hattie's parents saw her, she was planning to say she thought she'd left her bag here, if Barney saw her ... well, she hadn't worked out the details yet, but she knew that she wanted to scream and shout at him, gouge out his eyes. He couldn't expect to lay a finger on her best friend and get away with it.

She heard a splash of water, like someone diving into the pool and she froze. She'd come too far to turn back now. Peering around the corner she saw someone in the pool, head down, lazy strokes. He got to the end of the pool nearest to her, raised his head and shook it to get the hair out of his eyes. He looked more like a model than a schoolboy.

'I know you're there,' Barney said.

Beth could have turned and run but she was feeling bold so, instead, stepped out of the darkness. If anyone should be worried it was him, because she knew what he'd done.

'Beth, isn't it?' he said.

'Yeah. I'm Molly's friend.'

'Thought so. Why don't you join me?'

'I haven't got my swimming costume,' she said.

'So?'

He turned and began swimming back the way he'd come. Beth had expected some sign of remorse, a hint of shame. She put her hands in the back pocket of her jeans, trying to look casual, and her fingertips touched the tablets that Barney had given Molly earlier in the night. Molly had let him think she'd taken them but, instead, asked Beth to get rid of them for her. And that was exactly what Beth was intending to do.

The hot tub was bubbling gently and the lights changed from blue to purple to red. There were four cans of lager on the raised wooden surround. While Barney swam, Beth cracked open a can and placed all three tablets in it. She swirled it gently and the beer frothed over her hand.

'Are you getting in or what?' called Barney.

'Why don't you get out?'

She showed him the beer and opened one for herself.

Barney shook his head with a laugh and began swimming another length. She had to do something to get his attention so she put both cans down, undid her jeans and slipped them off. She noticed his head come up, knew he was watching her. She dropped her T-shirt on the floor and stepped into the hot tub in her underwear. It was warm but she still shivered like she'd submerged herself in ice-water.

He watched for a minute and then smiled and pulled himself out of the pool. There was no denying how beautiful he was, but beauty was dangerous. It disarmed you, sucked you in. Gorgeous people got away with so much. He walked towards Beth, tugging his red swim shorts up, and staggered slightly showing he wasn't as sober as he'd first appeared.

The wind blew a beer can across the lawn as Beth handed him the tainted drink, and he slipped into the hot tub.

'This is a nice surprise,' he said. 'I thought everyone had gone.'

'I had to get Molly back home, she wasn't feeling well.'

She watched him carefully but there still wasn't any concern for Molly.

'Father kicked everyone out,' he said. 'Which is good for us because we get some privacy.' He lowered his chin and looked up at Beth through impossibly long eyelashes. She noticed his eyes shift to her breasts and resisted the urge to fold her arms over her chest.

He still hadn't drunk any of his beer and Beth was starting to worry about what she'd got herself into. Apart from drugging his drink and giving him a piece of her mind, she didn't really have a plan.

'Cheers,' she said lifting her own beer to her lips. She was relieved when he followed her lead, throwing his head back and gulping.

He placed the can to the side of him and slipped closer. She tried to move away but he hooked a finger under her bra strap and pulled her towards him. She could smell the beer on his breath as he bent his head to kiss her shoulder. She shuddered and he smiled.

'No need to be nervous,' he said.

'Wait.'

'It's okay,' he said, running a finger down her neck and trailing it over her breast. He pushed her hair away from her face and kissed the hollow where her neck met her shoulder. His lips were warm and soft.

'No. Stop! I . . . I need the bathroom.'

He sighed and sneered at her. He picked up his beer and used it to point towards the pool house. 'In there,' he said. 'Be quick.'

Beth crawled out of the hot tub and struggled to put her top on as it stuck to wet skin. She ran to the pool house, her breath coming quick and shallow. She'd been driven by some sense of righting wrongs, of confronting the person who'd hurt her friend, but what had she expected to happen? Would she just look him in the eye and tell him what a bad person he was? That wouldn't help anyone. He wouldn't change. She'd let him kiss her neck, and part of her had liked it, even knowing what he was capable of. Perhaps he wasn't the monster, she was.

Beth watched as he drank, as he closed his eyes tapping his fingers on the edge of the hot tub as if he could hear music that no one else could. She should have left. Run all the way home. But her jeans were by the hot tub and she couldn't walk through town half-dressed. She'd have to at least acknowledge him on her way out.

Taking a deep breath, she pulled her shoulders back and walked towards Barnaby. He kept his eyes closed and she wondered whether he'd fallen asleep. As she got closer, she noticed his swim shorts discarded on the floor, and she felt sick. Sick for what he'd done, and for the assumptions he made every day of his charmed life.

'I'm going,' Beth said.

He opened his eyes but seemed to take a moment to focus on her. 'No you're not,' he smiled.

'I am. Molly told me what you did to her.'

'Is that what this is about? You two want to compare notes, huh?' He chuckled.

'That's not ... that's ... I know what you did to her and you won't get away with it.'

He drained the last of his beer and threw the can away from him. It rolled and fell into the pool.

'What did she tell you? That the bad man took advantage of the poor little girl? Give me a break.'

'She's been crying her eyes out. Don't you care at all? She could go to the police, you know.'

He lay his head back and closed his eyes. 'And who would the police believe? A girl like her. Or a boy like me?'

He belched but didn't cover his mouth. 'Now, are we going to do this, or what?'

Beth had never felt anger like it. Her fists clenched and her nails dug into her palms.

He didn't stir as she stepped closer and lifted the cover of the hot tub. It was heavy but it was on a cantilever and it slid up and down quickly and forcefully without her applying much pressure. He opened his eyes and started to sit up but the lid hit his head with a satisfying thud. Not enough to do any serious damage but enough to sting. She crouched and, while he banged on the lid, said, 'It's not nice when someone else holds all the power is it? Are you scared yet?'

'Fuck you!'

'Sorry, Barney, but you'll never get that chance. How about we start with an apology?'

'Yeah, right. I'm sorry your friend is a slut.'

Beth stood up, grabbed her jeans and struggled to get them on as she listened to him bang and swear. How long should she leave him there? How angry would he be when she finally let him out?

'How are you feeling?' Beth called. 'Those drugs you've been selling all night are now in your system. These ones though ... these are the ones you wanted Molly to take so she wouldn't put up a fight when you raped her.'

As Beth picked up her shoes a light came on in the house. It looked like Barnaby wouldn't be in there for much longer, and if she was caught here, she was the one who would get into trouble. Beth turned and started running across the lawn and out into the street. If Barnaby told them who'd drugged his drink and shut him in the hot tub it would come down to who the police believed. A boy like him, or a girl like her.

CHAPTER THIRTY-FIVE

DC Lowry Endecott

Lowry made the mistake of bringing a date to the wedding. She'd seen Mark three times over the past six weeks and hadn't planned to see him again. It wasn't even a conscious decision based on how much, or little, she liked him. She, quite simply, couldn't be bothered to make an effort. Dating meant buying new underwear. It meant pretending to be interested in everything someone said. It was compromising on which films you saw at the cinema. On the rare occasions she had some time off she needed sleep and some time for herself. She didn't know how she could fit someone else into her life without making big changes. Once before, she'd tried to fit herself around someone else's life and she'd learned the hard way that only led to disaster.

But in the days before the wedding, Lowry started panicking about being on her own at the occasion of the century. It wasn't that she didn't want to be judged for being single, it was more that she would appreciate the company. Someone she could hide behind if she got stuck with anyone she didn't want to speak to.

Part of the problem with being a detective in a small town was that people tended to corner you at events to tell you about the speeds that others drove down their road, or how their neighbour was refusing to cut back their leylandii. She didn't love the job enough to talk about it out-of-hours. And even if she did, she deserved a break, right?

Mark was nice enough. Not really her type, looks-wise. Shorter than her, which was a no-no from the start. On their first date, he'd worn shoes which looked suspiciously like they had a Cuban heel. But he was amusing and intelligent and wasn't over-keen, which was what she liked most in a man. And he wouldn't embarrass her at a wedding.

He didn't hide his surprise when she texted him to invite him to the wedding. He'd responded with Hi, this is Mark. Are you sure this text is for me?

Finn kept grinning at her as if he'd never seen her with a man before. To be fair, he probably hadn't. She'd made small talk, and introduced Mark to a few people she knew, and now they were sitting with very little to say to each other. The ceremony had been beautiful and the party was now in full swing. Most of Hellas Mill had turned up, not wanting to miss out on the free bar. A band was setting up, and the empty bottles were filling huge black bins behind the tent, yet Lowry couldn't quite relax.

Hattie had taken her advice about asking Beth to cater the wedding but it was a suggestion that Lowry would never have made if she'd known about the history between the two women. Lowry was alert, half-expecting everything to boil over. Beth was vulnerable and currently at a wedding where two of the women present had slept with her husband. Add alcohol to the mix and it was a dangerous cocktail.

Finn would be spending the next week honeymooning in Paris and Lowry would be in charge at the station. She'd tentatively said 'yes' to the new job in London but was waiting on the paperwork. She was relieved to have a new job lined up because, while Finn was away, there would be a new focus at work. And when he got back she'd be lucky if he didn't sack her on the spot.

From where she was sitting, Lowry could see Beth Lomas talking to a woman that she vaguely recognised. The other woman looked upset, drunk, and kept shaking her head. Miriam and Harvey were sitting at the opposite corner of the grounds from Beth and her friend. They weren't talking at all. Both of them had their gaze fixed on others who were having a better time than they were. If Beth was correct in her assertions that Oscar's affairs were only out of desperation for money then Miriam must have wealth that wasn't apparent and wasn't linked to her husband's. They didn't appear to be a flashy couple; no glinting diamonds on fingers, no designer clothes. They drove sensible cars and lived in a modest cottage off the main road. Lowry needed to find out how long the affair had been going on and when it had ended – if indeed it had before Oscar died. And more importantly, whether her husband knew about it before his brother's death.

Lowry wondered if Hattie would've invited Oscar if he'd been alive today. If he hadn't gone down the blackmail route, Hattie wouldn't have felt the need to confess all to her fiancé. Lomas could have been swanning around with the rest of them, looking over his conquests, smug that he was getting away with everything.

'Would you like to dance?' Mark asked her. The band had started playing 'Brown Eyed Girl'.

'Don't be ridiculous,' she said. 'I don't dance.'

'You do this evening.' He held out his hand to her.

'There's no one else on the dance floor, Mark.'

'Let's show them how it's done.'

He kept his hand extended and Lowry hesitated.

'Go on,' he said. 'I'm dancing with or without you. I've got some pretty wild moves and unless you're there to stop me, it could get messy.' He was grinning at her. A wicked spark in his eye. 'You'll be more embarrassed than me.'

Lowry hung her head for a moment. 'Oh, God. There'd better not be any pictures.' She took his hand and let him lead her to the dance floor.

CHAPTER THIRTY-SIX

Molly Ingram

'Whoops!'

Molly stumbled down the metal steps of the Portaloo and giggled. Never had a temporary toilet looked so posh. Cubicles and basins. Handwash and towels. She couldn't see Beth anywhere. She'd expected Beth to wait for her. Beth always waited. Beth was good. Beth was loyal. Beth was everything that Molly wasn't.

Molly didn't know how long she'd been in the bathroom. It had taken for ever to navigate the jumpsuit. It wasn't a practical outfit for narrow toilets when you'd already had far too much to drink, and your fingers became thumbs. She needed Beth to do up the top button for her.

'Beth,' she called as if she were summoning a dog. The thought of Beth bounding up to her made her chuckle.

She took a glass of something orange and alcoholic from a passing tray and drank it down in one go. She'd not expected it to be so difficult coming here today. Molly had often voiced the opinion that her past didn't define her, it didn't hold her back. She tried her very best to believe it too. She refused to be a victim, wouldn't blame the past for the mistakes she'd made in the present. Part of her had been . . . well, not exactly looking forward to being back at Wesley Manor, but she was cautiously curious after all this time. She wanted to confirm to herself that it was only a building. The place had no power over her. And, though she didn't believe in ghosts, she wanted to stick two fingers up to Barnaby and let him know that he hadn't broken her.

It was smaller than she remembered. Only a large house. In her memory, it had been part castle, part mansion. It had been her Manderley. The main reason for coming here today was to support Beth, but her own emotions were threatening to take over. Thankfully there was enough free alcohol to douse the flickering flames of painful memories.

She'd not spoken to Hattie since they'd arrived. They'd been shepherded into the kitchen where the help was, but now she had plenty of things she wanted to say to Hattie. For a start, she wanted to look her in the eye and ask her how she dared sleep with Oscar. Did she have no shame? Finn was a good man – one of the best – and he deserved to be treated better than that. Okay, so Molly didn't actually know him. Had never met him before today. But she would bet every pair of designer shoes she owned that he didn't deserve to have his fiancée sleep with the local factory boss. The whole family just took what they wanted without thinking of others.

Ah, fuck it, what was she thinking? She was no better than Hattie. Worse, in fact, because Oscar was her best friend's husband. They'd been so similar. They'd been so drunk. And now she'd found out that not only was Hattie a notch on his bedpost, but Miriam too. He was quite the Lothario. Yeah, well, where had that got him? Dead, that's where.

Another tray, another drink. Fruity. Pimm's. She fished the fruit and the mint out of the glass with her fingers and wiped her hand on her hip. Or borage. Wasn't it borage in a Pimm's? And if anyone would know that and track it down, it would be Hattie. Beautiful, rich and perfect. God, Molly hated her.

Molly had never been in the house even when she was at school with Hattie. Hattie used to go to the local private school but she'd been kicked out for reasons that Molly had never got to the bottom of. Some said there was a fire, others said she'd slept with a teacher. The only consensus was that she was a wild child and she'd done something so terrible that not even her parents' money could keep her in that school.

If Hattie was a pedigree then Molly was a mongrel. Everyone knew that Molly was the poor kid. The one with the dirty, patched up clothes. *Don't let her in your house in case she steals something.* Never quite good enough. Well she was good enough for Hattie's brother, wasn't she? Or was it because she had so little value that he thought he could take her? People like him thought they were entitled to the world. If he'd taken his time, just said some kind words to her, she would have given herself to him. But he was impatient. Entitled.

She'd gone willingly with him into the woods behind the house. He told her that the rest of them were children but that she was different. She was excited because he was the most gorgeous creature she'd ever seen, and he saw the worth in her. She imagined herself visiting his home, having tea with his parents in the drawing-room. She didn't even know what a drawing-room was, but it sounded like somewhere posh people drank tea. She imagined the gifts he'd lavish on her. The looks on everyone's faces when they found out that she was Barnaby Flint-Stanton's girlfriend. Molly Flint-Stanton had a lovely ring to it.

But Barnaby had other plans and he didn't care whether

Molly was ready or not. Afterwards, she'd found Beth and told her she needed to go home. They both cried because if it happened to one of them it happened to them both. Molly fell asleep, fitfully. Bad dreams and a spinning head. She thought Beth was sleeping on the bed opposite her but she'd gone back to Wesley Manor. Molly felt responsible for Barnaby's death. Yes, he shouldn't have done what he did but she should never have gone with him into the woods anyway. And it was Beth who risked losing her future by going to look for Barnaby to teach him a lesson. All because Molly was stupid.

'Hey!' Molly called to a passing waiter. 'Got any more of these fruit things?' She shook her glass at him but he didn't seem to hear her.

Bollocks to them. Bollocks to them all.

She wandered onto the lawn and let the glass slip from her hand. She didn't turn back for it. Didn't stoop to pick it up. That's what the hundreds and thousands of waiters were for.

The garden lights had come on even though there was still some light in the day. Thousands of fairy lights were strung between the trees, and candles smouldered in glass lamps. She could hear the band playing. Molly knew the song vaguely but the tune was more familiar than the lyrics. She tried to sing along but was a fraction late with each word. She laughed at herself and looked about for Beth. Instead, she saw Hattie coming off the dance floor, her hair artfully styled and a pink tinge to her cheeks. She waved to someone and started walking towards Molly. Or maybe she was heading towards the toilets. Either way, Molly stepped into her path.

'Hello to the blushing bride,' she said throwing her arms in the air.

'Hey, Molly. Goodness, I haven't seen you in such a long time. You're looking well.'

'You ...' Molly had no idea what to say next. You look beautiful? Or, you must be so happy. Instead, she said, 'You ... never liked me.'

Hattie's smile matched Molly's but there was confusion in her eyes.

'Don't be silly.'

'Never good enough, was I? You were there that night. I saw you in the woods. Who was that boy you were with? Would Mummy approve? Looked like rough stuff to me but then you and your brother both liked a bit of rough, didn't you?'

'You're drunk.'

'Yes, I am. But I'm still better than you. You saw what he did to me. You were there. You could have stopped him. But people like me don't matter to people like you, do they? You're not as special as you think you are. I know about you and Oscar. And guess what? You weren't the only one.'

Hattie seemed to be looking for someone. 'I have no idea what you're talking about,' she said.

'Oscar,' said Molly stepping closer to Hattie and losing a heel in the grass so she stumbled. 'Before you there was Miriam. Where is she? Look, there she is. Hey! Miriam!'

The other woman turned to frown at them.

'But you weren't the only ones. You were just the last on a long list. You were an afterthought because I got there first.'

She looked at Hattie closely, hoping to see some kind of shock there but Hattie wasn't even looking at her.

'Did you hear me, Mrs ... Whatever your name is now? I said I slept with Oscar Lomas first. Before he was yours, he was mine.'

When Hattie still didn't say anything, Molly turned to see what she was looking at. It took a second for her vision to sharpen, for her to make a face out of the shape standing two feet away from them.

'Oh, shit.'

Beth.

CHAPTER THIRTY-SEVEN

Beth Lomas

Once, when I was in my early twenties, I witnessed a car accident. It happened right in front of us when I was in the passenger seat of a car driven by Oscar. I remember it playing in slow motion. Literally. Everything slowed down and I knew what was going to happen before their brake lights even came on. I watched the car concertina, the people in the car shunt forwards, freeze, then jolt back again. I was already undoing my seatbelt to run to the wreck before the car had stopped moving. It took me for ever to get there, to unstrap the child from its car seat, to realise that the blood on its face had come from its mother. And all the while there was only silence. I don't remember a single sound but I can see the colour of the car's upholstery, the man standing across the street on his phone, and the time on the clock on the dashboard.

I suppose that's what shock does to you. It makes you step outside of your body and slows everything down while your mind catches up with your eyes. And as I stood in front of Molly and Hattie, I had that same sensation again; of time waiting patiently with an outstretched hand. Only this time I was at the heart of the wreck, the eye of the storm, and I was taking in everything around me. Hattie's open mouth, her hair coming loose. Molly's anguish, her unfocused eyes and the mascara smear on her upper lid. Lowry's concerned face as she strode across the lawn towards us as if she too could see what was unfolding. Miriam was sitting alone at a picnic table crying gently, a bunched-up tissue at her lips. Harvey and Finn, with loosened ties, were standing at the edge of the woods in the shadows, looking furtively around them.

I blinked and the world rushed back in. The music from the live band thudded through the night. A single raised voice, laughter, the punchline of a joke. And Molly shrinking in front of me. 'Beth. Let me explain.'

She reached out to touch me but I snatched my arm away and she staggered sideways, slipping out of one shoe.

'Please Beth. I can explain everything,' she said.

I stepped towards her and slapped her face. Hard. My palm stung and I could see the imprint of my hand on the smooth skin of her cheek. She cried out, but her shoulders dipped and she turned her face away from me and began to cry. I'd half expected her to fight back – I *wanted* her to – but she wouldn't even look at me now. Hattie put her arm around Molly's shoulders.

What was wrong with me that people could deceive me so easily? In front of me were two women who had slept with my husband, across the lawn was another. In the shadow of the trees were two men who were glad he was dead. Who knew how many others there were?

The music seemed louder, or perhaps it was because the guests were stunned into silence. A small group of people were watching us now, and for once I didn't cower from their gaze. I couldn't blame them for being curious. Let them look because this is what would happen from now on if anyone lied to me. I wouldn't take it anymore. I looked at their faces but most of them lowered their eyes. Not one person approached us to see what was wrong. Bystander apathy in action, hoping someone else would step in. And if no one was doing anything, well, at least they were doing nothing *together.* No one could be singled out for shirking their responsibility. Did they already know what would drive me to argue with Molly and Hattie on the bride's big day?

Molly had realised that Hattie's arm was around her and shrugged it off. 'Get off me. This is all your fault.'

'My fault?' She threw her hands up in despair.

Lowry had reached us now. 'What's going on here?'

Even in her pretty dress and her wedge heels she still looked like a policewoman. 'We've found lucky number three,' I said pointing to Molly. 'Another woman sleeping with my husband.'

Lowry looked at Molly and then back to me. Hattie folded her arms and turned away.

'This is the time,' I shouted to those in earshot, 'to come clean. If there's anyone else who's slept with my husband, now is the time to let me know, or forever hold your peace.'

People smirked at each other, lowered their faces, shuffled uncomfortably.

'No? No takers? So, it's just the bride, my best friend and my sister-in-law then? Good to know.'

'Shall we go somewhere we can talk?' Lowry asked.

I looked around me, at people I'd known most of my life, and they were suddenly strangers.

'I want to go home. And tell *her*,' I pointed towards Molly, 'that she is no longer welcome in my house. I never want to see her again.'

Stage Four of Grief

DEPRESSION

CHAPTER THIRTY-EIGHT

Beth Lomas.

'Thanks, love.'

I reached out my hand and stroked Honey's arm as she placed two cups of tea on the coffee table between Lowry and me. I'd given Honey a potted version of what happened at the wedding, though I told her that the reason Molly and I had fallen out was because we'd drunk too much. I wasn't protecting Oscar or Molly; I was protecting Honey.

'Where's Gabe?' I asked looking around the room as if I'd missed him hiding in a corner somewhere.

'Out. He didn't say where he was going.'

'I told him to stay home with you tonight. I didn't want you to be on your own.'

'I'm okay, Mum. Really.'

'That's not the point. Where does he keep sneaking off to? Has he got a girlfriend I don't know about?'

Honey shrugged. 'Not that I've noticed.'

'Can you do me a favour, sweetie? Can you give him a call and tell him I want him to come home straightaway?'

Honey stood up. 'He won't like it.'

'And I don't like the fact that he went out when I asked him not to.'

Honey walked out of the room lifting her phone to her ear and closing the door behind her.

'Sorry about that,' I said to Lowry. 'Every time I think I'm getting somewhere with Gabe . . .'

Lowry took a sip of her tea and said, 'You can keep your champagne. There's nothing better than a good cuppa.'

I groaned. 'I wish I'd stuck to tea at the wedding. I'm afraid I caused a bit of a scene.'

'I think that was your friend.'

'Ex-friend.'

I was lying on the sofa with a blanket over me even though the night was still warm. I'd changed out of my silk dress, putting on a long baggy T-shirt over leggings. I couldn't imagine wanting to wear that dress again because it would be forever associated with the day I thought I was putting the past behind me, but instead found that the past would never let me go. I was easy to dismiss, easy to overlook. A pushover. A laughing stock.

'Thanks for the lift, but you didn't have to drive me home. I could've got a taxi.'

'It was no problem.'

'You can go back to the wedding if you like. I'll be okay.'

Lowry shook her head and raised her cup. 'I'll head back in a bit. I don't think anyone will be missing me. It's okay.'

'He seems nice – your partner,' I said.

'Mark? No. I mean, yes, he's nice, but no, he's not my partner. It's only our fourth date. On our second, I arrested a shoplifter and he thought I enjoyed it a bit too much. In fairness, I shouldn't have shoved the kid against the wall for stealing an eyeliner. Maybe he's right, I can get a bit overzealous at times, and I was probably a bit too keen to intervene in your altercation with Molly.'

I grimaced. 'I'm so embarrassed. I drank too much, too quickly. I was worried about how people would react to the food and how I'd look in that ridiculous dress. Seems funny now, doesn't it? I went there wanting to look my best and came away looking my worst. I've never been in a brawl before.' I pulled my hand over my hair, smoothing stray hairs into place. 'I was already feeling emotional. It was difficult for me being there and, in hindsight, I should have done the job I was being paid for and then left. I was trying to prove a point, I guess. Seeing Hattie looking beautiful and knowing that my husband . . . well, it took a lot of effort to look like I didn't care. Molly and I had been talking about some things that happened years ago. It was painful to revisit it. And Molly . . . I've seen her drunk before, but never *that* drunk. It's my fault really, I should never have made her come with me. You see, when she was fifteen, we went to a party there and,' I paused. Was I ready to say this out loud? And to a police detective, of all people? 'She was attacked by Hattie's brother.'

Lowry placed her cup down and leaned forward. 'Do you mean that he raped her?'

I nodded, wincing a little at the word.

'And is this the same night he died?' Lowry asked.

'Yes. A lot happened that night.'

'Did Molly report it?'

I shook my head. 'It didn't occur to us at the time. Molly wanted it all to go away. I suppose she might have thought about going to the police the next morning but, by then, Barnaby was dead and it didn't seem like the right time to bring it up. He'd already paid the price for what he'd done to her.'

'Do you think that Molly had something to do with his death?' Lowry asked.

'No. Definitely not. We left the party and went back to my house where she cried herself to sleep. As angry as I am with her, I can put my hand on my heart and swear to you that she had nothing to do with that boy's death.'

'It was recorded as an accident, right?' asked Lowry.

'Yes, but it was his actions, the way he behaved that night that led to his death. No doubt about it.'

Lowry looked uncomfortable.

'Sorry,' I said. 'That probably sounds heartless.'

Lowry smiled faintly. 'I'm not here to judge. You don't have to explain yourself to me. Did I hear right that you were taken ill after that party and had to take some time off school?'

I sipped my tea and warmed my hands around the mug. 'Hmm. Glandular fever.'

'Glandular fever?'

'That's right.'

There was no way that Lowry could know what really happened that night, and there was nothing to be gained by telling her that I walked to the band-stand and lay down in it, waiting for the sun to come up while wondering if I was a terrible person. Beating myself up for not protecting Molly at the party and feeling sure I was going to be in big trouble once everyone found out that I'd shut Barnaby in the hot tub. I had no way of knowing that no one heard his cries, and no one had opened the lid to let him out.

When I found out what had happened something inside me broke. I didn't want to see anyone, became afraid of everything. Afraid of myself.

'Tell me about you and Molly. You've known each other for a long time?'

'We met on the first day of school and were really close

until she went off to university. Well, we were still close but it wasn't quite the same and she hasn't been back to Hellas Mill often. She's only here now because she has no other options. Her business has gone bust and she's lost her flat. When Oscar died, she was the first person I called. I thought I needed her. That she was one of the few people who I could rely on. Because, even though we hadn't spoken for a while, I thought she was the person who knew me best. We'd been there for each other through all the hard times. I couldn't think of anyone else I wanted to see. And now ... this. It seems that I am a complete idiot and everyone has been laughing behind my back.'

'Does it matter what anyone else thinks?' asked Lowry.

I thought about that for a moment. 'Obviously it shouldn't, but, yeah, it does. Anyway, given that I only managed to spot one of at least three affairs, you're probably thinking that I didn't know my husband very well.'

Lowry took a deep breath, ready to speak, but I held up my hand to stop her.

'But, you see, I did know him. I knew him better than anyone did. And all this has done has made me even more certain that he didn't take his own life. My husband loved himself more than he loved anyone else in the whole world. He also had the most self-belief of anyone I have ever met. No matter what life threw at him, he had this unerring belief that it would all work out okay because it always had. Self-belief can get you a long way. He wasn't depressed, Lowry. I know I missed a lot of what was going on with him but he didn't have depression. He took so much joy in life and he would always back himself to fall on his feet. Every day was a fresh start for him. He used to say that it was amazing that no matter how bad your day had been you got the chance of a do-over the next day. A fresh start every day to make the most out of life.'

'I don't know whether that's enough for me to ...'

'You have to admit there are many reasons that people would want him dead.'

'Yes, and that's what I was about to say. I don't think we have anything concrete to go on but, I agree, it needs looking into. I have to tell you, Beth, that after all this time, and the rain we've had, there'll be no physical evidence and I'm not sure what I'll be able to uncover. I can't promise that I can get you the answers you want.'

'It only matters that you believe me,' I said. 'At this precise moment, I hate my husband. It's not about getting justice for him – I couldn't care less about him – it's about getting justice for me. I deserve to know what really happened. I've been in the dark for too long and I'm sick of it.'

CHAPTER THIRTY-NINE

Molly Ingram

Molly lifted her head and tried to open her eyes. Holy mother of God. Neither of these things was a good idea. She placed her head back down gently on the pillow. She could hardly move for the pounding in her head and the rising sickness. She had that hollow anxious feeling in her chest where she knew that something terrible had happened. Her mouth was dry and her face tacky with saliva, or vomit. It was hard to know without proper inspection and she wasn't ready to be awake yet.

She listened.

No bird-song. No traffic noise, and yet, the glare through her eyelids suggested that it was daylight outside. She pulled her forearm over her face to block out the light streaming through the window. There was a humming coming from somewhere, and occasional clicks and ticks like a radiator coming to life. She wanted to go back to sleep but she *needed* to get a drink. If she could keep any fluids down. Lucozade. God, she could murder a Lucozade. On the count of three, she was going to open her eyes. One ... Two ...

No.

Not yet.

Another five minutes.

She breathed in deeply through her nose to surf the nausea, to breathe life into her fragile body. She felt as if she was made of paper. Crumpled. Insubstantial. And too easily screwed up and disregarded.

Her sheets smelled wrong. And it wasn't only her stale breath or the did-she-didn't-she whiff of vomit. And now she thought of it, the light from the window was all wrong too. It shouldn't be coming from that side of the room.

She opened her eyes then and squinted.

It wasn't her room. She gingerly turned her head to the right, scared that she was in bed with someone, but thankfully she was alone. Relief turned quickly to confusion.

'What the ...'

She pushed herself up to a sitting position and cradled her head. Could you die of a hangover? She looked about her. There was a tall, dark wardrobe. Matching wooden drawers. An old-fashioned sink in the corner with a mottled mirror above. A patterned rug on the floor. An oil painting of Dovedale on the wall. She had never set foot in this room before so why had she slept here? How? She looked down and noticed she was still wearing the jumpsuit from Hattie's wedding.

Dear God. The wedding. And here it came, the memory flood. Beth knew everything. Everything.

Molly slid out of bed and waited for the room to stop spinning before she took a step towards the closed curtains. She saw her reflection in the mirror and cringed in disgust. Her head hurt too much, her chest ached, and she couldn't stand up straight. She staggered, hunched over, to the window and opened the curtains a crack.

Beyond the window were hills. In front of the hills was a

wood, and in front of the wood was a white wedding marquee.

'Oh, God.' She groaned. She remembered the fighting. The shouting. Beth's face. She'd never seen her look so angry. The police were there, weren't they? Who called them? And Miriam too. Christ. Could it get any worse?

Molly remembered throwing up and then sitting on the cubicle floor, with her head on the toilet seat, for a little rest. She vaguely remembered a lot of banging and someone climbing over the top of the toilet stall. And then . . . and then, nothing. It appeared that someone had put her to bed in Hattie's house.

Molly looked at the antique clock on the wall. It was only five-thirty-five in the morning. If she was lucky, she could sneak out of the house before anyone else woke up. She shivered. Her stomach was squirming. She needed to get out of here, but where would she go?

She couldn't stay in Hellas Mill now. Not now that everyone knew what she'd done and what kind of person she was. Opening the window, she looked at the ground. It was too far for her to jump without breaking an ankle, or worse. She would have to go out through the door. First, she washed her face and drank from the tap. She braced herself against the side of the sink as she fought the urge to throw up. Her bag was on the dresser but she knew she didn't have enough money for a taxi. She'd have to walk. A conservative estimate was that it was three miles to her dad's house from here.

Molly put her bag under her arm and picked up her shoes. Opening the door she saw the hallway was empty and she tiptoed towards the stairs. With every squealing floorboard, she paused to listen for sounds of life.

At last, she was at the top of the staircase, and she moved as quickly as she dared. Desperate to get out, away from this place. How could Beth have left her here, knowing what Wesley Manor meant to Molly. Did she hate her that much? The answer was obvious and it made her feel worse than the hangover.

Molly pulled open the heavy front door and eased it closed behind her. It had been a while since Molly had had to flee a house in the early hours of the morning and she'd never fled from an empty bed. The morning was fresh and pink. A dawning of a beautiful day and yet Molly only felt dread and fear. Her feet ached as she hopped over the gravel drive, cursing rich people and their huge bloody houses and their unfeasibly long driveways.

She stepped onto the lawn as soon as she was able and started a gentle jog towards the gate. She paused by a large tree with her hand on her stomach.

'Where do you think you're going?'

Molly whipped her head up to look in the direction of the voice, and it felt like her brain rattled inside her skull. She put her hand to her forehead. Hattie was standing by the side of the house with her arms folded.

'Don't you think,' Hattie called, 'that we should have a little talk before you go?'

Molly bent over and threw up.

Hattie lent Molly some clothes so that she could change out of her jumpsuit and into something cleaner and warmer after her shower. Then the two of them sat in what Hattie called the Garden Room. The early morning sun had illuminated the golden carpets and dust motes swirled in the shafts of sunlight above the grand piano.

'I'm so sorry,' said Molly.

'You've already said that.'

'I know. But all I can think about is how sorry I am that I caused a scene. I could die. It was entirely my fault.'

'Yes, it was.'

'I don't remember what happened afterwards,' admitted Molly pulling her fingers through her wet hair to untangle it.

'I'm not surprised. You passed out in the toilets and Finn and Miriam put you to bed.'

'Miriam? God, as if she didn't hate me enough.'

'You dropped quite the bombshell. I don't think anyone knew about Miriam and Oscar. But they all do now. And luckily for me, that's all everyone was talking about. They either didn't hear Beth say that I was one of the select few, or they thought the fact that Oscar betrayed his brother as well as his wife was far juicier.'

Molly groaned. 'Oh, Christ. I'm such a disaster. I can never show my face in Hellas Mill again. I'm surprised Miriam didn't hold my head down the toilet.'

'I imagine she probably wanted to. Harvey stormed off. Miriam told me that he already knew about the affair but they'd agreed to work on their marriage. Of course, he didn't expect it to be announced to the whole village last night.'

'Don't,' Molly said. If her head wasn't hurting so much, she might have cried. She'd wounded her best friend in the worst way possible. What a terrible way to find out what Molly had done.

They sat in silence sipping on black coffee. Hattie hadn't asked whether Molly took milk or sugar and Molly didn't feel she was in any position to be choosy. She just wanted to drink her coffee and get out of here. Had she ever felt this

239

bad with a hangover? It was the argument with Beth rather than the cocktails that had poisoned her. Now Oscar was dead there'd been no reason to come clean to Beth. If she'd thought she'd feel better now it was all out in the open she was wildly mistaken.

It hurt knowing how low Beth's opinion of her must be right now, but this felt right. Everyone knew how twisted she really was, and she didn't have to pretend that she was a good person. The universe had righted itself. It was as if the powers that be had let her try to make something of herself, but at the end of the day she was back to being the poor, unloved girl who men used for sex. And the circle was complete. At least she knew her place.

'Shouldn't I be getting off before everyone wakes up? I'm sure that you've got to pack for your honeymoon. France isn't it?'

Hattie slowly took her gaze away from the garden as if her mind had been elsewhere and looked intently at Molly. 'Oh. Yes. The flight is tonight. Molly, you said something yesterday . . .' began Hattie.

'Please. Don't—'

'I'd not thought about it in so long but, you're right. I was there and I did see you and my brother.'

Molly felt like the blood was draining from her. She was lightheaded and heavy limbed all at once.

'I need to go home.' Molly stood up and so did Hattie.

'I saw you kissing and I left. I thought you wanted to be there. Though there'd been incidents. Rumours of him not taking no for an answer. Perhaps I should have checked that you were okay but I was . . . I don't know. Jealous? I didn't like him paying attention to you. He barely noticed me unless it

240

was to get to my friends. He wasn't even meant to be at my party but he saw an opportunity to sell drugs to my friends.'

Molly nodded and looked on the floor for her shoes. She didn't want to hear any more. She needed to get out, but Hattie stood between her and the door.

'It was the worse kept secret wasn't it? My brother the drug dealer. Everyone thought he was so cool, but I hated it. We used to be the best of friends when we were younger and then he discovered drugs and girls and I was a silly little inconvenience. But my friends . . . ? Oh, they were a whole new market for him.'

'I should go. I don't feel great,' said Molly. She tried to step around Hattie but the other woman put both hands on her shoulders and looked into her face.

'I don't know what I could have done differently. Should I have said something? I wasn't sure what was happening. I was just a child.'

'Don't.' Molly lowered her head and clenched her eyes against the tears.

Hattie put her hand on Molly's cheek and bent lower so that she could look into Molly's face. 'Molly? I'm sorry I didn't do something at the time. When Barney died no one talked about how detestable he'd been and I started to think that he'd been some kind of saint. Taken too soon. That's what everyone said, and it was so much easier to go along with.'

Molly hadn't realised how much she'd needed to hear that. It opened the flood gates and the tears began to fall. She crumpled into Hattie's chest, her hands covering her face, and let it out. Twenty-five years of holding it all in, wondering what was so wrong with her. It felt good to hear someone else acknowledge how bad Barnaby had been.

They stood like that as the sun stretched across the floor until Molly stood straight and wiped her face on the arm of her borrowed jumper.

'I don't know about you, but it feels good to address some of the things that happened that night. To get things all out in the open. And, to that end . . . There's something else I should tell you,' said Hattie.

Molly looked at her expectantly. 'Yes?'

'I saw a lot of things that night. After everyone went home, I couldn't sleep. I got up to get myself a glass of water and I saw that Barnaby wasn't alone in the garden.'

Molly put her hand to her mouth.

'I saw Beth running away,' said Hattie.

The door opened behind them and Molly flinched. Finn smiled at them sleepily and said, 'Come now, ladies, we're not about to have another bust-up, are we?'

He was in his pyjamas and his hair was sticking up at one side. He was wearing wire-rimmed glasses that didn't suit his face shape at all.

'Darling,' Hattie said. 'You're awake.'

She went to him and kissed his cheek as he slid his arm around her.

'I woke up and you were gone. I thought it was the shortest-lived marriage ever,' he smiled.

'Don't be silly. Couldn't sleep so went to muck out the horses. I found Molly trying to sneak out without so much as a coffee so I made her come and chat with me. You don't mind, do you?'

He looked at Molly. 'How's the head?'

'Not great. Look, I was saying to Hattie, I am mortified by my behaviour yesterday. I hope I didn't ruin your big day.'

'Nothing could ruin it. To be honest, we were all laughing

about it afterwards, weren't we Hats?' He was smiling but there was no amusement on his face. His eyes said he hated her; said that everyone had been laughing at her because she was a fool. Molly's face grew hot.

'Well, I'd best be off,' she said. There was no chance of getting Hattie to expand on what she'd said in front of Finn. The only question now was what Hattie was going to do with that information. She'd said it felt good to get things off her chest but how far would she go?

'Don't be silly,' said Hattie. 'Finn will drop you home, won't you darling?'

Molly was already shaking her head when Finn said, 'Babe, you know I would, but I'm possibly still over the limit from last night.' He looked at Molly, and she could have sworn he sneered at her.

'No. I'll make my own way home. I'll call someone to come and pick me up, but thanks for the offer. Have a lovely honeymoon and sorry again for what happened yesterday.'

Molly scurried from the house with a carrier bag containing last night's clothes. Once outside, she took deep lungfuls of air as if she had been holding her breath.

Hattie knew everything. She knew that Beth had killed Barnaby and that she and Molly had lied about it. If Molly hadn't brought up what happened that night, if she hadn't caused a scene at the wedding, all of this could have stayed buried. But now that Hattie was remembering what had happened that night and she felt the need to talk about it, Molly would have to do something.

Molly had to get as far away as possible. She had to get out of Hellas Mill. But before she did, she had to clean up the mess she'd made.

CHAPTER FORTY

DC Lowry Endecott

Technically it was Lowry's day off but, practically, such things didn't exist. She should have been sleeping off a wedding-sized hangover next to her date, but instead she'd sent Mark back to his own house and spent the morning planning who she needed to talk to this week while Finn was away. Which was how she found herself outside Lomas Lumber on a Sunday morning.

Harvey was waiting for her in reception, looking like he'd hardly slept. He was wearing shorts and a baggy jumper, the faint scent of toothpaste about him suggesting he'd not long woken up. The offices were impressive, not because they were modern or big, but because they reeked of hard work and passion. It felt like the factory had been here for ever and would outlast them all. It was a shame that Oscar Lomas had driven it into the ground.

'Nice to see you again, Detective Endecott,' Harvey said.

'Thank you for making time to see me on such short notice. I didn't expect you to open up the office for me on a Sunday.'

'Well, I was already here when you called so I thought it best to get this over with. Would you like to come through?'

Lowry followed him down a dark and narrow corridor

into a goldfish bowl of an office. It had glass sides and no privacy. Good for spying on the workers, she thought.

'Drink?' Harvey asked.

'No, thanks.'

'You wanted to talk to me about Oscar's affair with my wife,' he said, closing the door behind them even though there seemed to be no one else in the building. 'Please, take a seat.'

On the phone, Lowry had said she wanted to talk to him about the financial problems the company was having, but Harvey was too clever to believe that was all there was to it.

As he took a seat Lowry said, 'Yes and no. I want to talk to you about the pressures on your brother at the time of his death. I gather there were financial problems, and that three men were suing the company for unfair dismissal. And, yes, I'm also aware that he was having an affair with your wife. I suppose I'm wondering why you didn't mention that to me when you took me to Cloud Drop.'

'Well, the fact that you were still looking into what – to everyone else – was a clear suicide case, made me suspect you thought it might be murder. So, yeah, you could say I was reticent to single myself out as chief suspect. At that point I didn't think anyone else knew about him and Miriam.'

'Beth Lomas knew.'

Harvey rubbed his eyes. 'Well, it's not something she and I were likely to discuss, was it. If she's anything like me she'd want to pretend that none of it had ever happened.'

'Did you confront your brother about it?'

'Yes.'

'And?'

Harvey shrugged and turned his chair away. 'Well, he went

and threw himself off a cliff so maybe he had more of a conscience than I'd expected. But ... God, I don't know. He reacted the same way as he reacted to most things I suppose. Like it couldn't be helped. Like the affair meant nothing to him.'

'When was this?'

'Two weeks before he died.'

'And how were things left between the two of you?'

'Okay. Not ... not back to how they used to be, but we'd agreed to try and put it behind us for the sake of our family and for the sake of the company.'

'The day he died,' Lowry said, 'where were you?'

He shook his head. 'Not up Cloud Drop, if that's what you're getting at,' he said. 'I was here. I'm here every weekend trying to save this company.'

Lowry sat back in the chair and crossed her legs. 'Okay, so what can you tell me about the problems with the company?'

Harvey sat forward, glad to be on safer ground. 'Oscar took on contracts that we can't fulfil. We need a huge injection of cash in order to take more people on but, instead, debts have mounted up and we've been forced to let people go. Oscar was a law unto himself sometimes and didn't believe in following procedure. There was nothing wrong in making those redundancies but everything wrong with the manner in which he did it. It's caused nothing but trouble for us. We're not disputing that the correct channels weren't followed but they're angling after a payout that we're not in a position to give. They'll have to join a long queue of people we owe money to.'

'How bad is it?' Lowry asked.

Harvey chewed the inside of his cheek. He reached into the drawer by his right side and pulled out a grey folder and threw it onto the desk between them.

'We've been talking to the bank all week. Investors. Trying to save the company. We're working up severance packages for the workers now. I want to make sure they get their cut before our creditors do. Some of them have already been let go. We're fulfilling our current orders but there'll be nothing new. We're selling off old stock and then the debt-collection lot will be in to take our equipment. We should still be able to make something from the sale of the land and buildings but these things take time.'

'Can you tell me who the company owes money to?'

'I wish I could. I reckon I still don't know the half of it. We're getting invoices every day. There are a few unpaid bills for stock we've ordered and the delivery company hasn't been paid in six months. The bank won't lend us any extra money so, barring a miracle, it's the end of the line.'

'Why would Oscar take on contracts that you couldn't honour?'

'He wanted to break into the international market and had several promises of work, but nothing in writing. He had to expand the company to show that he could fulfil these orders and play with the big boys. He invested heavily, but the orders didn't appear. It was something we'd disagreed on. He wanted to expand the business and I was happy to keep it going as it was. I felt it had grown as big as it could get.'

'It's your company too, so why didn't you stand up to him?'

'It's not quite that simple,' he said. He played his fingers over the cover of the folder while he chose his words carefully. 'Oscar was very difficult to say no to. When he got an idea in his head, it was infectious, he had no doubt that he could succeed. And who was I to say that I was right and he was wrong? We didn't always see eye to eye, detective, but I loved my brother. Despite . . . everything.'

Lowry continued to watch him until he spoke again. 'I know you think someone killed him, but you are completely wide of the mark. My brother was a proud man and he hated the fact that he couldn't get what he wanted, so he did what all cowards do; he ran away.'

'From where I stand, he was getting exactly what he wanted,' said Lowry. 'Including your wife.'

Lowry expected him to lose his cool and get angry, but Harvey sighed.

'Well, that's where you're wrong, detective. Miriam made a stupid mistake but chose to stay with me. Oscar just wasn't used to being second best.'

CHAPTER FORTY-ONE

Beth Lomas

For the second time in quick succession, I dialled the number on the note pinned to the fridge door and listened to it ring.

'Come on. Come on!' I barked. Honey was pacing beside me, chewing on the end of her long blond plait.

'DC Endecott.'

'Thank God. I can't find him anywhere. He's been in such a state recently and, God, you don't think ... I mean, he wouldn't, would he? Should I call 999? Only I thought, seeing as you know everything that's been going on with us ...'

'Woah! Slow down. Who is this?'

'It's Beth Lomas. Gabe didn't come home last night and he's not answering his phone. His bed wasn't slept in. I didn't check. I just thought ... You see, I took a sleeping tablet. Stupid. Stupid! I thought he was in bed but I didn't actually go and look.' My voice was high pitched, breathless. This was worse than when Oscar went missing because, back then, I didn't think things like this could happen to people like me. Now I knew they could, and did.

'Okay. Let's rewind a minute. When did you last speak to him?' Lowry asked.

I reached out my hand for Honey and pulled her to me. 'He, um, so ...' I was having difficulty ordering my thoughts.

'He called after school last night asking if he could go to Josh's after cricket practice. They were working on a project together. I didn't even check. Christ … And then about, I don't know, seven-ish? He sent me a text saying he was staying there for tea. He's been staying out later and later recently. I fell asleep on the sofa and, when I woke up, I assumed he was already in bed.'

What kind of a parent did that make me? He hadn't sneaked out in the middle of the night, he hadn't even been home, and I'd not noticed. I'd been trying too hard to be the cool, understanding parent that I'd not set the boundaries he needed. I'd even thought about checking on him as he slept, but I was so very conscious of his personal space nowadays. Besides I was so very, very tired.

'Have you checked with his friends?' Lowry asked.

'I tried Josh's number but he's not answering his phone either. He's probably still asleep. I was wondering about driving over there now. I don't have his mum's number but I know where they live. I left it too long to report Oscar missing and he …'

Honey squeezed my hand, 'Mum. Don't.'

I was worrying her, but I couldn't stop myself. 'I don't know what to do. I thought the sooner you start looking for him … and if I go to Josh's now … God. What if someone's hurt him? The man, the one who was in my garden, the person who broke in – what if he's taken Gabe? It's all my fault. I should have left everything alone. I shouldn't have spoken to you about it.'

Lowry's tone was sharp. 'Don't go jumping to conclusions. We'll find him. Most of the time there's a simple explanation. I bet you'll find he's crashed at his friend's house and thought it was too late to call you. Stay calm, okay?'

'What if he's hurt? What if he's gone to Cloud Drop like his dad? We had breakfast together yesterday and everything was fine. Completely normal. We'd been getting on so well.'

'Listen, Beth. This is what I need you to do. I need you to stay calm. Make a list of his friends and then start calling them to see if they've heard from him. Stay at the house and I'll send someone round to be with you. Okay?'

I nodded even though Lowry couldn't see me. 'I'll be here.'

The phoneline went dead and Honey took both my hands in hers. 'What did she say?'

'That I'm to stay here. Call his friends. And calm down.'

'Right. But they are sending someone to look for him, aren't they?' She was terrified. Before we lost Oscar, she might have shrugged it off, but now she knew that it was possible for people you loved to die, there was no stopping the downwards spiral she was in. And in many ways, it was the same for me. A month ago, I'd have been worried, but not panicked. A month ago, I'd have known what to do. Or at least, Oscar would've. But a month ago, no one had killed my husband.

My world wasn't the same as it used to be. I wouldn't make the same mistake twice, and just assume that everything would be alright if I waited patiently.

'Mummy, what if something's happened to him?'

I pressed the heels of my hands into my eyes. I used to think I had everything under control but it was all a myth. I only saw what they wanted me to see. Or maybe I only saw what *I* wanted to see. The perfect life, the perfect husband, the perfect family. Blissful ignorance, but I couldn't say that anymore. The scales had well and truly fallen from my eyes. If I hadn't been so naïve, perhaps I could've stopped all of this from happening.

'I'm scared,' Honey said.

I took her face in my hands.

'I'm sorry, baby. I don't want to scare you. The truth is, Lowry's probably right. Gabe's been dealing with a lot of stress and he's probably just pushing boundaries. The most likely explanation is that he's slept at Josh's house.'

Honey put her hands over mine. 'Then why are you so worried?'

The phone started ringing and both Honey and I looked at it. I knew it had to be about Gabe. He would call on my mobile. Bad news called the landline.

'Answer it,' whispered Honey.

'I can't.'

'You have to.'

I reached out a hand. I couldn't ignore it, but I was terrified that this would be the one piece of news I couldn't survive.

'Hello?' I said into the mouthpiece.

'Beth. It's Lowry. Gabe is fine but he's . . .'

I turned to Honey. 'He's fine! She says he's fine.'

Honey put both her hands over her heart and looked like she could cry.

'But,' Lowry said.

'Yes?'

'But he's at the station. He's been arrested.'

CHAPTER FORTY-TWO

DC Lowry Endecott

Lowry hung up the phone and raised her eyebrows at PC Claire Sackler.

'Right. Beth Lomas is on her way into the station now. Should be here by . . .' Lowry checked the time on her watch, 'by nine fifteen.'

'If I'd known who he was I'd have called her already,' Claire said.

Lowry took her jacket from the back of her chair and shrugged it over her narrow shoulders, tugging at the cuffs of her blouse. She'd been in work for less than an hour and she was already feeling an intense desire for strong coffee.

She was relieved that Gabe was neither hurt nor had run away, but the fact that he was downstairs at the station – in custody – was just a different kind of headache.

'He wouldn't give us his name,' Claire explained. 'I didn't even peg him for a minor. Kids look older nowadays.'

This made Lowry smile. Claire was barely more than a child herself. What was she? Twenty? Twenty-five?

'What've you got for me?'

They began walking across the office, Claire half a step behind Lowry.

'Okay, so it looks like young Gabriel and his chums are

responsible for the burglaries round Hellas Mill,' she said. 'Three of 'em on bikes. Mostly shed break-ins. Bikes, fishing gear, loose change from cars.'

'Never expected it from Gabe Lomas,' Lowry said. 'Angry kid, sure, but petty theft? What's this about a stolen car, then?'

'This is where it gets interesting. Last night they decided to take it up a notch, didn't they? Broke into a house, stole a car, crashed a car. You'll never guess whose house it was.'

Lowry paused mid step and turned to her colleague. She didn't like the sound of this.

'Go on.'

'DS Greenwood's. Must've known they were on honeymoon but then, who didn't? Anyhoo, the kids were quite cocky by the sounds of it. The alarm went off but they'd worked out they still had plenty of time before a police car could reach them so they took it slowly. Hadn't banked on the fact the in-laws lived in a converted barn in the grounds though. So, old man Flint-Stanton appears with a shotgun and scares the bloody life out of them by all accounts. They panicked. Grabbed the car keys and sped off in the new Mrs Greenwood's BMW.'

Lowry shook her head. When the Lomases fucked up, they did it on a grand scale. 'Well, at least they've got taste,' she said. 'They could've taken the DS's Mondeo.'

'That might have suited them better, to be honest. The BMW was too much for them and they lost control and crashed into a tree.'

Lowry sucked in her breath sharply. 'Injuries?'

'One of them, the driver, is still in ICU. Punctured lung. Parents on their way to the hospital now. The other two are a bit battered and bruised. Minor lacerations. Your lad was trapped but, lucky for him, uniform spotted the car when they were responding to the break-in. No other vehicles were involved. Could've been a lot worse.'

'And Gabriel Lomas? What's he saying?'

'Well, that's the thing. He's gone from not saying a word to saying that he wants to talk to you – and only you.'

'Fine. I'll wait until his mum gets here and then ...'

Claire was already shaking her head. 'He wants to talk to you *before* his mum gets here. He says ... and these are his words not mine – he says he wants to talk to you about his dad's *murder*.'

'He called it a murder?'

'Yep. I thought this was a cut and dried suicide.'

'That's the official line, yes, but there are a few things that don't make sense, so we're just making sure that we've not missed anything.'

'Murder though?' said Claire. 'You don't expect that kind of thing round here, do you?'

'Could you do something for me, Claire? I'd love you for ever if you could get me a coffee. The stronger the better.'

The other woman nodded and raced off while Lowry stood outside the unmarked door. She shouldn't talk to Gabe without a lawyer present, or at least his mother. But it wasn't as if she was interviewing him. She was just going to pop her head around the door to see if he was okay and to tell him that his mum was on the way. That's all.

She pushed open the door of the family room but only stepped halfway inside. Gabe seemed smaller than before. Stripped of his bravado he was a scared little boy. He looked up at her with pink-rimmed eyes. Lowry, never maternal, wanted to give him a hug and tell him that it would all be okay. That he should treat this whole incident as a wake-up call to turn his life around. It was hardly surprising that he was acting out. His dead father had been sleeping with his aunt as well as others, his future was uncertain. He was angry. Who wouldn't be?

'Alright, Gabe? I didn't expect to see you this morning.'

He put his hand to his collarbone. Lowry guessed that's where the seat belt had cut into him. The very thing that was causing him discomfort had also saved his life.

'Do you know how Kit's doing?' he asked.

'That's your friend with the punctured lung, yeah?'

Gabe nodded.

'He's being well looked after. His parents are on the way to the hospital to be with him. He's lucky to be alive. You all are.'

'I didn't mean for this to happen,' he said.

'Your mum's on her way. My colleagues will want to talk to you about what happened last night and about the burglaries in the area, if you're up to it?'

He nodded again. He seemed resigned to it all.

'My colleague says you wanted to tell me something about your dad?' Lowry tried to keep her voice casual.

PC Claire Sackler came up behind Lowry with a coffee, forcing Lowry further into the room. 'Can I get you anything, Gabriel?' she asked.

'No, thank you.'

As the door closed Gabe said, 'I wondered about coming to see you before, but thought maybe, I dunno, maybe I should stay out of it for Mum's sake, but she's not letting it go, is she? Dad was hiding a lot of stuff from my mum, like all the other women and stuff.'

Lowry took a sip of her too-hot coffee. 'It was no accident

that it was Hattie's car you stole, was it, Gabe? You targeted her place.'

'Mum told me about Hattie and Dad last week. I wanted to trash that bitch's house, but then that old guy appeared with a gun. I hadn't planned on taking the car, but the keys were there and, you know ... It was her fault that Mum and Dad argued the night before he went missing but she gets her fancy wedding and goes off on honeymoon like nothing happened.'

Lowry cupped her hands around her coffee. 'Your mum's already told us about the affairs. We're taking it all into account, don't worry.'

'Well, anyway, that's not what I wanted to talk to you about,' he said.

'Are you sure you don't want to wait for your mum to get here? She won't be long.'

'No, I want to tell you now. I don't want to get her hopes up, but you can look into it, can't you? See, there was this bloke arguing with Dad a couple of days before he died,' he said. 'Me and Kit were cycling home from school. I didn't think much of it because I didn't actually ... well, you know, Mum didn't report him missing until later. This happened, like, the Thursday before he went missing.'

'What did you see, Gabe?'

'Dad was trying to get in his car and this guy had his hand on the car door keeping it closed. They weren't shouting but they were, like, intense. I thought he was going to thump my dad so I stopped at the corner and watched for a minute. The other guy walked off but said something like, "Saturday. No excuses."'

'And you didn't recognise him?'

'No.'

'Could it have been someone from your dad's work?'

'I don't think so.'

'What did the man look like, Gabe?' Lowry was interested now. She put her coffee down on the table and laced her fingers together, bending them backwards until they cracked.

'Don't know. I was mostly watching my dad. I'd never seen him look scared before.'

'Okay, so if you picture that scene for me. You're on your bike, cycling towards them. You can see your dad, yeah?'

Gabe nodded.

'Where's the other guy's head? Is it obscuring your dad's face? Does it come up to his chin? I'm trying to get an idea of how tall he was.'

'Same height as Dad, for sure. Wider though. He seemed to take up a lot of room. Quite stocky.'

'That's great, Gabe. What about hair?'

'Darkish. Maybe a bit grey. Not bald or anything.'

'Can you remember what he was wearing?'

'No. He was your average, middle-aged, white guy. Nothing about him stood out. I'd have paid more attention to him if I'd known he was the man who was about to murder my dad.'

Lowry spread the papers across the dinner table. Her printer was running out of ink and the bank statements were faint in parts. She'd gone over some of the lines in blue biro to make them stand out. She wasn't sure why she was even looking at Oscar's personal statements. His financial worries seemed to be confined to the business so there wouldn't be any clues as to who he'd argued with a couple of days before his death here. All transactions seemed standard. Car insurance. Cash. TV licence. Every couple of weeks he filled his car up at the same garage.

There was nothing else to find. At least, she was no closer to discovering who Gabriel had seen his father arguing with before he died. It couldn't have been Harvey because Gabe would have recognised him. She felt bad for even considering it, but could it have been her boss, Finn? He was a little taller than Lomas but the right age and build for the man Gabe saw. Of the men suing Lomas Lumber, Randall was too old, too small, but the others ... She was yet to question them. Perhaps she should make that a priority.

But what was it they were talking about? What had to be 'Saturday'? Money? Had Oscar killed himself before someone else did it for him? Was this person *telling* Oscar to kill himself on Saturday? Because, whatever it was, two days later Lomas was dead and there was no clear explanation as to why. Just because Gabe had seen someone arguing with his dad didn't mean that there'd been anyone with him when he died.

Lowry rubbed her eyes and sank into a chair. Not enough sleep, not enough coffee. There were disgruntled employees, cuckolded husbands and a jilted wife, any one of them had a lot to gain from killing him but she couldn't place any of them at Cloud Drop with Oscar on the morning of his death.

If Oscar was murdered, he must have known his attacker. He had met this person on his own either because he trusted them or because the meeting had to remain secret. Which would explain the stern words with the man by his car.

But why trek all the way to Cloud Drop? There had to be other places you could have a clandestine meeting which didn't involve waterproofs and walking boots. Why meet someone at a place where you could fall, or be pushed to your death?

Lowry grunted and scratched the back of her head. Nothing was making sense.

She started to tidy up the papers. She was getting a headache from trying to decipher the faded print. Mark had called her and offered to bring over a takeaway later. She surprised herself by being happy to hear from him and saying 'yes'. In fact, she'd said, 'Yes please!'

She wasn't planning on telling him she was moving to London until the contract was signed, and she didn't think he'd be particularly heartbroken. After all, he was only offering a couple of onion bhajis and a lamb bhuna, not romance.

As she scooped up the bank statements for the Lomas's personal account, she saw that there had been a couple of large withdrawals, £250 each. She placed the papers back down on the table and ran her finger over the lines of figures. Both withdrawals happened in Camborne, at a time when Beth was certainly in Hellas Mill. And, earlier, a smaller amount of fifty pounds. Before that, ten. It was a familiar pattern. These jerks took small amounts at first to fly under the radar before they took out the maximum amount that they were able. She picked up her phone and looked up the town. It was in Cornwall, roughly a six-hour drive away.

It wasn't exactly the motive for murder she'd been looking for, but it appeared someone had cloned Oscar's card and was making withdrawals.

Unless . . .

Hadn't Beth told her that Oscar's parents lived in Cornwall now?

CHAPTER FORTY-THREE

Molly Ingram

Molly was lying on her old bed, in her old room. The thin curtains may as well not have been there for all the light they kept out. The green cotton had faded over the years to the colour of grass at the end of a long summer without rain. Springs in the well-worn mattress poked her back, but that wasn't what kept her awake.

It had been three days since the wedding. Three days of Beth not returning her calls. Three days of Hattie's words making Molly's head spin.

I saw a lot of things that night.

Just as Beth thought that life was as bad as it could possibly get – a murdered husband, a disloyal friend – Hattie recalled that she knew enough to destroy what was left of her life. And all because Molly was stupid enough to bring up the night of Barnaby's death.

It's good to get things out in the open.

Molly had taken her old brown teddy bear from the top of the wardrobe and cuddled it as she'd lay staring at the ceiling. It smelled of mildew and cigarette smoke. It was big enough to use as a pillow, and one ear was tatty from years of her sucking at it in childhood. She pushed the stiff fur back from around its glass eyes. She wondered why her dad had kept hold of this one. There was nothing else of hers left in the house; no old books, clothes, or school reports. Perhaps there was a sentimental stitch in the old man somewhere. But for someone who never gave hugs or declarations of love, it was out of character.

Too often he was in his own world. If she could persuade him to go to a doctor, Molly was pretty sure he would be diagnosed with some sort of ... she didn't want to call it a mental illness but, without doubt, he reacted to the world in a different way to other people. He wouldn't leave the house, but she wouldn't say he had agoraphobia; he hated other people, but she wouldn't call him an introvert; he was devoid of empathy, but not a psychopath.

The television was always switched on and food was never far from the reach of his outstretched arm. He was one of those people you read about having to be taken out of the window by firemen because they were too big and immobile to fit through the door. He'd always been heading in this direction but he got worse after her mum died. She was the only person he was ever interested in and, once she was gone, any spark of love he had for life had died with her. For the longest time, Mum had been his addiction. He was a binger. He binge-watched television. He binged on food. He binged on his own company. He'd never shown Molly any affection and she couldn't blame him. She used to find his silences painful but now she was thankful for the freedom they afforded her.

She'd known what she had to do as soon as she'd left Hattie's house the morning after the wedding. All the long walk home she'd tried to come up with other ways to resolve the problem but she kept coming back to the same thing, the same person. It was something that only she could do. And she owed it to Beth to make everything alright. Hattie was threatening to bring it all out in the open, but Molly wouldn't let her. First Barnaby, now Hattie. The Flint-Stantons had ruined Beth and Molly's lives. Just when she thought they could start to put it all behind them, with a new business venture, a new shot at a fulfilling life, Molly ruined everything.

I saw Beth running away.

She disconnected her phone from the charger and brought up her contacts. Molly didn't know much about Frazer, which was safer for both of them. She knew that he was a loner, and she also knew that he did more than look moody and imposing in order to get people to do what he wanted. She hadn't expressly said 'don't kill Oscar' but she'd naïvely thought that had been implied. Goes to show how little she knew. The directions that she'd given him were to pay Oscar a visit and make him understand that, if he didn't pay up, the consequences would be a far greater price than the money he owed Molly. Frazer was to meet him somewhere remote. No witnesses.

Did she really believe that he would have *strong words* with him? How brainless could she be?

Frazer had either shoved Oscar off the cliff during a fight, or he'd scared Oscar so much that he'd felt he had no other choice than to jump to his death. And as a result, Beth's world had exploded. All because Molly had been drunk enough to sleep with him, and guilty enough to lend him money. It wasn't as if Molly didn't know that the things she did had consequences.

Hattie couldn't make trouble for Beth while she was on honeymoon, but Molly intended to make sure that she never got the chance to point the finger at anyone for what happened to her brother. Beth would never forgive her for sleeping with Oscar, and Molly didn't blame her, but perhaps Molly could do this last thing to keep her safe. What Beth did to Barnaby, well, it had been an accident, but it had happened because of Molly, and because Beth was a decent person who stuck up for her friends. Well, this time, it was Molly's turn.

She dialled the number and it went straight to voicemail.

'Hi. It's Molly. You did some . . . *work* for me in Hellas Mill? I understand why I can't get a refund. I'd like to employ your services again please. Similar situation as before in that I'd like the same end result. Call me back so we can discuss terms. You have my number.'

Molly hung up. She had nothing to lose. If the police traced it back to her and wondered what Molly's motive was, there'd be plenty of witnesses at the wedding who would vouch for the fact that Molly and Hattie had argued. It wouldn't take much digging to find that it was over a man. Her best friend's husband.

What could be simpler and more pathetic? Men had always been Molly's downfall. It started with Barnaby but it had ended with Oscar. Vijay had been an aberration. She'd accidentally met a good man who treated her well, but she didn't deserve him. She didn't deserve to be happy.

This time, she was prepared. She was already looking at how she could get her hands on the money Frazer would demand. She might have to take a loan with one of those unscrupulous loan sharks who advertised on daytime television as if they were doing you a favour. They didn't bother about credit checks and, by the time they'd want repaying, Molly would be long gone.

CHAPTER FORTY-FOUR

Beth Lomas

Gabe had spent most of the afternoon asleep. He was bruised and he was tired, but all that mattered to me was that he was safe and he was home. He was sheepish, apologetic, but I couldn't be angry with him. Maybe that would come, once I was over the shock, but we'd all made mistakes and I didn't feel in the position to judge.

He'd told me about the man he'd seen arguing with Oscar before his death, said that he'd only kept it from me because he knew that I'd see it as more evidence that Oscar had been murdered, when he was hoping I'd drop the whole thing. 'I just wanted it to stop hurting,' he'd said.

Lowry was going to look whether there was any CCTV in the area but the focus of my day was on Gabe and what he'd done. I'd known he hadn't been happy – even before Oscar's death – and it appeared that his anti-social streak had started around the same time as he'd seen his father kissing his aunt. He was happy to come clean about everything he'd done; the cars he'd broken into, the bikes he'd stolen and dumped, but we agreed that he didn't have to let the police know that it was him who vandalised his aunt's car. Some things could be kept between us. Loyalty should always be rewarded.

At the promise of homemade pizza he'd been lured into

the kitchen admitting that he could manage a slice or two if pushed. When the doorbell rang, he and Honey were choosing toppings, both of them more relaxed than I'd seen them in months. The three of us were in our pyjamas, ready to settle under blankets in front of an old black and white film. It was a family tradition from years ago and Honey had chosen to watch *Some Like it Hot*. It was one of our favourites – and Oscar had hated it. He said he found nothing funny about men dressing up as women.

I opened the door with a smile on my face feeling, despite all that had happened over the past few days, happy to have my family around me. But my smile froze when I saw Lowry Endecott on my doorstep. I had nothing against her personally, in fact, I'd go as far as to say I liked her, but I'd seen more than enough of her for one week.

'Oh, God,' I said. I couldn't take another setback today. I didn't have the strength.

'It's okay,' she said. 'Nothing bad. May I come in?'

Now that I was looking at her closely, I could see that she'd changed out of the suit she'd been wearing at the station, giving this the feeling of an unofficial visit.

'Of course, come in.'

She looked past me in the direction of the laughter coming from the kitchen. It was a lovely sound. Something I would cherish always. We had finally found our rhythm without Oscar. It was steady, and it was strong.

'We're just making dinner. You're welcome to join us?'

'No thanks. I've got plans myself, but I had to check something with you. Is that okay?'

We went into the living room but neither of us sat down. I'd closed the shutters, the film was ready to play, and the opening credits were paused on the screen, waiting to come to life as soon as we were all settled.

'How's Gabe?' she asked.

'Good. He's sore. Scared about what's going to happen next, and sick about what could've happened.'

'I can imagine.'

'Have you managed to get hold of Hattie and Finn?' I asked.

Lowry kept her voice low. 'No. I've left it up to Hattie's parents to tell them if they want to, but they've decided not to interrupt the honeymoon. They'll be back on Thursday night.'

'So soon?'

'The main event is later in the year, apparently, so this was just a short break.'

'Alright for some,' I said, trying not to feel bitter.

'Anyway, that's not why I'm here, Beth. Oscar's wallet. As you know, it wasn't found on the body.'

'Could you not call him "the body". He might have been a lot less than perfect, but he was still my husband.'

Lowry nodded once. 'You're right. And I'm sorry. I should've said, when we found Oscar, he didn't have his wallet on him.'

I nodded. 'Thank you. I was told that it could've come out of his pocket on . . . impact.'

'Right. Yes, right. I wanted to make sure there hadn't been an oversight and that you hadn't found it in the back of a drawer or anything? As far as you are aware, Oscar had his wallet with him when he disappeared, right?'

'He'd never leave home without it. What's this about? Have you found something?'

Lowry tilted her head to one side. 'Have you ever been to Camborne?'

'Camborne? Cornwall?' I looked away, thinking of the town where Esther and Vince lived. 'I don't think so. Oscar's parents live in Penzance, is it anywhere near there? We go to Cornwall every year on holiday but Camborne doesn't ring a bell as anything other than a name on a road sign.'

Lowry wrote something down in her notebook. 'Apart from his parents, does Oscar know anyone in Cornwall? Any business dealings? Friends?'

'Not that I know of. Will you please tell me what's going on.'

Lowry said, 'Money's being taken out of your bank account from cash points in and around Camborne.'

'How?'

'I don't know. Perhaps someone found Oscar's wallet, or maybe they took it from him. It might be nothing, but I'm looking into it all the same. When did his parents arrive from Cornwall?'

'You were here. It was the Sunday afternoon.'

'And they couldn't have been in the area earlier?'

'No. I phoned them at home that morning. It's four hundred miles away. Not the kind of round trip they can easily do in a day.'

Lowry scratched her nose and pursed her lips. 'And Harvey. Has he visited his parents lately?'

I shook my head but I couldn't know for sure what he'd been up to. 'As far as I know he spends all his time at the office. Do you have any idea how much money has been taken?' I asked.

'It amounts to about seven hundred pounds. It started a week after Oscar's death.'

'God, how stupid of me. I never even noticed.'

'You should be able to get the money back from the bank, though it might take a little while. It's easy enough to prove that it's fraudulent. The death certificate should do it.'

'Yes. Yes, right. Okay then. I'll call the bank now.'

'I'm going to request CCTV from those banks and see if we can get a look at who has been taking the money out. We have to hope they've been sloppy.'

'Sorry if I'm a bit slow on the uptake here – it's been a hell of a day – but are you saying that someone stole Oscar's wallet?'

'Looks like it.'

'But does that mean they killed him?' I sat on the arm of the sofa.

Lowry was shaking her head. 'All it means is someone is stealing money from your account and they might know something about how your husband died.'

Lowry's phone rang in her hand. She looked at the display, her eyes softening, but declined the call. 'Sorry. I've got to go, but I needed to check out the Cornwall connection. I'm not sure this is going to give us the breakthrough we want, but we can try.'

'No. I appreciate you coming round, thanks.'

I was aware that the noise in the kitchen had stopped. Gabe and Honey would have overheard every word. But that was fine, we'd promised not to keep secrets from each other from now on.

'Enjoy your evening,' Lowry said.

'Thanks. You too.'

I showed her out of the house and stood with my hand on the door. What were the chances of someone stealing Oscar's card and using it in the town where his parents lived? I didn't believe in coincidences, but I couldn't see how the Lomases could have a hand in the death of their son.

Could this have something to do with the debt-collector? The man in the garden, the break-in, the disappearing money. It had to be linked. And I was certain it was linked to Oscar's death too.

'Mum?'

I turned around to see Honey standing in the kitchen doorway, drying her hands on a tea-towel. Gabe stood behind her.

'What did the detective want?' she asked.

I walked towards her, past her, into the kitchen and opened the fridge. 'She wanted to ask me if I knew of any reason why money was being taken out of my bank account from Cornwall.'

Gabe chuckled. 'You pissed Nan off so much that she's nicking your money? Nice.'

I took the open bottle of white wine from the fridge door. 'Gabriel!'

'Who's doing it?' Honey asked.

'I don't know. But for the first time in nearly fifteen years, I've put my own hard-earned money in there and, after what I had to do to get it, there's no way I'm letting someone take that from me.'

CHAPTER FORTY-FIVE

Beth Lomas

'It was a rat,' I said to Gabe, pulling my collar around me.

'Squirrel,' he replied, not looking up from his phone.

'It had a long, thin tail,' I protested.

'Skinny squirrel,' he said.

I threw a tea-towel at him and went back to looking out of the kitchen window.

'It's gone behind the Cabin. Do they have nests?'

'Gabe!' Honey called from the hallway. 'We're going to be late!'

'At times like this, Mum,' said Gabe, 'Google is your friend. There's some ancient rat poison in the garage.'

'Is there?' I asked. I didn't like the idea of poisoning them, even if they were considered vermin. If I thought it would work, I'd have a quiet word with them and ask them to move along.

'Right.' Gabe stood up and lifted his battered bag from the floor. 'Got to go.'

'Straight home after school, yes?'

'Sure.'

'And wait for your sister.'

Again, I'd suggested he stay home for a little longer, and again he'd said *no*. 'I've missed too much already, Mum.'

He was right, but it should have been me that was saying that. We'd talked a lot, last night, about how he'd always thought he'd had time to turn his grades around and to decide what he wanted to do with his life but the last few weeks had shown him that he couldn't just close his eyes and hope for the best. He still thought he had a pretty good chance of making it as a musician but he'd decided that it didn't hurt to have a backup. Even if it was still an option when he left school, there was no way he wanted to join the family business.

I followed him towards the front door and made both him and Honey give me a hug and a kiss before I let them out of the house. I told them to be careful, though not of anything in particular.

'Can I have Amber over tonight?' Honey asked as she checked her school bag for her homework.

'Sure. As long as it's okay with her mum.'

'And can she stay for dinner?'

'Of course.'

I looked at Gabe, half-expecting him to ask if he could have someone over too, but one of his best friends was still in hospital and the other was, according to his mum, grounded for life. I'd told Gabe he'd be going nowhere without me for the foreseeable future, but I knew that wasn't practical. I was having coffee with Josh and Kit's mums this morning to discuss what we could do to support our kids, while also venting about how much we wanted to throttle them.

I had my hand up to wave them off, but before they'd even taken two steps Honey turned and asked, 'Are you ever going to make up with Aunty Molly?'

I let my hand drop to my side. 'I don't think so. She ...' I'd been thinking a lot about Molly and, the more I thought about her the angrier I got. 'She really hurt me and I don't know how to forgive her for that.'

'And Aunty Miriam?'

Both Honey and Gabe were watching me intently. 'This isn't the time to be talking about this, sweetie. You've got to get to school.'

'You said we could ask you anything.'

A faint breeze blew a strand of hair in front of her eyes and I stroked it away.

'Look, it's a little more complicated with Aunty Miriam because she's family. If Uncle Harvey has chosen to forgive her then, like it or not, I'm going to be seeing her around. That's one thing I'm just going to have to come to terms with somehow.'

From the way her brow creased I could tell she wasn't happy with my answer. 'I don't see why you can come to terms with what she did, but not Aunty Molly. I like Molly. She's fun.'

'Yeah, she is,' I said. 'But it hurts so much more when the person who lets you down is a person you trusted.'

Back in the house I picked up the pile of mail that had been sitting in the hall for days and headed to the kitchen. I had two hours before I went out for coffee and I had to keep myself busy until then. I sat at the kitchen table with the sun-light streaming onto the floor. I'd stacked dirty dishes in the sink. Oscar couldn't abide mess but, it turned out, I didn't mind. I used to be able to fill my days with housework and baking while the children were at school but it didn't seem to be a good use of time anymore.

Most of the letters were addressed to Oscar. I opened and smoothed them down to deal with later. Esther had already contacted most of these companies before the funeral, she'd left me a list somewhere. She'd urged me to forward Oscar's passport to her so she could cancel that too, but I found I couldn't part with it. His stern passport photo had made us laugh at the time.

Oscar's old debit card had been stopped. I'd set up a new savings account online last night and transferred the money from Hattie into it, before whoever was stealing money from me could get their grubby little hands on it. Today I was going to set up a website, or at least look into it. Gabe was going to design it for me and Honey was working on a logo. I was going to concentrate on cakes for special occasions rather than have the stress of catering for events.

I jumped as the doorbell rang, looking quickly at the clock, and feeling a prickle of fear. I stood and peered down the hallway, holding my breath. They knocked on the door with the side of their fist and the whole door shook. I almost ignored it, but then I had visions of accidents, of one of the children lying injured in the street.

'Yes?'

A man with a peaked cap had his back to me. 'Mrs Lomas?' he asked as he turned.

'Yes.'

'These are for you.'

He handed me a bouquet of flowers, beautifully wrapped, with a silver ribbon. I took them automatically but stood mutely as the man wished me a good day and disappeared off down the path to where a small blue van was idling at the kerb.

I walked backwards, turned, kicked the door closed behind

me. All the while, I held the flowers at arm's length. They were pink and white peonies.

Beautiful.

Familiar.

Identical to the ones I'd had on my wedding day.

I walked through the house, only now realising that today was my anniversary. I dropped them into the sink and stared at them. Was this someone's idea of a joke? Whoever sent them, knew us well enough to know that Oscar sent peonies every year on this day. But who would do such a thing? And why?

Perhaps, I mean, maybe … Could Oscar have ordered them before he died? He'd been an organised man and it was something he could have sorted months ago. Taped to the cellophane wrapping was a small envelope with my name on it. My hand was shaking as I prised it open. I didn't recognise the writing, but it would have been written by the florist. I blinked to bring the words into focus.

The note said *I hope you're happy now.*

If the sender of the flowers intended to unnerve me, they'd succeeded. I couldn't fight back, couldn't look them in the face and condemn their cowardice. I had to assume that the flowers had come from the same person as the congratulations card, because I couldn't fathom more than one person being this cruel to me. Though they weren't saying anything that my own treacherous mind hadn't already thought.

'Happy now?' My brain teased and mocked. 'Happy now that your husband is dead? You told him you'd like to see how life was without him. Well, you got your wish. Congratulations.'

Had it been me? Had I done this to us? Was that why I was intent on proving that Oscar hadn't taken his own life – because

I was so scared that he *had*? How would I live with myself if it turned out that I'd caused this? How would I face the children, if it was all my fault?

'Damn you, Oscar.'

I reached into the kitchen drawer for the scissors. One-by-one I cut the heads off the flowers. They fell into the sink with a thud, leaving thick naked stems behind. Not even Oscar's death was straightforward. I was sure that the man Oscar was seen arguing with was the debt-collector who'd been to the house, but these flowers, and the congratulations card I got before the funeral, made me feel like there was more to Oscar's death than punishment for an unpaid debt.

I didn't know what I wanted more – answers? Or to be rid of Oscar for ever? I needed both and now was as good a time as any to start. I dragged a nondescript box out of the cupboard under the stairs. It wasn't physically heavy, but the burden was substantial all the same. I pulled it behind me into the kitchen and sat down heavily next to it in a golden square of light.

Most of Oscar's belongings had been thrown away or boxed up and put to one side for charity shops. This was the last box that I had to sort and the worst of all of them. These were the clothes he'd been wearing when he died. I hadn't dealt with them immediately because I didn't want a reminder of his death though, at the moment, I scarcely wanted a reminder of his life either. To think of him alive meant to want him dead. Over the years his behaviour had caused me to doubt my own worth. But I'd always taken the easy option. Anything for a quiet life. And where had that got me? Life was as loud as it was possible to get right now. There was the screaming of grief, the wailing of infidelity, the screeching of a life being wrenched apart. The sound echoed into the vast expanse of loneliness that faced me now.

I stroked the lid of the box that Molly had put Oscar's things in. I'd put it off long enough. And not just opening the box of the last clothes Oscar ever wore, I'd put everything off. I'd put off dealing with the realities of Oscar's death and the fallout that came after. I'd put off making my own decisions and dealing with my own life, my own dreams. There were two things that I needed to do before I could move on from Oscar. One was unpacking this box and the other was scattering his ashes.

I took a deep breath. It was best to do it at a rush like taking off a plaster, so I flicked off the lid with my thumb half-expecting the stench of death to assault me, but there was something chemical about the aroma. It was the clinical smell of a morgue.

Oscar's boots were on top of the clothes. I wondered what he'd been wearing on his feet when they cremated him. What did Esther choose for him? Was he in his socks? I should have paid more attention.

I placed the boots on the floor by my side. They seemed too small, as if Oscar had been smaller than I'd remembered. The clothes were in a translucent bag. I touched the plastic as if I could picture his last moments by connecting with the clothes he'd been wearing.

I imagined someone's strong hands pushing him, and Oscar grasping handfuls of air, almost clasping the arm of his assailant, his fingertips glancing the material of their sleeve. I had a strong feeling that the money wasn't the only reason he was dead. Could either Harvey or Finn have been responsible? I knew how angry I was with the women who had slept with my husband and yet I didn't have the opportunity, the passion, nor the strength to hurt them. How did Harvey and Finn feel, when they found out about their partners' infidelities? And what would they do to the man who'd made a fool of them?

Gabe could've been on to something when he'd said that Oscar might've taken off his wedding ring because he'd been meeting a woman – or *thought* he was meeting her and instead, when he turned up, her husband was waiting for him at Cloud Drop. Did they speak to him first or did they rush him as soon as he walked into the clearing?

There was another bag in the box – small, made of brown paper like it held a sandwich from an artisan bakery. This was the one that I knew had Oscar's watch in. In fact, it was the only thing worth keeping. I would burn everything else in the fire pit. I would hand the watch to Gabe, but not yet. I'd wait until he was older, less angry, when the pain had lessened and forgiveness had taken hold. I took the paper bag out but put the lid back on the square box and pushed the whole thing to the back door. I didn't even want it in the house.

The paper bag was light in my hand. Everything was confusing to me. Boots that were smaller than I'd imagined, a watch that was lighter. It was as if I'd expected more substance to Oscar and was surprised when he turned out to be human after all. I reached inside the bag, with some strange notion that the watch would have stopped at the time that Oscar died, so I could pinpoint when he'd fallen from that cliff. I didn't look at it at first, just hooked my fingers under the strap and pulled it out. The wristband was black and rubbery, the watch face square and cheap.

It wasn't Oscar's watch.

Oscar's was chunky with a metal band, an emerald green face. Swiss.

'Oh, for God's sake.'

All that building myself up to finally look at his things and they weren't even Oscar's. It wasn't that I minded so much for myself, but there was a family out there who were missing their loved one's belongings. I'd have to call the funeral directors and explain the mix-up to them. Or, rather, get them to explain the mix-up to *me*. At least the clothes seemed to be Oscar's. I placed my hands on the walking boots and looked to the heels. They'd been worn down, as expected, but something wasn't right. I frowned. They were evenly worn. Oscar always wore down the left one first.

I took the boot with me and ran up the stairs. I was out of breath by the time I got to the attic room and flung open the door. In the corner were piles of neatly packed boxes. I pulled the lids off and toppled them to one side when I only saw clothes. At last, I found the box with Oscar's shoes in and grabbed a trainer. I put the sole of the walking boot to the sole of the trainer. The trainer was at least two sizes bigger. I picked his tan brogues up next and did the same. With the same result. I tried four or five different shoes until there was no doubt left in my mind. These were not Oscar's boots. And if these weren't his boots, and it wasn't his watch, was it even his body that they'd found at the bottom of Cloud Drop?

CHAPTER FORTY-SIX

DC Lowry Endecott

Lowry was searching through security footage from the bank at Camborne.

The video spooled at double speed, with her finger poised over the pause button. A steady stream of people approached the cash machine, paused, fidgeted and scurried away again. She kept her eye on the time stamp in the corner of the screen. Whoever used Lomas's card would be along any minute now.

Her mobile phone rang and she ignored it. She should have left it at her desk but it was from habit that she took it everywhere with her.

'Not now,' she said under her breath as she declined the call.

So far, the tapes hadn't helped her decipher who was taking money out of the Lomas account. On each occasion, it looked like the same man. Tall enough that he stooped to key in the pin number. Average build. When the weather was bad, he had his hood up. When it was good, he was wearing sunglasses and a hat. He knew what he was doing. His hat was plain, as was his coat. No logos. No distinguishing features. Lowry pulled up the cameras from surrounding areas but she lost sight of him as he ducked down alleyways or jogged into parks. Whoever he was, he didn't seem to drive to the cash points so there was no point in checking number plates.

Her phone started ringing again. She pressed pause on the screen. Forty-two seconds until the person she was after would walk into the frame. She didn't want to miss it but, now that her concentration had been broken, Lowry supposed she might as well answer the call.

'DC Endecott,' she said.

'Hi, Lowry, it's Beth Lomas.'

'Hi Beth. How are you?'

'Have you got five minutes?'

'I'm a little busy at the moment,' Lowry said glancing back to the display where a tall man in a dark hoodie was visible in the bottom left corner of the screen. One knee was cocked as if he was walking quickly, his hands already reaching into his wallet for his card, and his head down as he searched for it.

'It's important,' Beth said.

Lowry pushed her chair away from the desk and spun around so that she was no longer facing the screen. Delayed gratification they called it. Lowry had never been a fan.

'What can I do for you, Beth?'

'I wanted to ask about something that's been bothering me. About Oscar's death.'

'I'll help if I can. What is it?' Lowry asked.

'I was wondering how you were so sure that the body you found was Oscar's?'

Lowry pinched the bridge of her nose. Not this again.

'We've been through this haven't we, Beth?'

'Yes, I know, but humour me.'

Lowry tucked the phone under her chin as she looked up

to the ceiling and sighed. Too much police drama on the television. Everyone saw themselves as an amateur sleuth nowadays and thought they could tell the police how to do their jobs.

'Well,' she said as she brought the phone back to her mouth. 'We found his car in the lay-by near Cloud Drop. In it was his wedding ring. We . . .'

'Yes, I know that. But those are his *things*. I'm talking about the . . .' she paused as if she didn't want to say the next word. '. . . body. How did you identify the body? Physically I mean. Did you use dental records?'

Last time Lowry had seen Beth, the other woman had asked her to stop referring to her husband as 'the body' and now she was the one calling him that.

'That's the usual way of things. As I understand it,' she reached for Lomas's file, 'it was his brother who identified the body?'

'That's correct, yes. Harvey. He was with the rescue team and he was the one who found the body.'

'Of course. I remember now. Right. For starters, we have a positive ID.' She flicked to the right section of the folder. 'We tend to get in touch with the dental surgery for confirmation if there's any doubt at all.'

She stopped with her finger over the report.

Or not, she thought.

The dental report stated there was nothing to make them think that this wasn't Oscar Lomas. No dentures, or bridge, or gold teeth. Nothing there that shouldn't be there.

'Yeah, so, Beth? I'm looking at the report here and the evidence points to it being your husband, but there was no conclusive match with the dental records because . . .' Lowry was struggling to find the correct way to explain it to a civilian. She gave up and said, 'There was significant damage to his mandible and cranium.'

'Right,' Beth said. The word was dragged out as if she was toying with it. 'Right. But you don't actually *know* that it was my husband.'

'Well, yes, we do. Harvey identified him. There was no reason to doubt the positive identification, besides we found his phone in his pocket. You identified the clothes.'

'No. I didn't. I said he was wearing hiking boots but the ones that I've picked up from the undertaker aren't his. They're too big. The trousers are a thirty-four-inch waist but Oscar was a thirty-two. And there was a watch on the body but it's not my husband's watch, Lowry. These aren't Oscar's things.'

Lowry didn't want to dismiss what Beth was saying, but there'd be a simple explanation for these discrepancies. Beth and Oscar hadn't been close of late – by Beth's own admission – so she might not have paid attention to him putting on weight and needing bigger trousers. He had money problems – so he might have sold the expensive watch and bought a cheap replacement. The different sized boots though? Lowry couldn't explain that one.

'Perhaps,' Lowry began.

'And before you say anything else,' continued Beth, 'I've already called the Funeral Directors and they assure me these are the clothes that the body came in wearing. They take an inventory immediately and have talked me through what I should have here. It's exactly as they described.'

'Still. There could have been a mix-up?' Lowry said. 'Mistakes do happen and—'

'They're adamant that they couldn't make an error like that. What I'm saying is, if there's been a mistake,' said Beth, 'it was identifying that body as my husband.'

Lowry looked back to the computer screen, and to the man in plain clothes who, suddenly, looked an awful lot like Oscar Lomas.

Stage Five of Grief

ACCEPTANCE

CHAPTER FORTY-SEVEN

Beth Lomas

I looked at my watch as I locked the Cabin door. The rats were still scrabbling underneath the shed but, in the back of the garage, I'd found the rat poison that Gabe had mentioned. A quick internet search told me that the poison was made illegal years ago for containing strychnine. If I could have afforded it, I'd leave it to someone else to sort. And by *sort*, I mean to dispose of them however they saw fit, but tell me that the rats were living out their twilight years on a farm in the Cotswolds.

Honey and Gabe would be home from school in an hour and there was so much more to do. I'd cleared Oscar's things out of the Cabin. The sofa and the fridge had stayed and I'd fitted new locks myself. I'd even stocked the fridge with beer – alcohol-free – and I was looking forward to telling Gabe that the Cabin was his to have band practice in. I didn't care if they were used to being at Josh's. From now on, everything Gabe did would be under my watch.

I wanted to sell the house, but everything I'd read about grief advised not to make any rash decisions, and so I'd given myself twelve months to make a go of the catering business before we moved. There was part of me, though, that was scared to stay here in Hellas Mill. Because if Oscar was still alive, he could turn up at any minute and I couldn't cope with that.

Until I'd said it aloud to Lowry, I hadn't realised the repercussions of that body not being Oscar's. If it wasn't him, then Oscar was alive somewhere. Watching. Hiding. Oscar let everyone think he was dead and then had disappeared. He let us all grieve; left us to navigate the hole he'd left behind and sit through an agonising funeral. The children ... God, the children. How could he do this to them? He had ripped out their hearts and destroyed their lives, for what? Gabe was angry, stealing Hattie's car – and crashing it. Our son could have died, because of Oscar's lies. And poor sweet Honey had cried more than any child should ever have to. What would be worse for them – that their father had died? Or that he had only pretended to? Would it bring them any comfort to know that he was alive somewhere and this was the biggest, most elaborate prank he had ever played?

Dying should've been the worst thing that Oscar had ever done to them because at least it wouldn't be his fault. Pretending to be dead? Well, that was all on him. If he hadn't ended his life, he was going to wish he had.

I had been so focused on what – or who – had caused my husband's death that I had failed to see that he might not be dead at all. And then there was the other big question. If it hadn't been Oscar at the bottom of Cloud Drop, then who was it?

I had scoured the papers and the internet and couldn't find reports of any local men who'd gone missing in the last month. Bodies didn't turn up without names. He had to be someone. Lowry hadn't said she believed me but I heard the hesitation in her voice and, to her credit, she said she'd look into it.

I poured myself a glass of water and took a deep breath. He was taking the money from a bank in Cornwall. If Oscar was hiding out somewhere, it was there, and his mother would be helping him. She'd always told me they had an unbreakable bond. It was time to test that.

I dialled her number and waited.

'Hello?'

'Hi, Esther. It's me, Beth.'

Silence.

'I've not called at a bad time, have I?'

Esther took her time replying, but said, 'Not at all. Is something wrong? Is it the children?'

'No. Nothing like that. They're fine. Missing you of course. I do hope you'll come up to see us soon. I'd hate to think that the argument we had would sour your relationship with them.'

'Nonsense,' she said. 'They're my grandchildren, nothing would keep me away.'

'I'm so glad to hear that. Family is everything, isn't it? What wouldn't we do for our children?'

There was silence on the line and I worried I was pushing too hard.

'Listen, I'm sorry it has taken me so long to call you. I want to apologise. I'm sorry that we argued after the funeral. I ... It was a difficult time for all of us and I said things that I wouldn't normally have said. I hope you know how important you and Vince are to us all, and that you know that you always have a room here. I don't want the kids to lose their grandparents too. They've been through enough. Don't you think?'

'Yes,' she whispered into the phone.

'Good. Can we put it all behind us?'

'I'd like that.'

There was a moment of uncomfortable silence as I wondered how to talk about Oscar. 'So, how are you holding up, Esther? You know, about Oscar. I'm not sure I really asked you how you were when you were staying here. I think I was too wrapped up in my own grief and that of the children.'

'I'm ... taking it one day at a time,' she said. 'I've come to terms with the fact that nothing will ever be the same again. But, I do what I can. You?'

'Same.' I paused, ready to get to the real reason for calling. 'Esther, do you remember when you said that you didn't believe Oscar would have taken his own life? Do you still believe that?'

'No.' Esther's voice was strong again. Forceful. 'Ignore everything I said. I was upset and finding the news difficult to come to terms with. That's all. No. No. Vince explained all about the money problems. Harvey mentioned the ... their, um, relationship problems. And now it all makes complete sense. A proud man like Oscar, well, it would have all been too much for him. I see that now. We all need to move on with our lives. Time to look to the future.'

'Yes, I'm sure you're right. It does us no good to hang on to the past.'

She knew. I was sure of it. Esther knew that Oscar was still alive and didn't want me looking into his death. I wondered when she'd found out. Her grief at the funeral had been genuine, I was certain of that, so when did he get in touch? How did she react to her son coming back from the dead? I wished

I could have asked her, but for my plan to work she had to believe that I didn't suspect a thing.

'I've been at the bank most of the morning. Someone's been stealing money out of our bank account. Can you believe it? The card has been cancelled and I'm waiting for the money to be repaid but they won't be able to use that card again, which is something.'

'Yes,' she said. 'It's good you caught it before they took too much money.'

But I hadn't said how much they'd taken. She was either making assumptions or she knew exactly how much Oscar had helped himself to.

'Because the account is frozen for now, I've had to take out a load of cash to tide me over until this is all sorted. I feel quite nervous having such large sums of money in my bed-side drawer, but I don't know where else to put it. I've got an appointment on Saturday morning with a new bank, so I only need to keep it in the house until then.'

'Well, it's up to you what you do with your money.'

'Did you know that someone broke into Oscar's home office? I don't know whether Harvey mentioned it. Yeah, they took his laptop, but luckily Molly had had a clear-out for me and brought our passports and other important documents into the house. Makes you wonder if anywhere is safe anymore, doesn't it? I've got everything in the drawer by my bed now. Money, passports . . . the whole lot. I still haven't got round to cancelling Oscar's passport. I suppose I should do that at the weekend too.'

'If you remember, we did say that I would do that for you. Save you the job. Why don't you pop the passport in the post to me?'

'I wouldn't want to put you to any trouble.'

'Not at all, I did it when my parents died a few years back. Makes sense for me to do it.'

'That's very kind of you, Esther, but no, it'll give me something to do. I like to keep busy.'

Before Esther could respond, I said, 'Anyway, listen to me going on, this wasn't the reason that I called. I've got Oscar's ashes back now and, with your blessing, I want to scatter them on Friday. Would you like to be there when I do it?'

Esther cleared her throat. If these were Oscar's ashes, she'd want to be present. She'd been there for every step of his life. That she would be there for every step of his death was a foregone conclusion.

'No. He was your husband. You get to decide what to do with—'

'But he was your son for longer than he was my husband,' I said. 'Without you, there'd be no Oscar. You made him the man he was,' I said. I wondered whether Esther would hear the insult between the words.

'That's very kind of you to say so, Beth, but I don't think I can face it. Perhaps I can visit the place you scatter the ashes at some point, but I honestly don't think I could manage the drive at the moment. Vince hasn't been well. We're both suffering from colds.' She cleared her throat. 'What will the children do?'

'They don't want to be there. They're staying at friends' houses on Friday night so I can take my time remembering Oscar in my own way.'

Esther was quiet for a moment. If she thought it was odd that I was going to scatter the ashes on my own, she didn't say so. 'Where were you thinking of doing it? You know, scatter-ing the, er . . .'

'Cloud Drop,' I said immediately. It seemed apt that it should end there. 'It was somewhere that meant a lot to Oscar. It's where he chose to end his days, so I can't think of a better place, can you?'

CHAPTER FORTY-EIGHT

Molly Ingram

'Watch it!' a woman snapped as Molly bumped into her. She hadn't been concentrating on the pavement in front of her. Difficult to multi-task unless it involved drinking while feeling sorry for herself.

'Why don't *you* fucking "watch it"?' Molly retorted. Even to her own ears, her words were slurred. The woman looked at her with an expression part way between fear and disgust. Molly took a jerky step in her direction and the woman gave a squeak and scurried away.

Molly found it difficult to be around people today. Perhaps she was more like her dad than she realised. Everyone walked taller than her, bolder, owning the world and all those in it. Their narrow looks, hatred pouring from their eyes, showed her what they thought of her. Did they know? Everyone knew everyone around here, and gossip would have been delivered to doorsteps with the pints of milk and the newspapers, because Hellas Mill was the kind of place where time stood still. Molly the slut was back in town. She'd slept with her best friend's husband and her drink-loosened lips had reminded Hattie that she saw what happened at her birthday party. But that wasn't all that Hattie saw, and now Molly had one more chance – one last chance – to make it right.

She turned down a side street away from prying eyes, towards a path behind the houses that would take her to the park. It was quieter here, just a few yards from the main road and she was starting to relax when she heard footsteps coming up fast behind her. She quickened her pace, glancing over her shoulder, once, twice, trying not to make it look obvious, but could only see that it was a man with his hands in his pockets and a baseball hat pulled down low.

She felt cold, alert, and put her hand in her bag searching for anything she could use to protect herself from him. She felt the cool case of her phone, wondered whether she would have time to call for help, but she'd slowed her pace while she was focused on searching for a weapon, and the man was suddenly upon her. And just as quickly, past her.

Straight past, without looking at her, as if she wasn't even there. It was nothing. *He* was nothing. But the feeling that she was in danger was constant now. A current of dread and anxiety coursed through her veins. She used to be able to talk to anyone, fit into every social situation. It didn't always come easy and, often, it left her drained, but it had been many years since she'd felt so removed from everyone around her, knowing that, no matter where she looked, she didn't fit in. It felt like a lifetime since she used to wake each day, terrified, but now she couldn't imagine ever feeling any other way. People were dangerous. Not all of them, but there was no way of knowing where the real danger lay so it was better to treat them all the same and stay away from others as much as it was possible.

It wasn't like she hated her own company. Or, not until recently. Before she'd met Vijay, she could go the entire weekend without saying a word to another person from Friday night until Monday morning. Sometimes she'd talk to herself, or the television, just to prove that her vocal cords still worked, but she'd never minded or felt lonely. In the last six months, Vijay was the only person she saw outside of work or work-related dinners and parties. Molly liked spending time with him because he made very few demands on her and was easy to be around. They could sit side by side on the sofa and not even talk. Funny that she missed *not* talking to him.

Molly had reached the park, still with her phone in her hand in case she needed to call for help. Passing the band-stand she could see fresh graffiti. Similar in style and sentiment to the scrawls of the nineties. Someone was a slag. Someone was in love. All those *someones* thinking they were being original and rebellious, when it was the most obvious thing under the sun. She wondered about leaving a message for Beth here, scratched through layers and years of paint. An apology. An explanation.

She'd given up phoning Beth's home and mobile because every call went unanswered. If Beth was going to speak to her, she'd have to be tricked into it. Molly didn't have long, and she had to make Beth see how sorry she was. She wasn't even going to beg for forgiveness; she just wanted to apologise.

Over several text messages, she'd come to an agreement with Frazer. He'd do what she asked, for the same amount of money as last time. He'd let her know when he was in Hellas Mill and she had to be ready. It was lucky, he'd said, he already had plans to be nearby on Friday. The money was in her bag and she squeezed it to her chest. Part loan, part overdraft, part borrowed from her dad's account. There weren't many loose ends to tie up now. If she hadn't wanted to go to the bank, and if she hadn't needed to speak to Beth one last time, she wouldn't have left the house today.

She stopped at the bottom of Beth's path. Molly had never noticed how beautiful the house was before. The yellow roses twisting around the front door hanging heavy heads and casting the teal-painted door in shadow. This had always been Beth's dream. The house, the husband, the two beautiful children, and Molly had taken the husband away. She stumbled on the path but righted herself, rang the bell, and then used the brass knocker to knock twice.

'Beth!'

She rearranged her bag on her shoulder and tucked her hair behind her ears. She'd showered and washed her hair for the first time since rinsing off the residue of vomit the morning after the wedding. For Beth, she'd make all the effort in the world. She'd wanted Beth to see her sober, but she couldn't face her, or say what she had to say, without half a bottle of courage. If Beth would answer the door she was going to tell her everything. Frazer, the money, Hattie, *everything*.

Her hand trembled as she knocked again. Molly thought she could sense someone behind the door. She placed her hand on the glossy black wood.

'Beth? I know you're there. You hate me right now and I don't blame you. I hate me too, but please give me a chance to explain.'

Beyond the door there was silence but Molly thought she could feel Beth listening. She lay her forehead against the paintwork. 'Beth? I must have left you at least twenty messages. You are everything to me. I don't have anyone else. I'm not here for your forgiveness, I'm here because I haven't told you everything. There are some things you need to know. Things that you deserve to know. Oscar didn't leave you,

297

Beth. Not during the affairs, nor in life. He loved you. It was always you. And I always loved you, too, and I don't know why I'd do something so stupid, so hurtful. I'd take it back if I could. Listen, Beth. I don't believe Oscar died by suicide, and I know you don't either. But ... but I have proof, or ... information. And I can't tell the police yet because there's one more thing I have to do. But you're right, and even Oscar's death is my fault.'

She listened hard but there was only silence. Perhaps no one was there after all.

'Beth? If you're there, I know I've been selfish. Everything I did, I did for me. But what I'm doing next ... I'm doing it all for you, Beth. I'm going to make everything okay again. I promise you that, by the weekend, I'll have made everything better. This is me showing you that I love you. Don't think badly of me Beth. You're the only person whose opinion has ever mattered.'

CHAPTER FORTY-NINE

Beth Lomas

The smell of bacon frying dragged Gabe and Honey from their beds, and they were downstairs and ready for school without me having to shout or cajole. I'd been awake for two hours already, wiping the skirting boards, cleaning the downstairs windows, ironing. It felt like the light had pushed around the curtains before I'd even closed my eyes. There was too much riding on today.

'What's the occasion?' asked Gabe. The table was set with fresh flowers from the garden in a small crystal vase in the middle of the white tablecloth.

'Do I need a reason to spoil you?' I asked, putting a pile of pancakes in front of him.

'With bacon?' asked Honey. 'I told you, I'm vegetarian now.'

'I've also got fruit, yoghurt, maple syrup . . .'

'Fine,' said Honey helping herself to a hot slice of bacon.

'Why the change of heart?' asked Gabe.

'Sorry?' I said. 'Was that directed at me, or your sister and the bacon?'

'You. How come I'm grounded for life one minute but, the next, I'm allowed to go and stay at Josh's for the night?'

'Two reasons,' I said. I poured orange juice into tall glasses.

'Firstly, when I spoke with Josh and Kit's mums over coffee, we agreed that punishing you isn't going to make much difference. You went through a tough time and you probably need to get together to say, "Wow! Aren't we a bunch of idiots?" You're lucky to be alive. Secondly . . .'

I realised, too late, that I'd automatically poured four glasses of juice. 'Oh,' I said and sat down, staring at the surplus glass. 'Some habits . . .'

Honey put her hand over mine and squeezed.

'The lads are going to trip when they hear about the Studio,' said Gabe bringing me out of my trance.

I dragged my gaze from the glass which my treacherous mind was calling Oscar's.

'Oh, it's the *Studio* now, is it?' I asked with a smile.

'Well, yeah. All bands need a studio. You don't mind, do you?'

'Not at all.'

'The *Cabin* doesn't sound right, but I was talking to Kit last night and he was saying we should call our first EP Cabin Fever, or maybe it could be our new band name?'

Their band changed its name every couple of months. I'd given up asking but, last time I checked, they were The Twisted Frogs.

'Can I bring Josh round here tonight to show him?' he asked.

'Not tonight, love. Tomorrow? It's going to be a difficult day and tonight I'd like to be on my own with a glass of wine in the bath. Is that okay?'

Gabe's eyes were on the window. I couldn't remember the last time I'd seen him look this excited.

'What do I get?' asked Honey.

'You, my angel, get the entire top floor.'

'The attic?'

'Yep. We'll have to decorate it ourselves but there's no point keeping that space for guests we'll never have. Besides, it's turned into a dumping ground so you should make it yours.' I leaned over and tapped the tip of her nose. She beamed at me.

'Mum, you're the coolest!' She threw her arms around me and I almost cried at how easy it was to make the children happy. They needed to be seen and made to feel special. It was all I wanted for them, to realise how much they meant to me.

'You said there was something else,' Honey said. 'You said there were two reasons for letting jailbird Gabe go to Josh's tonight.'

Gabe playfully swatted at his sister's head.

'Right, yes. Ah, as you know, I'm going to scatter Dad's ashes today, and seeing as you don't want to be there when I do it, I thought I'd let myself have a full day of wallowing. That's okay, isn't it? I just want to get it done. Over with.'

I looked out of the window at the perfect blue sky. I noticed a furtive look pass between Honey and Gabe.

'Sorry. Did that sound too harsh?' I asked.

'No. It's not that,' said Honey.

Gabe took three long gulps of his juice and then said, 'The thing is, we feel bad about saying we didn't want to be there when you scatter the ashes. And when I say "we", you know I mean Honey, right?'

I smiled. 'There's no need to feel bad. I promise I'd say something if I needed you there.'

'Are you sure you want to do it on your own?' Honey asked. 'If you wait until tomorrow, we could go with you?'

'Oh bless you, that's sweet, but this is how I want it. Unless, that is, you've changed your mind and want to scatter the ashes with me.' I gritted my teeth. They couldn't change their minds because I had everything planned out, and it depended on me being on my own.

Honey screwed up her face. 'Nah.'

'Same,' said Gabe. 'I just can't get my head round Dad being in that urn. It's not really him, you know?'

'Yes,' I said. 'That's exactly how I see it too.'

CHAPTER FIFTY

Molly Ingram

At six o'clock the text message woke Molly up.

Will be in Hellas Mill by lunchtime. Leave money under bench at Cloud Drop.

By nine o'clock she'd hidden the money and was on her way back down the hill.

By eleven o'clock she was standing in the doorway of the lounge watching her dad.

She didn't think he'd miss her because his life was the same whether she was there or not. It wasn't that he didn't love her, but he managed perfectly fine on his own. She'd started off cleaning and cooking for him, but then stopped getting out of bed, and he hadn't even noticed.

He grunted at the television and scratched his stomach above the elastic waistband of his trousers.

'Need anything before I go, Dad?' she asked.

He grunted again and shook his head. 'You should go on this.' He pointed at the quiz programme on the television. 'You've always been the clever one.'

Molly stood up a little straighter. 'Do you really think I'm clever?' she asked, but her dad's focus was on the television again and he didn't respond.

She'd stripped the bed in her old room. The pillows were

back at the head of the bed and the duvet folded neatly. She polished and vacuumed, and opened both windows to air out the room. It was as if she'd never been here.

The flat would be sold off as part of her estate. Her dad would get anything that was left after all the debts were paid. Her recruitment consultancy was a limited company so she was pretty sure they couldn't touch the proceeds from the sale of the flat.

Molly wondered how long it would take for anyone to realise what she'd done. She was tidying up and saying her goodbyes but as far as her dad would know – for now at least – she was going back to London. And as far as anyone in London knew, she was back home in Hellas Mill licking her wounds. It could be months before anyone realised the truth.

'Hey, Dad?'

He didn't turn around. 'Take care of yourself, yeah?' She walked to his seat and waited for him to look up. He didn't. She bent and kissed his dry cheek.

'My sheets are in the wash.'

'Right,' he said.

She hesitated, felt like there should be more, but what else was there to say? She grabbed a bin-liner full of her clothes on the way out of the door and hesitated on the front door-step. Quietly so that her dad couldn't hear her she said, 'I love you.'

And then she heaved the bag over her shoulder and walked away.

Molly squeezed the last of her clothes into the big green recycling dome behind Sainsbury's. She was already sweating; dark grey stains bloomed at her armpits. She knew it shouldn't matter, and yet she was embarrassed for people to see how far she'd fallen. She'd made sure they'd all seen her ascent to designer clothes and independence, and now she wanted to hide away from them as she hurried from the car park dressed in the only clothes she owned. It was remarkably freeing to have nothing except the clothes on her back and the bottle of water in her hand. It was alien to her not having a handbag slung over her shoulder or a mobile phone to her ear. Her bag with her cards in it was on the top of the wardrobe at her dad's house. He wouldn't find it for months, perhaps not ever. Her phone was in the bin outside the railway station and the SIM card dropped over the side of the bridge into the river by the park.

She crossed her arms and kept her head down as the cars sped by. Motorbikes roared in her ears as the bikers took advantage of the good weather to head out to the Peaks. Lorries brushed past her and she felt herself buffeted by the wind. She had a vague idea of where she was going but was clueless about how long it would take her to get there. Her mouth was dry but she was saving the water for the pills that were in her pocket. She had to keep putting one foot in front of the other until, at some point, it would be her last step.

Part of her was saying she shouldn't do it, but her decision was made and she couldn't go back now. She had nothing to go back to. She had ruined so much for so many and didn't deserve to wake up to another sunrise.

Behind her she heard a woman call out but she didn't turn around. She had to keep her head down, had to keep walking. She'd considered taking her own life once before. It was after Barnaby died and she couldn't make sense of anything. And everything seemed to be her fault. Her fault that Barnaby had attacked her, her fault that Beth had killed him, her fault that Beth was in the hospital, her fault that her parents didn't care enough to notice that she was withdrawn and scared. That time, Beth's mum took her under her wing. All it took was for someone to notice her, to really *see* her, for Molly to realise that everyone has bad days that they think they'll never survive, but they do. What she'd give right now to have Beth's mum stroking her hair and telling her she was worth something.

'Molly? Wait up!'

This time Molly had to pause, and turn. She saw a woman waving and walking towards her. She almost ran away but her legs were tired, her mind too slow. It was the last person she wanted to see.

Hattie's face was flushed with trying to catch up with Molly. 'Didn't you hear me? I've been calling you.'

'Not now, Hattie.' She tried to back away but Hattie came closer.

'Are you okay? Because my dear, you look terrible.'

Molly looked wildly around her, for an escape route, for a reason to dismiss Hattie. She couldn't bear to look at the woman who would be dead before the weekend was out. She wanted to tell Hattie that it was nothing personal, but Molly had to protect Beth.

Hattie steered Molly into the shade of a beech tree, hands gripping her upper arm, and Molly flinched at the unwelcome touch. She turned her face from Hattie and put her hands over her ears.

Go away, go away, go away.

'We didn't get to finish our chat the other morning,' Hattie said. 'You ran off before I could explain.'

Molly closed her eyes. That's why she was having to do all this. The chat.

I saw Beth come back.

Molly hadn't been a good enough friend and she must make up for it. If she had to choose between Hattie and Beth, she would choose Beth every single time.

Hattie grabbed Molly's wrists and yanked her hands away from her ears. 'Listen to me, you stupid woman. What on earth has got into you?'

Molly cowered. 'Have you told him what you saw?'

She was focusing on a point over Hattie's right shoulder, but not looking in her eyes. *Not her eyes. Brown like Barnaby's.*

'Have I told who? Finn? God, no. What do you take me for?'

'It wasn't Beth's fault. She did it for me. It was my fault, not hers.' Molly pulled her hands free of Hattie's grasp and began pacing. In the shade, out of the shade, in the shade, and out again. Like strobe lighting.

'It wasn't your fault and it wasn't Beth's either. Not entirely. That's what I wanted to tell you. I knew you'd misunderstood, but I couldn't explain what I meant in front of Finn.'

Molly shook her head. There was no point going over it all again.

'Molly, let me explain.' Hattie pulled Molly's hands away from the side of her face and stared into her eyes. She lowered her voice and said, 'It was me.'

Molly tilted her head to one side.

'*What* was you?'

Hattie let go of Molly's hands. 'That night. I saw Beth close the lid on the hot tub. I could have helped my brother. I saw everything.'

'I don't understand.' Molly was sweating heavily and her mind was slow to process what she was hearing.

'You were right. My brother wasn't a good person. He was the reason I was suspended from my previous school. I covered for him so he didn't get kicked out just as he was about to take his GCSEs. He let me take the blame for the drugs, and my parents saw me as the failure. The embarrassment. He ... he was never going to change. And then ...' Hattie put her fingers to her lips as if steadying herself. She cleared her throat.

'When I saw Beth ... well, she'd always seemed like a genuinely good person. I'd never heard her say a bad word about anyone and ... that's when I thought that maybe I could guess what Barney had done to you. There had to be a good reason why she'd come back to confront a boy who was older and stronger than her. And it was that instinct to protect her friend, wasn't it? To get ... not revenge, but, oh, I don't know. Justice maybe. Like, why should he get away with everything? Why did he get to cruise through life while everyone else had to live with the consequences? I could have helped him, Molly. But I chose not to.'

Molly shook her head. 'You couldn't have known how it would turn out.'

'I did.' Hattie's eyes were wide, her voice low. 'I sat and listened to him banging on the lid of the hot tub. It was my fault.'

'But it was Beth who closed the lid,' Molly said. 'If she hadn't ...'

'No. Listen to me.' Hattie stepped closer to Molly. 'If that lid had been closed when my father had found Barney, don't you think there'd have been an investigation? How would anyone expect Barney to have closed it himself?'

'It was windy that night. Maybe it ...'

'Not windy enough to close the heavy lid of a hot tub,' said Hattie. 'I opened it. When he went quiet, I opened it. And, in case the death looked suspicious and the police started an investigation or something, I wiped the cans so that Beth's prints wouldn't be on them. I knew what I was doing.'

'You've never told anyone?' Molly whispered.

'No. My parents would never forgive me.' Hattie swallowed hard and tears trickled down her cheeks. She wiped her chin with the back of her hand. 'I'm not proud of it, but I can't change what I did. I just ... I just wanted you to know that it wasn't Beth's fault. When people ask why I haven't had children I usually tell them I like my life too much the way it is. But that's not true. I worry about passing on my genes to a child. I'm not a good person, Molly. I sabotage everything good in my life. Sleeping with Oscar was just that. Sabotage. I know Finn loves me but maybe I was trying to see how much. Whether he would put up with me at my worst. And he's still here so perhaps I am worthy of happiness. And I'm trying to make amends for what I've done. Truly I am. New starts all round, yeah? Will you let Beth know what I've told you? I don't think I could face ...'

Molly shook her head. 'She's not speaking to me. She won't answer my calls, won't answer the door.' Molly bit the dry skin on her lips. 'She hates me.'

Hattie lowered her head. 'I'm sure she'll come round. You two ... well, just don't let Oscar come between you, yeah? He was always jealous of your close bond. He would have loved the fact that Beth is on her own now with no one to turn to. Right, I need to get on. Look, truly, I'm sorry about everything.'

Hattie had regained her composure but Molly was losing what was left of hers.

'Are you okay?' Hattie asked. 'Can I give you a lift somewhere?'

Molly shook her head. 'No, I need to be on my own.'

'Okay. Well, if you're sure?' Hattie started to walk away and then paused. Turned. 'You know, you're a good friend to Beth. Give her some time, and she'll soon realise how important you are to her. The kids too. Be patient. Don't give up on her yet. I don't think she'll listen to me, but I'm happy to talk to her if you think it might help.'

Molly watched until Hattie was out of sight and then crouched in the dirt and let her tears darken the dry soil. The relief was huge. It wasn't her fault. Barnaby had never been a good person and she wasn't the only person he'd hurt. And more than that, Beth hadn't killed anyone because of her.

All those years of blaming herself, of feeling responsible for Beth's breakdown, they'd been wasted. Perhaps if they'd come clean about what had happened at the time, it would all be behind them now.

She looked up from where she was hunched in the dirt. She felt a little light-headed. This new reality would take some adjusting to. Hattie had done a good job of looking like she was gloriously swanning around and getting on with her life after her brother's death. It gave Molly some comfort that she wasn't the only one who'd let that night cast a shadow over her entire life. Beth wouldn't be in trouble because Hattie couldn't go to the police without implicating herself and so there was no need for Frazer to . . .

Shit.

Frazer.

Molly stood up and ran back to the road. Hattie was nowhere to be seen. Molly reached in her pocket for her phone, she needed to tell Frazer to stop, but her hand only closed around the bag of tablets. The phone wasn't there. She looked into the distance, realising that her SIM card would be halfway down the stream by now.

Fuck, fuck, fuck.

The money. If she could get to the money before Frazer did, he wouldn't hurt Hattie. She had no time to waste.

She cast wildly around her. She had nothing, no money, no phone and she had no idea how to get to Cloud Drop before Frazer did.

'Please,' she said to a passing woman, 'could you—'

'I don't have any change, I'm sorry.'

'No, I—'

But the woman bustled away.

'Excuse me?' She put out her hand towards a man pushing a pram.

'No,' he snapped and increased his pace as if to keep the baby safe. They thought she was begging for money. Her clothes were dirty but, even so, it shocked her that she had become someone to be ignored, shunned. In her work clothes and blow-dried hair they would all have stopped to hear her out, but not anymore. She was one of the invisible people now.

She looked up at Wilders Pass towering above her, its impressive rocks were a fortress protecting the town. She'd climbed up there once already today and now she'd have to do it again. Molly crossed the road and began running.

CHAPTER FIFTY-ONE

Beth Lomas

It was a glorious day. Washing was line-dancing in the breeze. School shirts and bedding were gleaming white under the summer sun. It was only a few weeks until the children broke up from school and they had a whole summer ahead of them. I couldn't wait to have them to myself. We'd talked about exploring the south coast together this summer with little more than our bikes and a tent.

I'd lied to Esther about there being money and passports in the bedside drawers. But, if I was right about her, she'd have told Oscar and he wouldn't be able to resist the lure of a pile of money and a passport to get him out of the country. It must be torture for him, remaining hidden. He was a man who liked to be in the spotlight.

Our house was show home spotless. I'd taken all the photos down, and anything that had once belonged to Oscar was long gone. I wondered about leaving the doors unlocked because at least then I wouldn't have to pay for the replacement of locks or windows when Oscar came, like I knew he would. In the drawer by my side of the bed I'd placed a note which said, 'Nice try. Did you really think I'd leave that kind of money lying about?'

As soon as the children left for school, I baked a peanut

butter cake. Topped with chocolate, caramelised nuts, and sandwiched with dulce de leche. It was Oscar's favourite, but the rest of us hated the taste of peanut butter. This would be the last time I ever baked one and so I took my time over it, remembering how Oscar said it was the cake version of a Snicker's bar. He'd eat the whole cake to himself over three days. I didn't know how he managed it.

Weighing and measuring brought me a simple sense of comfort. I'd followed this recipe so many times that I knew it off by heart. I took a knife out of the drawer and left it by the cake.

Everything was ready.

And now all I had to do was wait for Oscar.

CHAPTER FIFTY-TWO

Molly Ingram

Every time a car went past, Molly tried to flag it down. Some of them slowed to get a better look at the mad woman, but no one stopped.

She went off the main road and started up a little-used pathway that you wouldn't know was there if you hadn't lived in Hellas Mill for years. She had tried so hard to not be the Hellas Mill estate girl. The one from the council house who kept getting nits. The one whose parents never turned up to sports day, or parents' evening.

And look at her now, back where she started and still ruining everything. She could never be anything other than what she was.

What if Frazer had already picked up the money? Should she have gone to Hattie's house or the police station instead? Stupid. She was stupid. Why hadn't she thought of that first? But she was so close now to Cloud Drop and it would take her too long to get back down the ridge and across town to Hattie's. She had to hope for a miracle. God knows she was due one.

CHAPTER FIFTY-THREE

DC Lowry Endecott

Lowry had spent the last few days going through everything she knew about Oscar Lomas, and it didn't amount to much. Now that Finn was back from honeymoon, she'd run out of time to uncover anything else.

She slid all her reports and notes into the top drawer of her desk. Out of sight but not out of mind. She could see why Beth thought Oscar Lomas was still alive, but it was probably someone having fun at Beth's expense. The flowers, the card, the person in the garden, and the break-in. Somebody was angry that Oscar was dead and they blamed Beth.

The phone on Lowry's desk rang once and she snatched it up.

She listened as PC Claire Sackler spoke into her ear. She got to her feet but felt like she'd left all her blood behind in her seat.

'Sorry, Claire, can you repeat that?'

She hoped, prayed, that she'd heard her wrong. This couldn't be happening.

Lowry looked up as Finn Greenwood walked in through the door. 'Y'alright mate?' he called.

Finn was looking tanned in an open-necked white shirt. Lowry should have known he wouldn't be able to keep away, especially following the break-in and the wrecked car, but she didn't expect to see him now. She didn't want to be the one to tell him.

Lowry didn't even thank Claire, nor say goodbye. The phone left her hand and she walked towards Finn in a daze.

'Finn,' she said.

'Missed me?' he said with a grin. 'Good to see the station is still standing. I wasn't sure about coming back at all. You should've seen the place we were staying.'

Lowry already had the car keys in her hand. 'We need to go.'

'Where? I've only just got here.'

'Beth Lomas's house. An ambulance is on its way.'

CHAPTER FIFTY-FOUR

Beth Lomas

I parked the car in the lay-by just as Oscar had done. I was – without realising it – recreating the day that my world fell apart. It was another warm day with storms forecast for the coming week. The Spanish Plume, the papers were calling it. The heat was too oppressive for me to move quickly and, as soon as I got out of the air-conditioned car, I felt my body grow heavier. There were no other cars on the road, but I could see two Lycra-clad cyclists moving my way. I locked the car – something Oscar had failed to do – and began walking. I had a backpack slung over my shoulder with the urn and Oscar's passport in it.

If I was right about him faking his death then he would see the note in the drawer and, thanks to his mother repeating all I'd said to her on the phone, would know exactly where to find me. If he was as arrogant as I thought he was, he would meet me at Cloud Drop. He wouldn't let anyone outsmart him, especially not his pathetic little wife. He wanted that money and he wanted the passport – why else would he have broken into the Cabin that night? Of course, I could be wrong, and Oscar really was a pile of dust. In which case, I would scatter his ashes and put this all behind me; accept that my husband was dead and move on.

I lowered my head as the cyclists passed but they didn't pay me any attention. As I went through the kissing gate to the field beyond the road, I glanced back at the car. If I was right, then someone else had been here on the day that Oscar disappeared. Another car would have been parked behind Oscar's; perhaps the one he'd used for his getaway. The person who'd been driving that car was the person Harvey had found at Cloud Drop. I expected that same car would once again be parked behind Oscar's but, this time, my husband would be behind the steering wheel.

When Oscar and I were first dating, we often used to come out to Cloud Drop. It wasn't an easy place to get to. It always felt like our own special piece of paradise, sitting there, looking out over the fields and listening to the rumble of the waterfall. The climb over Wilders Pass seemed steeper now, my legs not used to the exertion. Sweat was trickling between my shoulder blades already.

I pulled myself up the hill using tree trunks and rocks, pausing every five minutes to catch my breath. The pack on my back felt like it was getting heavier. My shoulder was aching now. I shrugged the bag over both shoulders to spread the burden, even though I knew it would make me sweat more. One last push.

These last few weeks had opened my eyes to the reality of what my husband was capable of in pursuit of money. Oscar had killed someone who'd got in his way. For the first time I realised the danger I could be putting myself in. If Oscar had killed the last person who'd confronted him how would he react to me doing the same?

My hammering heart was only partly due to the exertion of the climb as I emerged in the clearing at the top of Cloud

Drop. I dropped the backpack at my feet and sank onto the bench. It took a while to get my breathing under control, and for the sweat to dry on my skin.

I reached into the bag for the urn and gave it a little shake. It was surprisingly heavy. I still hadn't been able to trace anyone who'd gone missing in the last month near Hellas Mill. Certainly, no one who could have been mistaken for Oscar.

Listening to the waterfall, I waited for my husband. I thought of the good times we'd had, but also of the times when I should have realised he would eventually let me down. Though the signs were there, I could never have foreseen this.

I looked at the urn in my hand, still finding it hard to understand how Oscar could have killed another person.

I tapped the top of the cylinder as if to wake it up. 'Who the hell *are* you?' I asked.

There was a scuffling behind me and a voice said, 'Who the hell, indeed.'

His voice, once so familiar, sent a shudder down my spine. I couldn't turn to face him. I was right to believe he was still alive, though the confirmation brought no satisfaction.

'Hello sweetheart,' I said as lightly as I could. 'Nice party trick.'

Oscar moved forward until he was level with me. Both of us were looking out at the view rather than at each other, but I could see the shape of him out of the corner of my eye. I almost reached out to check he wasn't a ghost, but I kept my hands on the urn.

'What trick's that?' he asked.

'The one where you rose from the dead.'

He chuckled. 'You should see me turn water into wine.'

Part of me wanted to throw my arms around him and say how much I'd missed him and how much it had hurt when I thought he was lost to me for ever. And the other part of me wanted to push him, kick him, and slap him. What had he done? Why had he done it? I wanted to scream at him, to rage, but instead I swallowed and kept my voice as measured as possible.

'Don't you think you're overestimating your abilities a tad, darling? I mean, you're not as clever as you thought, are you? Even a simpleton like me worked out what you'd done.'

Oscar scratched behind his ear. 'What would you like? A medal?'

I could hear his sneer between the words.

'I'll settle for an explanation,' I said. 'Why did you do it?'

I was aware of Oscar looking down at me but I didn't return his gaze. I was desperate to stare at him, to touch his face, to see the truth in his eyes but I couldn't stay strong if I allowed myself to be mesmerised by him again. He'd always had an inexplicable power over me. And even now, I longed for him as much as I hated him.

I was at a disadvantage with him towering over me but I wasn't going to stand in case he used the momentum to tip me over the edge of Cloud Drop. I'd never been physically scared of my husband before, only scared of disappointing him. Now I could see what a mistake that had been.

CHAPTER FIFTY-FIVE

DC Lowry Endecott

An ambulance was blocking the road in front of Beth Lomas's house as Lowry came to a halt. She hadn't even switched off her car engine before Finn was out of the door and running up the pathway.

People walked by, slowing, trying to spot something that they didn't want to see but couldn't help looking for. Lowry moved towards the door where a uniformed police officer stood. She could see thick droplets of blood like ticker tape over the tiles. She averted her eyes. There was a huddle of green-backed paramedics in the kitchen trying to save a life, an urgency to their movements.

Lowry tiptoed carefully around the blood, not wanting to compromise the crime scene. The kitchen floor tiles were glossy white and the pooling blood looked almost black. She wanted to scoop it all up again and put it back. How could anyone lose this much blood and still be alive?

'Can you give us some space, sir.'

'But that's my wife,' Finn wailed. 'That's my wife!'

Lowry tried not to look at Hattie. One leg was bent up behind the other. A shoe had come off showing her orange painted toenails. There was a knife handle sticking out of her striped top. Lowry looked away, forced herself to take in the rest of the scene. There was a cake on the kitchen side with a slice missing from it, crumbs littered the kitchen work surface.

What else? There were fresh flowers in a vase on the table, the draining board and taps were gleaming silver. The house was cleaner than Lowry had ever seen it. This could be helpful in terms of finding prints. The only thing out of place was the body of her friend on the kitchen floor.

The patio door was open, red crescents from where the front of a shoe or boot had stepped in Hattie's blood, were stamped across the floor. Wide strides.

Okay, she thought. *That's it. Keep looking at it like it's a crime scene. No time to get sentimental.* She took two deep breaths and swallowed. She could taste the blood in the air.

Why was Hattie in Beth Lomas's house? And where was Beth? The neighbours who ran the B&B next door called the police when they'd heard screaming. They said they'd seen Mrs Lomas leave the house a couple of hours before. They couldn't be sure that she hadn't returned, but her car wasn't there, and it was a different vehicle that was seen speeding away up the alley behind the house, knocking into the bins.

The paramedics were performing CPR on Hattie while Finn watched on with his hands knotted in his hair. Pacing. Lowry felt like she was underwater. She wasn't part of this scene. Merely a spectator. No one had noticed she was even there. She slipped out into the garden and saw that the back gate was open. She walked towards it and looked into the alleyway. There was nothing to see. Nothing obvious anyway.

Lowry looked back to the house at the first and second floor windows, she didn't want to see what was happening in the kitchen. On the first floor the curtains had been pulled from their pole. She jogged back inside, and past the scene of carnage, to the bottom of the stairs. She tapped the uniformed officer on his shoulder.

'The upstairs has been checked, yeah?'

'Yep. All clear,' he said.

Lowry went up the stairs, two at a time, careful not to touch the bannister in case they could lift any prints off it. The bedroom door was open and the room beyond it was a mess. Not that she was one to talk, her room was always a mess of dirty clothes and clean clothes yet to be put away, but this was different. This was a room which had been torn apart. A lamp lay on the floor, its shade dented, a curtain was sliding from its rail. Drawers were open and pillows had been thrown on the floor. Lowry took a step inside the room. There were no empty cups, no dirty underwear, this was a room that, until recently, had been spotless.

She kept coming back to Hattie, why had she been here of all places on the day after she came back from her honeymoon? Beth and Hattie hadn't been friends. Beth had only been at the wedding because she had provided the catering and Hattie had been grateful. Perhaps she felt a little guilty and wanted to show how they could put it all behind them. No more secrets.

Lowry took another step into the bedroom and kicked a crumpled-up bit of paper. She bent to open it, careful to hold as little of it as possible. It said, 'Nice try.' It looked like the note had been torn in half but she couldn't see the other piece of the puzzle.

She backed out of the room and turned to see Claire Sackler coming up the stairs.

'Anything?' Lowry asked.

'We got hold of the kids as they were coming out of school. They've gone to a friend's house. The daughter says their mum was scattering their dad's ashes this afternoon.'

'Without them?'

'Apparently.'

'Have you managed to get hold of Beth?' Lowry asked.

'Phone's off.'

'Do the kids know where she was scattering the ashes?'

'Up at Cloud Drop.'

Hearing voices from the hallway below, Lowry looked down to see Hattie being wheeled out of the house. One of the paramedics appeared to be holding a drip above her. Her eyes were closed and she had an oxygen mask over her face. Lowry swayed and said a silent prayer. *Don't you dare bloody die on me, Hattie. Don't you dare.*

CHAPTER FIFTY-SIX

Beth Lomas

'You'd have enjoyed your funeral,' I said. 'Lots of people turned up.'

I looked at the urn in my hands. It didn't appear that anyone missed him, so perhaps the turnout was better than he would have expected.

'So I hear.'

'How did you know about the funeral?' I asked.

'Mum told me.'

'She knew? Even at the funeral, she knew? God, I was so blind.'

Oscar took his sunglasses off, folded them, and put them in his pocket. I noticed that his hands were dirty. 'No. Not then. I never planned to involve Mum at all but it became ... necessary. If I'd known I was never going home again ...'

I thought he was going to say that he would have kissed me one last time. He would have held me close, told me and the children that he loved us. But instead he said, '... I would have packed a bag and grabbed my passport.'

I closed my eyes. There was no point in pretending that Oscar was somebody he could never be.

'When did Esther find out?'

'A couple of days after the funeral. Gave her a bit of a shock when I turned up in her garden in Cornwall.'

'And I suppose she was the one who told you I was scattering the ashes here today.'

He nodded.

'What about Vince?' I asked.

Oscar shook his head. 'Still doesn't know. He'd have grand ideas about me turning myself in.'

I felt sorry for his parents. Esther knew he wasn't dead but she also knew that he couldn't be a part of her life anymore. I'd do anything to keep my children safe, but covering for them if they'd killed someone? Helping them leave the country? A life on the run would be no life at all. I don't think I could do it.

'Mum called you one night,' he said.

'Did she?'

'She wanted to tell you everything. I took the phone off her and hung up before she could say a word.'

The silent phone call had been Esther. It was nice to know that she'd wanted to put me out of my misery, that she wasn't completely heartless.

'Why have you come back, Oscar?'

'Passport and money, of course.'

'A bit risky, isn't it? What if someone spotted you? Aren't you scared I'll go to the police?'

'And tell them what? That I'm back from the dead? They'd never believe someone like you.'

Someone like me. It was so close to what Barnaby had said when I'd threatened him with going to the police. Why did everyone underestimate me?

'Talking of passports,' said Oscar. 'It wasn't where you said it'd be.'

'Of course. Stupid of me to think you'd come back to apologise to me and the children. Don't you miss us at all?'

He pursed his lips. 'Don't, Beth. Don't. This hasn't been easy for me. I'm trying to make the best of a bad situation.' He massaged a spot on his stomach and winced. 'I need the money so that I can leave the country and start again. Thanks to you putting a stop on the card I had to throw it away. Useless.'

He looked different, but I supposed that was the point. He had a red-flecked beard now. I'd never seen him with more than a couple of days' growth before. It didn't suit him at all.

He'd lost weight, looked skinny, but strong. His bare arms were lined with veins and sinew but they were as pale as if he'd been living underground for the past month. The clothes were different, too. Not the colourful ones he usually favoured but bland, everyday clothes. Pale blue jeans, dark grey T-shirt. Only his walking boots were familiar.

'Gabe and Honey think you're dead. How are they meant to make the best of this?'

He went quiet and so did I. I was talking to my dead husband, only he wasn't dead. It was difficult to make sense of my feelings. The anger that he'd done this to us, the relief that I wasn't going mad, the knowledge that – after today – I'd never see him again.

'So what now?' I whispered.

'I need my passport.'

'And then?'

He scratched his chin. 'You know I can't tell you that.'

I nodded. I didn't want to know anyway.

'Was it you that I saw in the garden the night of the funeral?' I asked.

'I went to get my things from the Cabin but someone was in there and I had to come back once they'd gone. I realised I couldn't keep sleeping rough much longer so I went to Mum's.'

'I thought my mind was playing tricks on me.'

'I almost said something to you, tried to explain,' he said.

'You did?' Despite myself, my heart lifted. I realised that I needed to know that he hadn't walked out on me without a backwards glance, that I hadn't been disposable.

'But I knew that you'd get hysterical and beg me to stay.'

'For God's sake, Oscar! Is that what you think of me?'

'Don't take it the wrong way,' he said. His voice was soft now and he sounded more like the man I loved. 'All I mean is, you're not practical, I knew you wouldn't have let me walk away again. For what it's worth I do miss you and the kids.' His mask slipped for a moment and he looked vulnerable, genuinely full of regret.

I looked away from him and folded my arms around the urn. I couldn't go to him. Couldn't fall for this again.

'How are the kids?' he asked.

I almost didn't tell him. He gave up his right to know how the children were on the day he walked out. But the truth would show him exactly what he was responsible for.

'Gabe was arrested for breaking and entering, and joy-riding.'

'What?'

'He stole – and then crashed – Hattie's car. Any idea why he chose her car in particular, Oscar? Kit was in ICU with a punctured lung. Josh needed stitches. Gabe's lucky to be alive.'

'Christ. Why weren't you keeping a better eye on him?'

I stood up, incensed. 'How is this my fault? I thought you'd killed yourself because of a row we'd had over your affair with Hattie – one of many, I soon found out. Oh yes,' I said seeing his eyes widen. 'I know all about Molly and Miriam too.'

Oscar scratched his ear and I caught a glimpse of his laconic, one-sided smile. 'And then,' I said, 'I started to think you'd been murdered and I owed it to you to find out who'd done this to you. I was devastated, and even getting out of bed seemed like a huge achievement at times. I've been doing my best but I was a bit distracted, Oscar. Maybe you should be asking yourself *why* Gabe's been playing up. Anything spring to mind? Any reason why our beautiful son should be lashing out? I suppose you can't see what this has to do with you, can you? Can't you see the hurt you caused when you . . . God, what am I meant to call it? Died? Because you didn't, did you?' I took a step towards him. He was sweating and his pallor was waxy. He pushed his fingers into the side of his stomach and bent at the waist.

'Whose body was it, Oscar? Who did we cry over?'

I held the blue container out in front of me. 'Whose ashes are in this urn?'

'No one,' he said with a dismissive shake of his head. He grunted and wiped the sweat off his forehead with the back of his hand.

'He was somebody, Oscar. He must've had friends, and family. We need to let someone know.'

'He was a hired thug. Molly paid him to rough me up. He was scum of the earth and I bet no one's missing him at all.'

The confusion must have shown on my face because he laughed and said, 'You don't know everything then? You don't know that Molly would've been happy if it really had been my body at the bottom of Cloud Drop. She must be loving all this.'

'You ... Well, you used her, so ...' I was struggling to grasp the fact that my best friend slept with my husband and then paid someone to go after him. 'How do you know that Molly hired him?'

'She lent me a bit of money and I would've paid her back if the deal hadn't fallen through. She threatened me and said that, unless I coughed up, her business would go under and she'd take me down with her. Next thing I know, this thug turns up demanding I paid what I owed, or else.'

Oscar blinked rapidly and his mouth twitched.

'So, what, you ... talk me through what happened. You brought him up here and then you killed him?'

'That wasn't my intention. Me and Harvey—'

'Harvey?'

'I told him that I had to meet this guy. Thought if he saw us together he'd be intimidated and leave us alone, give us more time, or something. It affected the business so it affected both of us.'

'And then what?'

'This guy was strong but he wasn't fit. His legs were weak from the climb. I hit him as soon as he appeared and he ... Honest to God, he collapsed. He shouldn't have gone down like that. He hit his head and I panicked. I mean, who wouldn't? He was just lying there. Honestly, I was going to call the police, tell them it was an accident but Harvey had a better idea. I took his stuff, replaced it with mine, took his car keys, his phone, and we just ... we rolled him over the edge. I thought the body would get sucked into the caves but he got stuck on the ledge.'

He stared into the distance for a moment as if searching for his conscience, and not finding it. He shook his head and smiled. 'I'd forgotten to put the wedding ring on him though, so I left that in the car. I got in his car and drove and drove. I slept in it and used his debit card on small transactions that didn't need a pin. It wasn't as difficult as I'd expected. In fact, I started to enjoy the freedom.'

'What was his name?' I asked.

'Who?'

'The man you killed.'

'God knows. He didn't give me his business card. I had no way of knowing whether I'd get away with it. I just wanted some money and my passport so I could leave the country before anyone realised what had happened.'

How could this be the man I'd loved for half of my life? He was completely detached from me, from his life, from the fact that he had killed and lied and broken all our hearts.

I sank back down on to the bench and let out a long breath. 'You could have told me what was going on. I would have helped you. Instead you've destroyed so many lives.'

'Can't be helped,' he said kicking the soil with the toe of his hiking boot. I looked at his leg, it seemed to be trembling.

'Why did Harvey help you and say that the body was yours, Oscar?'

Oscar didn't say anything.

'Oscar? Why would Harvey cover up a murder and help you get away? He knew about you and Miriam. Surely he wanted to kill you, not help you.'

'He made me see that this was my chance to walk away from all the mess I'd made. Not just the body, but the

331

business, the affair. He was thinking clearer than I was. He told me what to do and I just did it.'

I was surprised that Harvey would have supported Oscar to do something like this and then it struck me. 'He wanted rid of you, didn't he?'

Oscar nodded slowly. 'He said he'd kill me if he ever saw me again. If I disappeared, he'd make sure he was first on the scene and identify the body as mine. He said it would be better for everyone if they thought I was dead.'

I looked at the urn in my hand. A nameless man, without a proper burial. I was sad for all of us.

'I can't believe you slept with Miriam,' I said to Oscar. 'Harvey's your brother. Hattie says you only slept with her for the money. You can't tell me that Miriam was about money too.'

'I don't think you want to know the truth,' he said with a wry smile. His face softened and I saw something I'd never expected to see.

'Oh, my God. You're in love with her.'

'We had a connection. Harvey's an idiot. He'd do anything to keep her, including lie about a dead body as long as I never contacted Miriam again.'

'How long's it been going on for?' I asked. 'Actually no. I don't care. Here,' I reached for the black rucksack at my feet and threw it to him. He caught it but the force of it made him take a step backwards. 'Your passport. Harvey had the right idea. Leave Hellas Mill and never contact me or the children again. I thought I had to prove that you didn't die by suicide so that I could be free of the guilt of not noticing how much you were struggling. But I'd rather everyone believed that, than face the shame of the kind of man you really are. I hate you Oscar. I hate everything you stand for. I wish you were dead, so let's go back to pretending that you are.'

Oscar snorted as if he found everything I said amusing, but I could tell he was taken aback by my willingness to let him go.

'There's a bag by your side,' he said pointing to my feet. 'I believe someone has left it there for me.'

I'd not noticed it when I'd first sat down. I reached for it as I asked, 'Who else knows you're here?'

'Don't worry,' he said. 'They think they're leaving it for someone else. Mistaken identity, that's all.'

'I don't understand,' I said.

'What's new?' he sneered. 'Why can't women keep their noses out? All these questions. Turning up where they're not wanted and demanding answers. Threatening me with the police. I can't be held responsible for what happens when they poke their noses in where they're not wanted. I don't take kindly to being threatened.' He bent over with his hands on his knees and grimaced. He spat on to the ground at his feet.

'What are you talking about?'

He turned to look at me but I wasn't sure he was seeing me. His eyes were distant and troubled.

'What is it?' I asked.

'Hand me the bag,' he snapped, straightening up.

I held out the bag but didn't let go even when he reached for it. We stayed that way for a moment, me seated, him standing, both with fingers grasping the bag. In my other hand I had the urn. It was almost too big to hold comfortably in one hand but I gripped it as if it was the only person here who was on my side.

Oscar yanked the bag backwards suddenly and I was pulled to my feet as it left my grasp.

'If you'd left the passport in the Cabin, or if it had been in the drawer where you said it would be ... Well, I'd be on my way by now and we would never have had to do this. Her blood is on your hands. It's you who made me come back.' His face contorted as if he was in pain.

'What are you talking about? Whose blood? What have you done?'

'Why do you assume it's my fault?'

Oscar stuffed the carrier bag into the rucksack and flung it onto the ground behind him. I took a step towards him to plead with him to tell me who he was talking about, but he grabbed my wrist and pulled me towards him.

'Let go of me,' I said. His breath was bitter and I turned my face away.

'Ideally they'd never have found that guy's body.' He stepped closer to the edge, dragging me with him. 'Bad luck that he hit that ledge and got stuck there. If he'd hit the bottom he wouldn't have been found. I thought it would be obvious that he wasn't me but good old Harvey played a blinder, didn't he?'

'What about the suicide note?' I asked.

'The what?'

I'd said all along it wasn't a suicide note, and the confusion on Oscar's face only confirmed it.

'You left a note saying "sorry".'

'I'd forgotten about that. No. That was ... that was something else.'

'Then what was it?'

His grip loosened but he didn't let go of my wrist. 'When

I wrote it, I didn't realise I wouldn't be coming back. I was sorry you'd found out about the affair. I wanted you to forgive me.' He shrugged and then continued, 'I couldn't afford a divorce as well as everything else.'

My fury boiled over and I tried to shake my hand free so that I could slap him.

'You piece of shit!'

Oscar gripped my wrist tighter and bared his teeth like a wild animal. I spat in his face and he grabbed me by the throat. We stayed like that a moment, but I didn't drop his gaze. I wanted him to know that I saw him for what he was. He pushed me closer to the edge of the cliff. Still, I didn't drop his gaze. I was clinging on to the urn as if it was a life jacket but it couldn't save me now. I lifted my chin. 'I'm not scared of you, Oscar.'

He smiled and pulled me to him. And then he whispered in my ear, 'You should be.'

CHAPTER FIFTY-SEVEN

DC Lowry Endecott

Harvey was waiting for Lowry at the bottom of the track to Wilders Pass. 'Thanks for meeting me here,' Lowry said.

'What's this about?' he asked. 'Couldn't it wait?'

'Can we talk as we walk?' Lowry motioned up the hill and began her ascent. 'Everyone's tied up dealing with this incident but support should be here soon.'

'What incident? I don't think I quite understood your message.'

Harvey hung back a little, looking nervously at the summit. Lowry didn't have time for caution. 'We have to move quickly,' she said. 'Come on.'

'Won't you tell me what's going on?'

Lowry ignored his question until he'd caught up with her and was walking level with her shoulder.

'I'm looking for Beth.'

'Beth?'

Lowry sighed. She didn't want to waste her breath by answering questions.

'There's been an incident at her house. I need to find her to check that she's okay. Her children believe she's gone to Cloud Drop to scatter her husband's ashes.'

'Are you sure? I'd think she'd tell me if that was her plan.'

Lowry stumbled and Harvey put out an arm to steady her.

'Really? Didn't realise you two were on good terms at the moment,' she said.

Harvey's face reddened. 'Well, it's Miriam that she's furious with, not me.'

'None of my business,' said Lowry, 'but might she be a bit pissed off that you knew about the affair and didn't tell her?'

'I didn't want to hurt Beth,' Harvey said with a defensive tone. 'I didn't think she could handle any more shocks.'

'It's not your job to decide what Beth can and cannot handle. She's stronger than you think. At least, I hope that's the case.' Lowry stopped for a moment and blew hard. There was still a long way to go and she hoped that Beth hadn't done anything rash.

Harvey looked down at his feet but said nothing. They continued in silence for a few minutes and then he said, 'Hold on.' He grabbed her arm and forced her to face him. 'You said there was an incident at the house. Are the children okay?'

'The children are fine; they were at school. It was …' Lowry almost didn't say, but there was a small chance Harvey could shed light on why Hattie had been at the house. 'Hattie Flint-Stanton has been stabbed. There was no one else at the house when the ambulance arrived.'

'Christ almighty! You don't think that Beth did it?'

'I don't even know whether Beth was there, I don't know if she was hurt, I don't know whether she's up Cloud Drop right now contemplating ending her life in the same way as her husband did. That's why we have to find her, and I'm not sure I can get to the spot again without you.'

'Of course.' Harvey suddenly picked up the pace and left Lowry behind. As she struggled to catch up, she heard him say, 'Sorry. I hope I didn't seem difficult when you first arrived. Having a bad day. Nothing compared to ... well,' he sighed. 'Miriam is leaving me, or has already left me, I suppose. Last time I saw her she had her bags packed and was about to head to the airport. It seems an old flame is back in town. Someone she thought she wouldn't see again. That's lucky, isn't it?'

Lowry wasn't very good at knowing what to say in these situations. 'I'm sorry to hear that.'

'No, you're not, though I appreciate you saying so. I guess it was on the cards from the moment she fell in love with my brother. I never could compete with Oscar.'

'Surely a dead man isn't much competition,' Lowry said.

Harvey frowned. 'You'd be surprised.'

CHAPTER FIFTY-EIGHT

Beth Lomas

I felt Oscar's body tense and I adjusted my grip on the urn that I was clutching to my chest. Before Oscar could move, I smashed it into his jaw. He staggered backwards and let go of me. The lid came off and fine grey ash arced through the air. I moved away from the edge, panting, while Oscar blinked his eyes hard. He was holding his stomach even though it was his face that had taken the impact.

My heart was beating hard but it was a feeling closer to exhilaration than fear. I'd had enough of being controlled by him. I'd never felt so powerful.

'Beth,' he croaked, 'I don't feel good. Something's not right.'

I placed the urn on the bench and stood as tall as I could while Oscar crouched with one hand on the ground keeping him steady.

'You don't expect me to feel sorry for you, do you?'

I noticed, for the first time, how his hair was disappearing at his crown. It was damp at the nape of his neck, either from the exertion of the climb or from the discomfort in his body. Because I knew exactly why he was in pain. I knew better than he did, what was happening to his body. Perhaps I should have felt guilty, but it was too late for that now.

'How was the cake?' I asked.

He spat on the ground. 'The what?'

'The cake, Oscar. I assume you had a slice because you can't resist your favourite, can you? You've always loved peanut butter. Never could understand the appeal myself. I prefer something lighter like a lemon drizzle. I made it easy for you, I suppose. I even left out a knife. Sorry it wasn't perfect. I should have let it cool more before I covered it in chocolate, but I was in a bit of a hurry. I knew you'd eat it anyway.'

He clenched his fist. 'Beth, what's happening to me?'

'According to Google – I mean, where would we be without the internet, huh? – so, I googled it, and it turns out rats love peanut butter. Do you remember I told you I'd seen a rat in the garden? Well it looks like there's a nest behind the shed. You can hear them scrabbling around.'

He grunted. 'And?'

'Sorry. I'm getting off topic, aren't I? So, anyway, it turns out that peanut butter is a really good way to disguise the taste of rat poison.'

He was breathing heavily. 'What have you done?'

I walked over to him. 'I suppose I could have given them the peanut butter straight from the jar, right? But this way seemed more ... well, I thought I could kill two birds with one stone. Or, in this case, two rats. Of course, I couldn't be sure you'd eat it. I decided to leave that to fate. What kind of person breaks into a house and cuts themselves a slice of cake? I made it to deal with our terrible rat problem.'

I was surprised at how calm my voice was, and how weak Oscar looked.

'The rat poison has strychnine in it. Illegal to buy now, of course, but that poison has been lingering in the back of our garage for more than ten years. I bet you wish you'd got rid of the rats when you said you would, huh? Do you suppose there's such a thing as an antidote?' I looked away over Cloud Drop as if I was considering that for a moment. 'Even if there was, we're a long way from the hospital here.'

'You wouldn't.'

I crouched down next to him. 'I haven't done anything wrong, Oscar. I baked a cake with rat poison in it so I could feed it to the vermin that live behind the Cabin. I told the kids what I was going to do, warned them not to touch it. Really the question is, what have *you* done? I couldn't even be sure the poison would still be potent after all this time.'

Oscar grunted; his whole body convulsed. There was a trace of spittle at the side of his mouth.

'And even if it did work, I didn't know how long it would take. There was always a chance you wouldn't make it up here in time, because I couldn't search "how much poison should I put in a cake to make sure my husband dies roughly an hour after ingesting it?" on the internet. That kind of thing could get me into a lot of trouble.'

He lashed out and grabbed me around the neck. I fell on top of him and he turned over like a crocodile's deathroll towards the edge of the cliff. I could feel the thunder of the waterfall underneath my back.

'You bitch,' he said.

'You lied to us, Oscar. You had affairs, you betrayed your brother. And then you killed an innocent man. You let us believe that you were dead. Because of you, Gabe has been arrested. Because of you, Honey cries herself to sleep every night. All I did was bake a cake. You once told me it was the only thing I was good at. I always think it's best to play to your strengths. Don't you?'

Oscar tightened his grip around my neck, unsure at first and then with more force.

My arms were outstretched, fingers shaped into claws as I grabbed a handful of the ash and flung it in Oscar's face. Instinct brought his hand to his eyes and he loosened his grip on me. I scrambled away from him but he grabbed my leg and pulled me towards him. His eyes were wide and bloodshot.

'Am I going to die?' he whispered. The words almost got lost behind the roar of the waterfall but I could see in his face what he wanted to know.

I nodded.

He twitched and spasmed and then looked at me and smiled. 'Then you're coming with me.'

'Oscar, no!'

He started pawing at me, pulling me towards the edge, inching his legs over the drop. For myself, I'd fight him, but for my children I was willing to kill him. I wouldn't leave them without a mother too. I bent one leg and brought my heel down onto his nose. He blinked hard but still didn't let go. I reached for his hand and started peeling his fingers back, digging in my nails as I did.

'Get. Off. Me.'

I heard someone call my name and felt a hand on my arm. For a moment I couldn't work out what was happening.

'I got you,' the voice said as I felt them grab handfuls of my top and start wrenching me backwards.

'Molly?'

'Help me,' she said, but she was sliding towards the edge too. I kicked and squirmed but Oscar was holding on. Molly let go of me and stretched for the urn on the bench. She flung it past me and I heard it hit its target. Oscar let go with one hand but his right hand was still clamped around my ankle. I half turned and his eyes met mine. There was fear and panic. For a moment, he looked like my husband again, a man who I'd loved with all my heart. His fingers were slipping, his eyes widening. I saw the moment he decided to let go. Instinctively, I reached out to save him, but as I clasped his wrist, he let go of me and, without making a sound, he was gone.

Gone.

He was there, and then he wasn't. All I was left holding was his watch.

Molly dragged me away from the edge and we clung to each other. I half expected to see Oscar reappear, but we were alone. I manoeuvred so that I was lying on my stomach and dragged myself to the edge. I looked down into the thundering water below, but there was no sign of him.

For the second time, Oscar was dead.

'I killed him,' I whispered.

'No, babe,' said Molly stroking my hair. 'You can't kill a dead man.'

CHAPTER FIFTY-NINE

DC Lowry Endecott

Two people were coming down Wilders Pass. They were clinging to each other, swaying and stumbling. Immediately Lowry knew that one of them was Beth and started to rush up the hill. She tripped, and fell to her knees, cutting the heels of her hands. Harvey helped her stand up again.

'Y'okay?'

'Yes,' she wiped her hands on her trousers. 'Look! It's Beth. Jesus, I didn't realise how worried I was. Who's that with her?'

'Don't know. Is it Molly?' Harvey squinted at them.

Lowry raised her hand in greeting but waited for them to get closer before she spoke. She'd been so concerned that Beth was going to harm herself, that she hadn't planned what she was going to ask her about Hattie.

'What are you doing here?' Molly asked.

'Are you okay, love?' Harvey asked Beth. 'You don't look great.'

Beth shrugged but didn't meet his eye. Molly squeezed her friend's hand.

'We've been trying to reach you,' Lowry said.

Beth's eyes widened. 'Oh God, it's not the children?'

'No, they're fine.'

Beth seemed to collapse against Molly who gripped her

tightly. Lowry noticed that Beth had dirt under her finger-nails and soil on her face. Molly was a far cry from her usual well-turned-out self too. Her clothes were dirty and she had a black rucksack slung over her shoulder.

'Then what?' asked Molly. 'What's wrong?'

Lowry directed her response to Beth. She wanted to see her reaction.

'Hattie has been stabbed at your house.'

The two women looked at each other. 'Hattie?' repeated Beth. 'But ...'

The shock and pain on her face seemed genuine. 'Is she okay?'

Lowry shrugged. 'She's in the hospital. Lost a lot of blood.'

'Oh, God,' Molly said. 'But she'll be okay, right? What was she ...? I mean why was she at the house? I don't ...'

Beth looked at Molly. 'I can't cope, Moll. It's ... it's too much.'

'Is everything okay?' Lowry asked them.

Beth and Molly ignored Lowry. 'It's alright, Beth. At least, it will be. You let me deal with this, okay?'

Beth shook her head and said to Lowry, 'It's Oscar.'

Molly put her arm around Beth's shoulder. 'Don't, Beth.'

'I'm done, Molly. I've had enough.' She rubbed one eye with the back of her hand and levelled her gaze at Lowry. 'You see, the thing is, I've just thrown ... That is ... Oscar.' Her voice was trembling. 'He's gone. I baked his favourite cake and then I ...'

Harvey stepped between Lowry and Beth. He obscured her view for a second and Lowry had to step to the side to see Beth's face.

'So you've thrown his *ashes* off the cliff,' Harvey said to

Beth, putting his hand on her shoulder. 'The detective was telling me how you'd gone to Cloud Drop to scatter his ashes.'

'Harvey, you don't understand,' said Beth wiping her eyes with the heel of her hand.

'No. I really do,' Harvey said. 'It's a terrible and final act of goodbye, when you realise he can never, ever, come back. That you will never get the answers you wanted because ... well, the dead can't talk, can they?'

Lowry looked from Beth to Harvey. There was something in the way that Harvey was talking, almost like he was trying to hypnotise Beth.

'Yes,' said Molly. 'Yes, that's right. The dead can't talk.' She was speaking as if this hypnotism thing was working.

Lowry shook her head. 'Can someone please tell me what is going on?'

'Isn't it obvious?' Harvey said turning to face Lowry and blocking her view of the women once more. 'Beth has been to scatter Oscar's ashes and it was all a bit much for her, as you can imagine. Lots of ... ah, mixed emotions. Great to see that she and Molly have made up now though. Lovely to see.' He smiled a smile that didn't seem at all genuine. 'Shall we make our way back?' he asked.

'What the hell is going on here?' Lowry demanded.

'Well,' said Molly. 'As Harvey said, Beth and I have been scattering Oscar's ashes and saying our final goodbyes. Beth is overcome with emotion.' She squeezed her friend's hand.

Molly's eyes challenged Lowry to say anything else. Lowry shook her head and extended her arm down Wilders Pass. 'After you. Did you see anyone else on your walk?'

Molly looked at Beth. 'Did we?'

346

'No,' said Beth. 'I don't think we did.'

Lowry caught Beth looking at the watch in her hand. 'What's that?' Lowry asked.

'Oscar's watch,' Beth replied.

'I thought you said that the watch you had wasn't his?'

Beth took a deep, shuddering breath. 'I was wrong. I was wrong about everything.'

EPILOGUE

I didn't go to Hattie's funeral. I couldn't bear it.

I thought I'd been so clever, luring Oscar back to the house to expose his lies, but Hattie had paid the price for my mis-judgement. Molly says she was only there that day to tell me about the part she'd played in her brother's death. To stop me from feeling so guilty.

It didn't work because now I felt guilty for her death as well as her brother's.

I can only imagine how surprised she must have been to come face-to-face with a man who was meant to be dead. We'd never know what she said to him, but it was enough that Oscar felt he had to shut her up.

It was still difficult for me to accept that my husband was a killer. Twice. If I'd realised the truth about Oscar sooner, maybe Hattie would still be alive. No one has been arrested for her murder. For a while I was their best suspect because the only fingerprints found in the house were mine, the kids', and Oscar's . . . and God knows, dead men can't kill.

The children had alibis and so did I, though I was initially a suspect due to my erratic behaviour when Lowry found me that day – and the fact that almost fifty witnesses had seen me argue with Hattie on her wedding day. Molly swore she'd been with me the whole afternoon and my neighbours confirmed they'd seen me leave the house at least two hours before they'd heard Hattie's screams.

With nothing else to go on, the police seem to think that Hattie's death was linked to the previous break-in. They think she disturbed the burglars and they attacked her with the knife that had been used to cut the cake, which I fed to the rats as soon as I was allowed back in my house. Lowry was still looking for the owner of that bloodied footprint. She said she wouldn't rest until she'd found the murderer and so, she'd turned down the chance to move to a new job in London. She's not going anywhere until she's got justice for her friend. Finn has stepped down from his duties for the time being and Lowry is acting Detective Sergeant. I have no doubt she'll do a great job, but I wish she'd stop watching me in that intense way of hers, as if she's trying to read my mind.

Gabe has been given community service for stealing the car. He's lucky and he knows it. He's a different person nowadays. We're a lot closer and, when we speak of Oscar, it's with fondness as we rewrite our memories of him. I thought he'd been keeping his feelings bottled up but, he's played me some songs that the band have written recently, and they were all about dealing with loss and grief. They have their first gig next week.

Where the rest of us seem to have aged in the last couple of months, Honey has regressed. She's started sleeping in my bed, and never wanting to leave my side. Molly has suggested that she might need counselling but, for now, I think she just needs her mum. And I am glad of the company. She is still her sunny, beautiful self but she is more aware of death than any child should have to be. We're in the process of moving to a new house. It's difficult to walk through our kitchen and not imagine you can still smell the blood.

That deal that Oscar had been working on finally came through. He was right to be optimistic. All the debts have been paid, including the money owed to Molly, and the business is looking healthier than it has done in years. Though Molly has moved in with Vijay she turned down his marriage proposal. She said he should try again in a year or so.

I've rented premises for my catering business from the monthly dividends I get as a shareholder of Lomas Lumber. Harvey and I haven't told each other what we know. It's best not to have our worst fears confirmed, and also, there's a phrase I've learned recently – plausible deniability. If Oscar's body is ever found, Harvey can honestly say he knew nothing about it.

I had a moment of panic when his wallet turned up a few miles down the valley, snagged in leaves and twigs in a river, but there was no other trace of Oscar. Lowry had to admit that it meant that the body that had been found a few weeks prior had been Oscar's. Seeing as there was no cash card in the wallet, Lowry suggested someone had stolen it prior to Oscar's death, and chanced their luck.

Harvey and Miriam have separated. When Oscar didn't turn up at the airport, Miriam went back to Harvey with her tail between her legs, assuming Oscar had gone off without her, only to find that Harvey wouldn't take her back. She and I had one, final, showdown. A huge argument that seemed to shock her more than me. It was Miriam who'd been behind the congratulations card and the flowers. She blamed me for having driven Oscar away. At first, she believed I'd driven him to his death but, even when she found out he was still alive, she was furious with me for ruining everything. Every year Oscar had her organise those flowers from him for our wedding anniversary. They were the only romantic gesture I could remember yet the only involvement he'd had was to order someone else to arrange them.

I don't know how to explain how I feel about what I did to Oscar. I'd like to say I feel guilty about poisoning him. But I can't. I tell myself that I didn't really do anything wrong. That cake was for the rats and I didn't know for certain Oscar would come back to the house and then help himself to a slice. That was on him. *His* choices led to that.

I should be heartbroken that I let him fall to his death, but he was trying to kill me so all I did was save myself, and ensure Gabe and Honey weren't left without both parents. It's as if we've rewound to that day when Lowry first told me they'd found a body at Cloud Drop.

Esther and I speak regularly but Oscar is rarely mentioned. I assume that she thinks he's left the country. It's kinder to let her believe that Oscar is alive and well, and living abroad, than know for a fact that he's dead. Though, she must have made some assumptions about Oscar being back in Hellas Mill and the body of Hattie being found in our kitchen. Perhaps she's started to see his true colours. Certainly, she's a lot kinder to me now.

I still haven't worked out who died in Oscar's place. That car Oscar had taken had been stolen so it was a dead-end in terms of finding out who Molly had hired. At least I have a first name now, thanks to Molly, and a geographical area in which to search. I can't believe that no one knows who he is. I don't know what I'll do if I find out that Frazer has a family and friends who are missing him, but I'll try and help them out somehow, be their guardian angel. Because Frazer turned out to be mine.

It could have been worse – it might not have happened at all. I could still be sleepwalking through life, controlled by a man with his own interests at heart. But I'm a firm believer in fate, and Oscar Lomas got what he deserved.

Oh, and I no longer have a problem with rats.

Firstly, thank you for reading this book. While I have your attention, I wanted to say that I have tried wherever possible to deal with the issue of suicide with utmost sensitivity, but I'm no expert. I'm grateful to the Samaritans for their guidance on how to depict suicide in literature. I have personal experience of losing a friend to suicide, so it's something I really tried to get right. To anyone who is struggling, I beg you to reach out.

The shocking truth is that every four minutes someone in the UK tries to kill themselves and every hour and a half someone succeeds. The World Health Organisation states that on average around one million people a year die by suicide. That's one death every forty seconds. Please get help if you are struggling, or know of someone who is.

Free at any time, from any phone, you can call the
Samaritans on **116 123**.

Or please check out some of these amazing charities:

www.Samaritans.org
www.papyrus-uk.org
www.mind.org.uk
www.nspa.org.uk
www.thecalmzone.net

Thank you
Jo x

ACKNOWLEDGEMENTS

I love this part of a book – both writing them and reading them. It never fails to astound me how many passionate people there are in the book world who champion authors like me and I'm grateful to get the chance to say *thank you*.

I am lucky to have Imogen Pelham as my agent. She is often my first reader, my sounding board, and the voice of reason when I'm having a wobble. I can't thank her enough for everything she does for me. And my editors have been nothing short of amazing. Jade Chandler and Sara Adams at Vintage in the UK, and Lara Hinchberger and Deborah Sun De La Cruz at PRH Canada, have been insightful and patient as I've worked to bring out the story I wanted to tell. And of course, there's a lot that goes on behind the scenes, and for that I want to thank everyone who has been involved getting *What His Wife Knew* over the finish line.

Hats off to the amazing writers I'm lucky to call friends. Never has there been a more supportive bunch. To The Ladykillers, The Doomsbury Group, and CS - thank you for keeping me relatively sane and making me laugh. Also, a special thank you to The Writers' Flock. When I set up the group during lockdown I thought I'd be helping YOU, but I hadn't realised how much I would learn from you all.

Thank you to everyone who organised online events during lockdown, to libraries who tirelessly champion books, bookshops, bloggers, reviewers and, of course, to YOU. If no-one bought my books I'd still write them, but I'd be pretty sad about it. So, thank you to everyone who has read this or any of my books. You know you're my favourite reader, right?

Again, the incomparable Rachael Hodges read an early draft to advise me on police procedure. Thank you, Rachael – and sorry for the parts where I ignored your advice to suit the story. Any mistakes are entirely mine, but you already knew that.

My family, as ever, have been incredibly supportive. So, the largest thank you is saved for James, Alex and Danny. I hope you know how much you inspire me and how much your support matters. I wouldn't put it past any of you to write a novel and outsell me within minutes but, for now, thank you for letting me be the tortured writer who is still in her PJs at three in the afternoon.

Love, always x

The author would like to thank everyone involved in the publication of *What His Wife Knew* in the UK.

Editorial
Jade Chandler
Liz Foley
Dredheza Maloku
Sara Adams

Copy editor
Laura Gerrard

Proofreader
Alex Milner

Design
Dan Mogford

Publicity
Mia Quibell-Smith

Rights
Jane Kirby
Lucy Beresford-Knox
Rachael Sharples

Sales
Justin Ward-Turner
Sasha Cox
David Heath

Cara Conquest
Nat Breakwell
Christina Usher

Marketing
Kate Neilan
Mollie Stewart

Operations
Claire Dolan
Alex Cutts

Finance
Ed Grande
Jérôme Davies

Contracts
Gemma Avery
Alice Johnstone

Production
Polly Dorner

penguin.co.uk/vintage